The Companion of Lady Holmeshire

By

Debra Brown

World Castle Publishing

Debra Brown

This is a work of fiction. Names, characters, places, and incidents are products of the author's imagination or are used fictitiously and are not to be construed as real. Any resemblance to actual events, locations, organizations, or person, living or dead, is entirely coincidental.

World Castle Publishing
Pensacola, Florida

Copyright © Debra Brown 2011
ISBN: 9781937085377
Library of Congress Catalogue Number 2011930708
First Edition World Castle Publishing July 15, 2011
http://www.worldcastlepublishing.com

Cover Artist: Fantasia Frog Designs
Editor: Teresa Welch of Wild Iris Communications

Dedication

Dedicated to my Mother, who learned that my book would be published just on time.

~Chapter 1~

A Servant Girl's New and Quite Extraordinary Life

Chilly winds filled a once-shining black carriage. Over many miles and due to the dry conditions of the week, it had acquired a uniform coating of dust. Warming stones had gone cold on the journey from London to northern England, and Miss Emma Carrington pushed them from her feet as she huddled, shivering on her seat. Exhausted from the bumping and jostling, the changing of horses and the searching for meals in frightening and unfamiliar places, Emma sighed with relief and relaxed her tight shoulders as she traveled through the last village. Holmeshire, the center of her childhood memories, was the home of her many friends.

A short ride remained, though it seemed eternal, out of the town and up the hill through an intimidating, ivy-covered stone gateway. The carriage ascended the hill to an old masonry castle, which was this night set beneath a large moon. Built as a stronghold in the years of Scottish wars, the fortress' cold, formidable appearance was deceptive, for the warmest hearts in

Britain dwelt inside.

The horses came to an impatient stop at the first edge of the house, wanting their feed and water. Emma took the coachman's hand to step from the carriage. He hoisted her luggage off its top. In fine London dress, she hurried to the heavy servants' door, turned her great key and pushed her way through.

She shushed the man carrying her cumbersome case as most of the domestics had gone to bed, but someone watched from a window in an old watchtower now filled with beds. Eager proclamations rang from that chamber to the next through the servants' wing, and night-capped revelers poured into the stone kitchen. Emma removed her warm winter wrap and hung it near the door, smiling and exchanging excited nods.

"Miss Emma," said the delighted scullery maid. "Are you really here? Look at you, all fancy." Emma, the former housemaid, felt quite out of place in the ringlets and refined dress, the multitude of petticoats and the soft, tended hands of a London beauty. She blushed and hugged the young girl.

She regaled when a hefty man snatched her and spun her about below tin-coated copper pots and iron utensils, which hung from a rack. "Put me down," she said with a laugh. "Have you not grown up in all this time? London society will never accept me if they hear of this." She sighed, knowing they never would regardless. She dreaded facing the coming Season.

The cook appeared and snapped a rebuke. "Put her down, lad, before everything crashes to the ground. You have hit her boot on the table leg. Those are high-priced boots you will be payin' for, and I'll take the table out of your hide. Besides, the rest of us cannot get our arms about the lass. Emma, girl, you were gone too long."

Barreby the butler, still fully dressed in the adjoining pantry, had been auditing the silver serving dishes. He smiled when Emma arrived, and shook his head at the carrying on. He closed and locked a cherry-wood hutch and hurried up two flights of stairs to notify the sleeping countess, The Lady Winifred Holmeshire, that his Tiger Lily had arrived.

Emma glowed as even the countess came down to the kitchen to join the celebration which had produced the cake, puddings and tea prepared for her companion's return. Emma curtsied and accepted the lady's warm words of welcome. "How happy I am to be home," she told Lady Holmeshire, and turned about in a dignified way to show her the beautiful gown.

The lady sat in the kitchen for the reunion that had burst through the thick of night and ordered that bottles of fine wine be brought from the cellar for all to share. Emma enjoyed seeing the servants relish their first taste of an expensive bottle. She spoke of her training in the ways of refinement. "I was terribly hard to correct," she said. "I am best seen with a scrub brush and broom."

She listened as they asked about her time spent away. They went out infrequently, she replied, and focused on music and languages in the house. She learned to sleep past five in the morning, though it was oh so hard to do, she told them, her eyes widened and shaking her head. Teasing and hearty laughter continued for two hours. Emma had, after all, returned.

At long last, a night-robed footman, tired and tousled of hair, brought Emma's belongings up to the elegant room that awaited her. She would love to stay and never return to London, but Lady Holmeshire had made other plans.

Emma had been happy in service, for though Lady

Winifred lived the leisurely life of a countess, she had a place in her heart for humanity. A butler had been chosen to maintain order amidst laughter and guard the welfare of the lowest maid.

A new, framed mirror under candled sconces showed Emma the condition of her dark hair and olive complexion. *Dusty*, she thought—dirty, dreadful skin it was for a lady's companion. She sighed with disgust and wiped off the traveling grime. At least a bonnet had protected her hair. She stepped back on long legs to analyze the new clothes she wore, so above her station in life. Would these clothes hide the truth?

In her soft, new, feather bed she closed her eyes and drifted to the pleasures of times past on Holmeshire Hill. She'd enjoyed a climb in the fragrant breeze as a girl. She'd loved watching animals amongst the trees. She loved autumn, when the fallen leaves offered themselves as colorful stepping-stones. The oaks and yews of Holmeshire were her childhood friends. Before her need for an income required her to go into service, she had spent free hours alone on the hillside, sketching twisted branches and their pleasing foliage.

Emma woke to see some of her works hanging on the old walls of her new room, delighted to find them framed during her absence, a gift from the lady. It touched her heart. The countess was good indeed. Emma could not fathom this kindness—but her companionship would quiet the lady's loneliness. Surely, she determined to be a loyal companion.

Emma threw open the lined velvet drapes that blocked the morning light and looked about her well-scrubbed room. In the past, she had many times cleaned the slate fireplace that now warmed her after a silent housemaid's early endeavor. As a maid herself, Emma had washed the wide-plank floor, oiled the four-poster bed and polished the brass when guests were to be accommodated. She had wiped down the single leaded-glass window and had been in awe of the inspiring, misty view it afforded. Ruins of an ancient monastery at the foot of the hill were visible through naked winter branches. She had often paused her scrubbing to absorb it, and now it was hers to enjoy.

She left the warmth of the fire and dressed herself as best she could in one of the lovely gowns that had been made for her while she was yet in London. She wrapped herself in a blanket and rushed across the hall to the lady's room to perhaps waken her. She found her up and dressed, however, the housemaid having cared for her needs with the lady's maid gone.

"Good morning, Emma. So, you are awake after that long ordeal. I thought you might sleep all day. Did you sleep well?"

"Milady," she said and curtsied, "in that huge bed? The lot of us could have slept as comfortably there as do angels in the clouds."

"I am sure your trip tired you enough to render you unconscious, with or without the lot of them. Breakfast is served, and I am ravenous. Let us go down and eat."

Emma unwrapped herself and exposed her unfastened clothes. "How am I to do up my corset, ma'am? I cannot go down this way."

The countess laughed and turned Emma around. "I shall enjoy pulling this thing about you, as I recall your having done once to me. Mmm." She laughed and pulled on the cords. She tied them and patted Emma's dress into place. Emma feigned inability to breathe, grasping her throat as they walked out the door.

Woolen paths led the chatting women to the breakfast room. The day's first meal had long been served in this eastern chamber lined with large mirrors to brighten the winter mornings. Winnie's Shropshire Spaniel joined her as ever to lie at her feet.

Emma poured her tea at the sideboard and watched it spin into her cup as she reflected in awe on the changes of her life. Raised in the village, she had arrived at the castle to serve as a housemaid eight years before. Winnie had taken a liking to her and chose her as companion for the many years of widowhood ahead. A squire's wife, Mrs. Carrington, had raised her with genteel ways, and Winnie had sent her to London for further instruction.

"We must let the kitchen know of your preference for breakfast and tea," Winnie said.

"I did create an unforgivable stir in that kitchen over foods in the past, ma'am. I'm convinced the cook cannot forget."

"They did not give you just dry bits of bread and water, according to my orders?" Winnie pretended to be surprised.

Emma laughed. "No, ma'am, they do not take orders downstairs, I'm sorry to say. But I am sure cook will never ever fuss over the likes of me."

"She shall do her best to change her view of you, Miss Emma, and do her best to please. You are to be treated as a lady."

"I feel they may find it disagreeable, my elevating myself, though they do know it is according to your wish. I am privileged to be made so comfortable, ma'am. I do not know how I shall repay you for making a lady of me." Her face betrayed both pleasure and discomfort as she ran her hands down her sides to display her exquisite, well-fitted dress. "I am, you know, quite above my place."

"You shall keep me engaged and relieve the loneliness I have felt while you were in London and

Wills has been gone. I hope to never feel so forsaken again for the rest of my life. And Emma, Elizabeth will return later today and bring her sister to become your lady's maid. The girl has finished her seamstress' apprenticeship with her mama. She will be a novice of a lady's maid."

"Milady," Emma said, her eyes widening, and she asked, "How could I have a maid? I do not deserve a lady's maid, ma'am. Even noble ladies do not have such until they marry."

"Are you saying I should sit and wait alone every morning while you struggle with your hair and then do up your corset as I did today, young lady?" She leaned toward Emma and nearly whispered, "I know it is not done. I do not always do what is done. Shhh."

Emma struggled to overcome the disparity. She admitted she loved the pampering. Clasping her hands to her chest, she paused to absorb the thought. She savored a sip of tea and asked, "Which sister of hers is it, ma'am? Do you know her name?"

"Of course I do. It is Anne. Barreby has checked everything about her. She has an excellent reputation. And....so that you understand, you are to treat the servants as if you were never one of them."

"Oh, ma'am, they will think I am affected."

"Well, then, they will be correct. You are to be a lady."

"Yes, ma'am." Emma shifted in her seat.

"Allow me to see your confidence. Did Miss Wathem teach you nothing?" Lady Holmeshire straightened and set the example. "You must sit properly, despite me." She nodded her head sharply.

"Yes, ma'am," Emma conceded, and she straightened up her shoulders against her velvet chair.

Winifred, Lady Holmeshire, had come from one of

the oldest and most powerful families in Britain. Growing up in grand Streybourne Manor near Wales, the daughter of a duke, perfection had been required. Her parents, now living in London, had spared no expense. There were music masters, literary teachers and riding lessons. There were painting, languages, refinement and of course her governess, Miss Wathem, to bring it all together. And what a success—with her natural elegance and good will, she had come to be the belle of all balls and the most sought-after hand in the country.

After accepting countless invitations and meeting young noblemen and even royals from far and wide, she had accepted a proposal from the 6th Earl of Holmeshire, by name, Tristan Bradley. She had married for love and brought a good deal of money to Holmeshire Hall, a castle older and smaller than her childhood home. Among the happiest couples in British society, their first and only child was Wilfred. Wills was sixteen when his good father died and he became the 7th Earl.

As mistress of the house, widowed at thirty-six years of age, the countess had managed well on her own to all appearances when her son went to Eton. Alone, she had entertained and visited out. She had painted and ridden and written beautiful letters.

At last she was to have a companion. This perfection and grandeur were to be pushed into and rubbed off onto this housemaid, the lovely Emma. Miss Wathem took her in and taught and trained and dressed and styled her.

"Can I bring you some eggs?" Winnie asked, as she maintained perfect posture while ignoring protocol.

"I think just this scone and tea today, ma'am. My jostled stomach is not ready to tolerate more." Emma looked up and peered out the small window where the scenery caught her eye for beauty. "We should send this countryside off to some artist for painting."

"Yes, it should indeed be painted," Winnie said. "But I fear it would not travel well. It would not fit into even the monstrous crates we have stacked in the north wing. Wills has sent an entire wing full of wooden boxes. He has asked me to be patient and not to open them and decorate before his reconstruction of this dilapidated castle."

"How extensively will he rebuild?"

"He will not tear down walls, that I know. He is to simply make them strong and, I do hope, beautiful again."

"Do you know what it is that he has sent?"

"No. His letters did not reveal much of it. It has all arrived from Rome, so quite surely we will be doing something classical."

"Roman, like Miss Wathem's house—I love it. The swirling marble and beautiful art—I shall simply adore it." Anything Wills might do would please Emma. Handsome and responsible, he had caught her eye as a child, but she had kept her distance as it was, of course, impossible.

"Dear Miss Wathem. How happy I was when her fortune came in," Winnie said. "Such a lady she is. And I cannot wait to show you the new home of Her Grace, my sister Helena." Winnie spoke with admiration of a mansion in Belgrave Square, London. "She has darker colors indoors than I, but that is less bothersome when you have large windows. There are some few walls here that I could safely knock down to add windows. Our home is built to withstand a siege."

"Though, of course, you have never endangered your life making enemies," laughed Emma. "This fortress is secure, notwithstanding that the battles of Scotland, at the nethermost regions of the hill, might arise from their sleep in history. Then, with no lord of the castle present, we should undertake to slay the lot of them ourselves."

Winnie chuckled. "You see why I have dressed you to sit upstairs, my dear girl? You amuse me so. But I shall have enemies quite soon, and not just those opposed to my bringing you along to tea."

"I do dread that, ma'am. I wish you would repent of the intention, though you make it clear that you do not intend to spare me." Emma sighed, perplexed at the countess' determination on the matter. "But we have discussed that aplenty. As for the matter of décor, your many mirrors do bounce light from the small windows about the house. You are brilliant. It surely does help. You have magnificent fireplaces, as well, to brighten things here."

"They do not do enough to alleviate the horrid cold of the north in this stone fortress. Sometimes I wish we had a cozy little home as they do in the village where the fireplace could warm the whole room. Should it not be for this multitude of petticoats, we would both freeze." Winnie shivered the more for thinking of it.

"Those homes are small enough to heat despite the drafts, ma'am, only should there be wood or coal enough. Some of them must save it to cook their evening meal, and even for that, at times, there is no wood." Could her empathy, in some way, help?

"I confess to not knowing enough of the people's needs in the village. I recall that Mrs. Carrington took you on her visits to the poor while you were growing up. Did you find many people greatly in want?"

"Some, yes, ma'am. Winters are difficult in Holmeshire, especially during these last years, as I have heard when in town."

"You should tell me more of it, Emma. It is time I use my influence to invite some restraint into society and to persuade gentlemen and ladies to take more action on behalf of their fellow man. I believe Wills intends to take the matter up when he is seated in Parliament. Thus we shall have new enemies, as I said." Winnie's sweetness became firm determination, and she formed her hands into a steeple.

"It would be the kindest thing, ma'am, if the people could keep warm and be provided with a bit more meat and bread. They are employed in Holmeshire Village during the summer, better than many in London, I dare say, but they must save as the cost of food is so high. In the winter, some do not have enough. They must look out for each other."

"Those without enough look out for each other. And their betters do not notice their want for all the dinners we attend. It is time that should change. That, then, is my intention—they will have better means to provide for themselves. We must create more work that they may have more food and coal in the winter. I must talk to his young lordship, should he ever return from his travels."

Barreby stepped in to inform the women that Elizabeth and Anne had climbed the hill and entered the house. "Shall I send them up for you to meet Anne, ma'am?"

"Let us move first to the sitting room," Winnie replied. "We will be ready in fifteen minutes. Have Elizabeth show Anne the arrangement of their quarters for now." She turned to Emma. "They shall spend their lives together here. Is it not nice when sisters can be together?"

***

In London, Lady Genevieve, the twenty-year-old daughter of the Marquess of Breyton, long promised to the Earl of Holmeshire, stepped from a carriage after her mother into a spacious park filled with towering trees. Her parasol up to divert a light rain, she strolled recounting their diary of upcoming dinners and leisurely teas. The ladies waved to friends on horseback, promising to join them soon for a ride on their estate. Genny's mother questioned her on the names of plants and expressed delight at her daughter's recall.

"Indeed, Mama, did you think I failed to listen?" Genny objected. "I shall have you know that I am most serious about my education and shall make Lord Holmeshire an excellent wife."

"I do hope these lessons will assist you in cultivating that hill, darling. Someone must bring it under control."

"I altogether agree, Mama. It must be improved. I wish his lordship had a finer home for me to administer. A fortress indeed—how did I come to be so fortunate? At least our children shall be safe if some ogre rises from the moors. Remind me, please, to post a lookout in each tower."

"Her Ladyship, The Countess of Holmeshire is a woman to admire. I surely would not have taken the place on. But I'm sorry, darling. I do not mean to discourage you."

"Never mind, Mother, I am determined to live in London. Papa will give me Chenbury, and I shall refuse to live in the moors."

"And in that case, my dear, I shall come to visit."

Watching a man release pigeons into the air sobered the marchioness. She recalled a fearsome incident they had experienced during a respite to beautiful Bath. Feeding birds in the resort town, they had noticed a man watching Genevieve for the second time in a day. Lady Breyton again expressed fright. "We must be cautious, Genny, as we do not understand the purpose of the man who was observing our actions in Bath."

"Mama, there was a different man watching us Monday, when I went out with Auntie."

"Monday this week? Then it must be you they are watching, and not me."

"Yes, but he was ever so different. This man was thin. He was also a gentleman, quite well dressed like the first man."

"He was thin, Genny? It surely was a different man. I can't imagine why there should be two men watching you, and I am utterly terrified."

Genevieve looked about through the manicured wintery scene and turned back to her mother. "Hush, Mama, I saw him again. Just this very moment—he rode past, staring at us. Let us go, Mama, do hurry."

"Um, where, dear, which coach?" Her mother took a step back and rubbed the back of her neck.

Genny froze and dared not point. "Let us go, please Mama, and let us go now." Her pleading ended abruptly, for whether Lady Breyton believed her daughter or not, Genny had determined they must leave. She took her mother by the hand and pulled her along, dropping her parasol to wave for the coachman. The girl's conviction persuaded her mother, and she, too, took up her skirts to rush over the lawn and through lush flowering bushes.

In the carriage traveling homeward, the women exchanged anxious thoughts. "This is so incomprehensible, Mama. Why would they be following us?"

"I do not know, Genny. We must talk to Papa today. There shall be no more delay if you are certain. You must be accompanied by our biggest men. Do not leave the house without them. This is most distressing."

***

On the other side of London a young earl walked over a plank and the swirling waters below to exit a ship from afar. Adjusting his balance to the solid land under his feet, he saw an approaching acquaintance, his solicitor.

"Mr. Wentby," he said, looking at the ground and lifting his feet up and down. "How good that you have come to meet me as I set foot on English soil again. I say, though, this English ground does not behave. I had no trouble with Italian soil as I boarded the ship. What could be wrong here? I say," he said, looking at the man. "What spy has sent you?"

"My Lord Holmeshire. I meet you by coincidence. I am here to fetch my mother-in-law."

"Ah, do have a pleasant visit with the dear lady, then, sir. I am home at long last after my travels on the Continent. Pray do not notify my mother, as I wish to see her delight when I burst into the house, and I must spend time in London before I return."

"I shall leave the surprise to you, then, sir. Tell me, please, have you decided when you will approach Chancery on the matter of the little boy?"

"That matter attempts to assail my peace of mind, sir, but I brush it aside. Nicholas will be best cared for in my home, and I do not wish to complicate the matter. Any opposition could but prove detrimental to the welfare and happiness of the lad."

"I shall leave that to you also, then, sir. I can only advise and hope you do not encounter a disaster that I

20

must untangle."

"And I thank you for your daring to do business with me, Wentby. They tell me I am a bit of difficulty. My mother rolls her eyes when I approach, though surely her governess once forbade such a look upon her face."

"Forgive my opinion, sir, but I am certain the poor woman cannot prevent reactions that come from deep within. Having had your acquaintance, myself, I...."

"A woman stands behind you, sir, preferring not to interrupt as I have done to escape the expected flattery. Could this be the lady you are here to greet? You must introduce me."

"Ah, it is, sir."

Wills nodded a friendly hello.

***

Winnie sat as near as possible to the fire on the slate hearth seat. "I suppose the maids will not mind where I sit. Do you? You have arrived with your head filled with Miss Wathem's corrections. Helena would love to misbehave and sit here with me. I absolutely must warm myself." She pulled her cording-trimmed gown further from the blazing fire. "Elizabeth tells me that Anne works wonders with hair—yours will be most elegant."

"You are known for your style, ma'am. The maids will be a good pair." Emma, by now, felt quite at home.

The door opened, and Barreby announced with great pride, "I have locked up the breakfast tea service and silverware. Elizabeth and Anne, ma'am."

The girls stepped in with Elizabeth in the lead. The elder Lizzy had cared for and taught her siblings with a firm hand. The ever meek Anne had learned early in life to do as her sister said, "so Mama could sew," and was now to spend her life in service under her commander's direction. She followed Lizzy in, hiding as long as she could. She curtsied, barely glancing up afterward, for which she was immediately chastened. Her hesitation exposed her newness to such a frightful position.

Emma was impressed by Winnie's renowned patience. The first correction was for her obsessive butler. "Remember not to report on the silver when you announce persons, Barreby, no matter who they are. You may go." His deep sigh indicated how difficult it would be to comply, for his thoughts, day and night, centered on protecting the house and its treasures.

"Elizabeth," Winnie said in welcome. "Bring your sister here. Do not be shy now, Anne," she said as she peered around Lizzy, "there will not be time for that."

"I'm sorry, milady." Anne stumbled over herself, entirely without confidence.

"'Milady' at the first meeting of the day," Winnie told her. "And then it is ma'am for the remainder of the day. This is my companion, Emma. She is to be waited on now, Elizabeth, especially by Anne, and addressed by you both as ma'am."

Anne curtsied again, and Emma blushed but knew better than to decline.

"Acquaint yourself with Emma's needs and preferences as soon as possible, Anne. Make sure her room is warmed in the winter at the right times of day. The housemaids should know how to manage, but do make sure of it. You will need to develop an air of confidence, as you will be over them in matters relating to Emma's room and personal effects. Do you see where the excellent education from your hardworking Mama has placed you? Be certain to listen carefully to directions from the housekeeper and learn well from your sister. The two of you will be able to enjoy the comforts of your quarters, send money home to your parents and save a bit. I am sure you will be very happy here. You see, I instruct your superiors to be compassionate."

"Thank you, ma'am," Anne said and curtsied.

Elizabeth nudged her sister, frowned and whispered in a severe tone, "Too many curtsies, and do not fidget." Anne's eyes opened widely, and she held her breath.

"Provided you earn your keep," Winnie continued.

"I will, ma'am!" she exhaled.

"Emma, do you have questions for either of the girls?"

"Yes. Anne, it is good to see you so fully blossomed," Emma said, proud of little Anne, "and how is your family?"

"Oh, thank you, ma'am. We are happy to be well, all of us, and so grateful that both Elizabeth and I are in service and can help our parents. Mama stitches on her dresses late into the night, you know, if she has candles, and Papa wishes to pay for an apprenticeship for little Fredrick someday. The younger girls are learning stitchery and doing hems for Mama. I'm grateful to be here." She could speak when required, as long as the listener was familiar and friendly.

"Yes, we all have things to thank God for, myself I am sure more than most," Emma replied. "It is good to hear of your family's well-being. I do hope that Freddy shall have his apprenticeship. It is admirable and commendable that you will help with that."

"Thank you indeed, ma'am."

"Be off then," Winnie ordered. "Elizabeth, do teach Anne privately. It will spare her embarrassment. And Anne, be ready for Emma this evening."

"Aye...yes, ma'am." Anne watched her sister and

followed her manner a bit too carefully until they were out of sight. Winnie chuckled, and Emma covered her mouth to hide her amusement.

"She will grow into this with me, ma'am, perhaps faster than I."

"You will both do very well. Now, let's hear you on the pianoforte."

They whiled away their morning, Emma grateful to be settling in. Comfortable with her mistress, she displayed some of the artistic improvements that Miss Wathem had made. They talked about the former days, before her stay in London, when Winnie had asked Emma to take breaks from her housekeeping to sit and converse. Of all the servants, Emma knew that only she had dined with her ladyship. At lunch they considered further tutoring, to begin in September, and discussed thoughts about how her world would change in so many ways.

Days drifted by as Emma learned to be waited on and fussed over by her former fellows. She tried to be over Anne, showing her where to place things, how to part her hair, where to lay out her clothes, but Emma curtsied on one occasion when Anne was about to depart. Anne fled from the room aghast, not knowing quite what to do, and Emma called her back to try again. "We are both just learning, aren't we?" she giggled.

One evening she kissed the pantry maid on the cheek when surprised with her beloved jam and scones. "We just could not eat one without you, Emma...ma'am..." the girl said, "and so I sneaked up the stairs." Nothing could go too amiss, Emma thought, for though Winnie ran a good house she often did so with a wink and a look away. Happily, the housekeeper knew when to frown, and when there were guests in the house, no excuse could be made for trouble or neglect in the least.

~Chapter 2~

A Pleasant Reception By the Lord Himself

Every afternoon at two o'clock, Nicky was brought down the stairs to visit the two adoring women. The bouncy little gentleman had been brought home along with a nanny and installed in the nursery by Lord Holmeshire when he once returned from his travels. The dear boy could not be raised by his father, Wills told people, and Wills had sworn to raise the child as his own.

Nicholas had now been at the castle for well over half of his two years of life and had no recollection of any other home. Peals of laughter rang through the halls, manifesting his happiness. He was amply hugged and kissed by the Holmeshires, and now by Emma. Aristocratic constraint was, to some degree, happily lacking in this home.

Emma would peek in on Nanny Gwyndolyn Bowen and little Nicholas on the sly. She thought Nanny Bowen to be quite stern and would steal a treat away to Nicky from the tea table, once handing something off as the three passed in the hall. Nicky nearly gave the misdeed away with a laugh.

Days and activities passed happily for the ladies. Messages went out to other lords and ladies. Replies came in and arrangements were made. From time to time someone paid a call, or Winnie and perhaps Emma went out to visit. Dismal winter dragged on, but this afternoon was different.

"How can it be so lovely in February?" Winnie said, looking toward the windows. "What shall we do with the warmth and sunshine? It is such a treat. We could take Nicholas out to play. Shall we?"

"That would be nice. The ground will be muddy, but we can stay on the tiles. I'll send for him and have a few toys brought down." Emma rang the bell. A footman arrived, and the message was delivered. They sent for wraps and waited by the western door. Finally the little one appeared, his excitement barely contained.

Nanny admonished, "Now, Nicholas, slow yourself down before you take a fall." She pulled a cap over his crop of hair.

Winnie added, "We are eager to go outside too, young man, but we do wish to keep our noses in place on the front of our faces." Her anxious and hopeful dog ignored the thought and knocked the boy down trying to join in the outing.

Properly bundled, Nick peered out between hat and scarf. He would surely retain his health. He rose to his feet, clapped his hands and jumped a bit. He pulled the women toward the door. "It sunny, lady, so we goes outside."

The door was opened by Barreby. The ladies and Nicky stepped into the welcoming sunlight onto a terrace enclosed by meter-high stone walls. Wisteria hugged the walls from below and drooped inward over the tops. Emma and Nicky played nursery games. He ran about, throwing his Australian boomerang, laughing heartily and delighting Emma. They scurried down the stairs and set up targets to shoot from childish bows. The dog retrieved stray arrows, having failed at her arduous searching far and wide for a bird to carry in. Nicholas ran and played with the dog while Emma, bent over with laughter, cheered them on.

Time passed, Winnie watching from a bench until they all began to tire.

"Look dere," Nicky cried, pointing a little hand toward the road, "Who dere coming?" A carriage, drawn by two trotting black horses, had created a swirling cloud of dust.

"Oh my," cried Winnie, taken aback. "Could it be Wills?" She came to life and rushed past the mossy stone walls down to the walk leading to the front of the house. She stopped at the edge of the grass to wave, and burst into a petticoat-hampered run—forgetting to set an example. Emma and Nicky followed her around the building toward the courtyard where the fatigued horses had slowed to a halt. Wilfred stepped out of the coach onto the cobblestone passage and waved both hands with his irrepressible smile.

Wills, always well-mannered if a tease, was a whirlwind of goodness, class and changeable moods. He was generous, impetuous and brilliant. "Look at you, Mama," he shouted, "I knew you would be outside waiting for me in the cold. I forgot to inform you that I was back in the country, did I not, but you would have been all blubbery about that. And there's my favorite bit of a chap, grown so very much. And look, Emma has at last returned. What a fine day." He had a huge smile for the former maid.

Servants had assembled on the sheltered front stairs to welcome their master home, and the women at last reached the approach. Winifred could not contain herself after ten months apart from her son, and whirled around on the courtyard, holding his hands.

Little Nick did not remember his benefactor but knew this was a special occasion, and he bowed at Emma's direction like a very big man. Emma told the lad, "This is his lordship, Nick, and you will be like a son to him. He is caring for you, and you must obey him. He is Wilfred Bradley, Earl of Holmeshire, and you have been named Nicholas Bradley. You may call him sir."

"Sir," shouted the tot, and he ran around to hide behind Emma's skirts, but was pulled out to stand at attention. Wills returned a snap to soldierly stance.

"And there you all are," Wills said, turning with cheer to his household, "I am sure that I missed every one of you. I have brought some miserable little gift for all. And it is a good job I brought extra crushed baubles, as I see a few new faces."

He stretched back in discomfort with his hands on his hips. "I shall be so grateful when the railways come this way. One can stand up as you roll along the countryside on the trains—they roll so smoothly. Can you imagine? I have been on a few, you know."

The family entered the house, Emma leading Nicky by the hand and turning him over to his tigress of a nanny, who pulled him back outside to dust him off. Footmen with heavy wooden trunks came through the door from the carriage and struggled their way up the stairs. "Did you happily receive my crates from Italy, Mum?" Wills asked. "I sent thirty-two to be exact."

"I am afraid we did, Wills. It was happy work hauling them all up this hill, and we hid them in the back wing so the menservants could forget what we put them through. Now, what do you require before you can sit down and tell us about your travels?" Would Winnie ever let go of his arm again, he wondered?

"Mother, I wrote you every detail of everything I did. You have had two or three particular letters a week until I was in London, and then I had much to accomplish. I can elaborate, but I am most eager to show you the things I sent home. I presume you were civilized and did not rip the crates open? Now, will you have time for that after I have some rest and fill my stomach?"

Wills turned to the waiting butler. "I'll want one…no, two of Cook's roast lambs on my plate today. Tell her she must change the menu for me. I suppose I should have written ahead. But I wanted to make sure everyone pined away and waited for my return to throw matters into confusion."

Barreby kept his countenance as serious as he could sustain. "Cook knows she must make double the amount when you are home, milord."

"Barreby, have dinner served as early as possible," Winnie interjected, rolling her eyes. "Whatever is already being prepared. We shall sit there in the bit of remaining sunshine and have tea immediately." She threw a chastening glance at her son. "Wills, I surely had planned nothing today but to watch you tear through your crates. But first we will hear of your journey. Now, do prepare yourself for tea and meet us there."

The women went to the vast, curved and cushioned seat under the window of the sitting room. Emma loved the pleasing mix of French provincial scenic prints and the prevailing fourteenth century stone of the architecture. A round table was brought to the area.

A footman carrying tea service and delicacies on a tray above his head entered and presented his offering to the ladies. He rushed about adjusting the room to suit Wills' preference. The servants loved and respected their master.

Emma asserted, after Winnie's request, that she did not wish to play the pianoforte this day. "Oh no, ma'am, I could not possibly with his lordship here." She blushed at the suggestion, but when reminded that her position was changed she promised to attempt to overcome her modesty soon. She felt conspicuous for being at tea when Wills came and sat down. Charmed by his presence, she felt lowly and did her best to be invisible. She received immediate attention.

"Emma." Startled, she looked up.

"Yes, milord?"

"You are back. It seemed so long." He poured water and drank the glass straight down. Winnie poured him a burgundy to savor while they talked.

"It was a long time, sir. But it had to be. My person was to be adjusted entirely. I had to learn arts and languages, you see, and something tolerable of elegance. It was a bit of overwhelming commitment for a scrub maid."

"And how did you put up with old Miss Wathem for so long? She must have fussed about polishing you to a bright shine. I am sure you could not have even lifted your hand correctly and had to be trained in it. And did she teach you which words to choose in order to keep your little mouth looking pretty? A lady ought not pronounce the wrong words and have her cheeks puff out, can she? And I hope you know you cannot blow out a candle and must use a snuffer?" He blew into the air, puffing up excessively, but soon returned his attention to her.

"Oh...so many things I could not improve on. I am a poorly chiseled bust, and nothing can be done to make it right."

"Then we must hide our laughter. Or should we laugh aloud and correct you?"

"Correct me, please, sir, here at home, or I will be made a fool in company. And they shan't forgive it as you do."

"You are right. They surely will not. I shall not enjoy Mama's exposing you to the fangs of society. It does indeed have fangs, you know. Only this house is exempt, and I believe you should not be dragged out of it. Mother, apparently, cannot fathom going into society without you anymore, and so I suppose you will attend her."

"I will learn to face the lions. And I am thankful for your generosity. I nearly dwell in heaven here."

"And when will you call me Wills? Should she call me Wills, Mama?"

"Your lordship…I could not."

"Perhaps later. I shall insist someday. Mama, tell me about yourself now."

"Myself. Well, dear Wills. I was abandoned, you know, these ten months since you left until Emma returned." Winnie tapped her fingers on her saucer. "Let me think. I went to London and made an accounting of things, of Emma and Miss Wathem, of family there and such."

"And you went to glut yourself at dinners and spend my fortune, I am sure. I do hope you bought me something quite entertaining. And you were seen at the palace, I know."

"Yes," she said with a big smile. "I was invited when the queen learned I was visiting Helena and His Grace. It was a surprise, you know, to be asked to visit Her Majesty at short notice. Actually, it was a great surprise to be invited or thought of at all."

"Because of not knowing her well, I am sure, Mama. Everyone is charmed that she wishes to acquaint herself with the nobility now." His eyes widened at the sight of some chocolate, and he reached for a cup. "A shame it is, the way she was kept from people nearly until she was queen."

Down went the chocolate, and there was a pause for savoring it with proper manners before he continued. "Emma, you remember we went to the coronation and afterward the ball. I danced with Her Majesty, and you know, she played at liking Albert better. Strange it was, as he did not attend, and I was all charm and presence. Mama didn't talk to her much, did you, Mama? But we shall go to town before Parliament opens. I hope to be invited to the palace to visit Her Majesty myself. I must be proclaimed her favorite lord before I am seated in the House. And I am eager to see how she feels about our grand intentions."

Wills looked several times at the spread of food, but had not yet finished talking. He turned to Emma and said, "Kings invite us to visit because the crown owes us much, you know. Or at least His Majesty, King William, said they do. I take his word for it. It was all before my time. It is quite likely in the endless volumes of history books, should you care to check."

Winnie interjected, "It is indeed, Emma. My father was a hero of the Napoleonic Wars. He did wonderful things, though he claims to have been having a bowl of beans at the time. That is his humor for you. Lord Breyton was honored as well. Breyton saved one of the regent's dear friends from sure death. There was no end to the displays of appreciation for it as long as he reigned. Helena and I attended endless parties where Papa and Breyton received honors. They were, in time, bestowed titles for their trouble and regal properties after the regent became king. His Majesty was quite improvident."

Wills nodded and picked up the story. "When Caroline of Brunswick was alive my Mama was barely tolerated by the prince despite the honors heaped upon my grandfather. He hated his wife, you see, and lived apart from her. Mama and Aunt Helena were friends of their daughter, Princess Charlotte of Wales, and on rare occasion accompanied her to visit her mother. The regent was in quite a rage about it. The daughters of the Duke of Streybourne at the home of the hated Caroline of Brunswick, can you imagine? We were quite surprised when his disdain for Mama and Aunt Helena faded—enough so, in fact, that he allowed the Duke of Trent to marry Helena. You shall meet him soon if you have not already. Have you?"

"No, my lord."

"Well, all that to do with George IV is done, and Her Majesty has begun her reign. What a change it has been. The throne went from one old man to another for decades, and now it has gone to a young woman. I have applied to marry her, you know, but it is not likely to be, as she has her eyes elsewhere," he joked. "Had she met me sooner, she would have forgotten Albert, and I would be king, would I not?"

Winnie looked to heaven, rolled her eyes and agreed. "Perhaps we will see her in London, and Albert will be told to remain in Saxe-Coburg-Saalfeld, but remember that you are engaged to be married. Your pretensions are for naught. Your future with Lady Genevieve is tied up and concluded, and you must comply. I apologize for it, but we were quite unaware that a queen would become available. Being nephew-in-law of a duke may not have qualified you for the position, in any event." She became serious and sat forward. "Have you begun to pay calls on your fiancé, Wills?" She leaned forward. "She has been waiting since age four and is beginning to feel like an old maid." She emphasized the number of years. "It has been a seventeen-year wait for her thus far."

"Yes, well her mother ought not to have told her so young, Mama. It puts a girl into a romantic state of delirium. I hear she played with dolls—me and her." Wills shook his head, crossed his arms and slumped back in his chair.

"We told you at a young age also, you know."

He shook his head. "And I threw a muddy stone at the apple tree for it. Boys are proper."

"I hope your mood has changed a bit?"

"Well, she is beautiful. I cannot help but see that. But as I said—romantic delirium." He leaned forward, picked up an imaginary rock and threw it at a gold-framed mirror, which relieved the problem temporarily.

"And how does that display itself?"

"At the balls, Mama—she watches me." He pulled at the high collar of his shirt, and flicked his gaze upward. "She once dropped her handkerchief in my line of sight. I was under obligation to retrieve it which of course led to a useless conversation regarding the rain." He shook his head. "Why should a gentleman have to pick up a handkerchief unaware of its condition? And her friends eye me with suspicion. At Canbury Lodge my rifle went missing, and I found her friends had propped it next to her chair. " A wretched look crossed his face. "I was forced to claim it, and do you think I could get myself out the door? They surrounded me while the hunting party got on their horses, and this time we discussed the beloved sun. She may have been quoting Shakespeare—do not ask me, but she does that. I wanted to get to my horse. This marriage...I can wait until I feel ready, can I not? I want to do some things, to not be...tied down with things. At least not her sort of things." Wills glanced at poor, concerned Emma and then looked back, listening to his Mama.

"Genevieve may fear that you do not care for her. Consider how that could affect your happiness together when married. You must prepare now to have a happy home."

"I wish one could marry whomever one liked best, you know. Like timid little housemaids turned companion and dressed up. One might hurry a bit faster. If only I could ask Papa for a change in the arrangement." He smiled and winked at the chagrined Emma.

"Wilfred, behave," Winnie sighed. "You will embarrass poor Emma. It was not your father's doing, you should know. It was entirely between the king and his favorites, your grandfather and Lord Breyton. Your father and I truly did not wish it. But it is quite a tangled matter with inheritances, entitlements and politics. You or she could undo that by refusing to marry, I suppose, but many things are involved—many important contracts. Breyton has no son, so he is all the more determined to have grandsons by you and Genevieve who will receive all Prinny meant for him— your inheritances and his. When the title was created, it was made to be passed through Breyton's daughter as it was clear he would never have a son. There is no one to take Breyton's title unless Genny has sons, and he at one time saw himself as the first of a long line. He tried to pass a law that the title of marquess be passed down perpetually. It would secure his name in the history books."

"Yes, that is the intent. Lord Breyton must go down

in history. He must be the first of many Marquesses of Breyton. What better stud for the purpose than the grandson of another great hero of Waterloo?"

"I am sure you can make yourself and Genny perfectly happy. It is a matter of developing the determination. Both of you must, you simply must. When you visit her more often you may come to love her. You must look for her pleasing qualities. I visit there, and she is a truly lovely girl. She is gentle, has a wonderful singing voice and is well educated."

"All that she ought to be. I am sure we will find much to bring us together. Some things, by degrees, you know. But for now—"

"The Season in London begins soon. You will be seated in Parliament this year. Emma and I are to visit Handerton within the week of arriving, and you have been invited to join us."

"Oh, Emma was invited." A great smile appeared and Wills' tone lightened measurably.

"At my request."

His dutiful spirit returned, and with it, thoughts of consideration for Genevieve. "Of course. Of course I will join you. But I must return to Holmeshire for a week during Parliament's sessions. I am eager to start on this monstrous castle, Mama. I have such plans. The fellow is coming in a month and—"

"And Genevieve should be here for it."

"Mama." Wills' head dropped.

"She is to be mistress of Holmeshire Hall and should have her say. She will entertain here and raise children. She may wish to make changes in the antediluvian servants' quarters, you know. Since you are making major improvements and not simply decorating, it should be done together, should it not?"

"So I may not have my castle my way, then, you

are saying."

"It certainly seems it will all be Roman, will it not? Married life, though, requires compromises. You must adjust to that. It is not according to the law of Britain, but it is to the law of happiness. She will give you heirs to care for your holdings and preserve the family name. You are the last male in the family, you know—both our family and Breyton's. Someone must inherit everything from the two of you. It is as though no one in your father's family, mine, or Breyton's can bear any boys but you. You are everyone's son. And I had no spare." She sighed, but thought better of reminding him further of the weightiness of his position. "You will be surprised at how much joy and pride you will have from your little ones."

"I am sure I will, Mama." There was some hesitation as he considered his direction. "I will go with the two of you to Handerton. And I think we should bring Nicholas. Genevieve must know of him. Besides that, he should not spend his entire life in the nursery, should he? Not at all. He is full of energy. I've been a boy, and so I know better than you. Old and wise does not win in every case. He must see the world."

"He is young, Wills. He will see the world when he grows a bit. Handerton is not much for a child to see, anyway. There are no children there. What would he do?"

"Gwyndolyn can see to that. That is what nannies are for. Genevieve needs to know I have this child, does she not? Do I have no say at all in my life? Of what use is it to be an earl?" Wills cocked at his mother and gave her a stern look. "Don't forget I am an earl. I must make use of the power it bestows upon me and drag my child about where I wish."

"Of course you may decide the matter, darling. I

must let you be grown."

"And be an earl, Mama."

"Indeed. We shall inform them that you have accepted their invitation and Nicholas will be coming along. Now, tell us about Italy?"

Barreby opened the door as if to announce a king. Behind him was a cart, piled with items covered with a richly embroidered, black cloth. His expression asked if Wills was ready. He then stood sober.

"Yes, yes, bring it all in, Barreby. Mama, Emma, I have brought gifts for you both." Wills then realized he had forgotten someone. "And Nicky, we should retrieve him, as his gifts are on the cart as well. Barreby, could you send for little Nick?"

"Yes, sir. I will be in with everything when he arrives," Barreby replied. Off the butler went. Within minutes Gwyn brought the child, and Barreby the cart. "Your valuables are safely locked up, sir."

"Fine, thank you. You take such care of things for us. Nicky, come sit here, my boy," he said, pointing to a leather-covered ottoman, "and see what I have brought you aaaall the way from Italy. But you must learn patience, so first we shall see what is on the cart for Miss Emma." Nicky puckered up his chin, but recovered to bounce on his seat while he tried to contain himself. Such a trial it was, enduring admonishment to sit and watch and see what she was to have. Wilfred felt around on the occult mound and looked under one end.

"Ah yes, here we have it." He turned the cart around and rolled it nearer her. "Look here, Ems. Something every lady requires."

"I am not a lady," she admonished, "but I am delighted that you thought to bring me a gift."

"Well, do not tell Mama. She is quite set on you

being a lady, regardless of the details. We must play along." He peeled back the cloth and exposed a block of white marble, skillfully carved with drawers and doors. "It is for your jewelry."

"Oh," she gasped. "It is amazing—exquisite!" She opened a drawer, and then a door. An enameled crane popped out of the space within.

"You can hang necklaces over its neck." Wills was ever so pleased with the artisan bird.

"Oh, my lord, I have never seen anything so beautiful. I will find a use for it, certainly, though I have never had jewelry but for my ring. Thank you."

"Check the case thoroughly," Wills prodded her. She continued to open doors and pull drawers, each with a brass handle, and each with velvet lining in harmonizing colors. Her eyes opened wide when she unlatched a tall door, for hanging within it was a gold chain with a ruby in a leaf-shaped pendant. "My Lord Holmeshire—how beautiful—oh, how very thoughtful of you," she cried, attempting to extinguish feelings for the man as his gift fanned the flames. "A maple leaf with…a ruby, is it not? I have never had even the smallest stone."

"Well, now you do have the smallest stone. Wear it with some of those luscious dresses that Mama has ordered made for you. Wear it to Handerton."

"I will. I surely will. How can I thank you?"

"Most of all, I should care to see you smiling. You are starting a new life with us. Let us all be happy. Do you promise?" She smiled and nodded decided agreement.

"And now, Nick, have you been patient and good?" The wide-eyed boy nodded in the affirmative, but had no intention of moving from the ottoman for fear of losing everything. He did lean as far forward as possible without tipping off, staring at the covering and blinking his enormous eyes. Everyone laughed. Wills felt about under the cloth and, after a pretense of fighting it, pulled out a carved wooden box. "What do you like to play with, lad?"

"Balls?" Nicky tested out. "Or, or, or what?"

"What about books, Nicky? Do you like long, dull law books with no drawings?" A look of disappointment came over his little face. "No? You must learn to like dull books, as you will be sent away to school someday, and I shall expect you to do brilliantly. Well, then, do you like apple peelings? A box full of apple peels?" Nicky recognized the game and stuck out his lower lip. He nearly laughed, but the wait was all too painful. "All right, then, Nicky, how about horses?"

Wills opened the lid to reveal padded sections, each containing a beautiful horse, each in its own stage of canter, gallop or rearing. Nicky's eyebrows went up, and he stared at the intricate figures in shades of marbled brown. "You cannot play with these, of course. They are for your bookcase when you are a great scholar. So—I have also brought another horse for you." He pulled out a hobbyhorse with a bronze-studded leather bridle and a luscious mane. The tot squealed with delight and forgot he was sitting still. He and the horse were off about the room with Emma hustling along behind, admonishing him where necessary to make sure no heirloom was destroyed.

Wills turned to Winnie. "And now, Mama...oh dear, I must have forgotten about you. Here I have for myself a fabulous new embossed leather rifle case. It has my name on it. And look, a set of dominoes like none you have ever seen. Black and white marble with little stones. I do love to look at dominoes sitting on the shelf. But nothing for you."

"Well, then, I shall shop for myself."

"Oh dear, we cannot have London emptied of goods, can we? I shall concede the dominoes. And I think I must check under this cover again." Wills pulled off the fabric with a flourish and exposed a rectangular gilt box, just two inches high, covered with the gold over-laid image of a man.

Upon close examination, Winnie, in awe, found a carving of Wilfred himself. "And now open it, please, Mama," he directed. "But stand it like this first." He pulled it up on end with the statue's feet down. She delayed while she studied every part of the image and the trees behind it. It was dressed sharply, and each of the four corners was decorated with the Family Arms.

"Do I dare to open this box?" Winnie knew what she had long wanted, and so did Wills. In one motion, opening the cover, she flew into a standing position and gasped, "Oh, yes!"

The equestrian and his guard returned from Ascot to see what inside the box had created such rapturous response. And there it was. "I've waited so long, you stubborn boy who would not sit for a portrait."

"I was busy, Mama, and I had the time there. It was planned all along, anyway."

"It takes my breath away, your father standing there beside you. How dear you are." A subtle image of his father was part of the background as though he stood behind and to the side of Wills. "I never realized you took that portrait of him along."

"Why do you think I hung it in such a secluded place, Mama? It was so you would not know when I took it. You would have never allowed that, would you? But I took care of it. I was most severe with the footmen and have returned it in one piece." Wills pushed the cart aside. "Tomorrow we shall look at the boxes in the north wing, Mama, but for today, I have changed my mind. I want to rest."

Winnie sank to her seat, her astonishment stealing her strength. They all sat down. Nicky, thankful not to have a boring book, fed his horse a muffin. Emma had dreamy eyes, thinking of wearing her pale amethyst dress and new necklace at Belgrave Square in London.

~Chapter 3~
Nostalgia and the Slumping Slate Chapel

On the land below Holmeshire Hill to the south was an ancient village. Pasturage and woolen mills lay on the outskirts, inland from the dangerous moors. On each end of town hung rusted iron-framed signs declaring its name, "Holmeshire." Old and new buildings were crowded together along narrow, rutted streets, all of which opened to the cobblestones making up the village square.

Villagers bartered what little they had. Farmers traded crops. Spinners, weavers and fabricators worked the heaps of wool into yarn and goods, but sales in these times were painfully slow, and shops struggled to keep their doors open. The blacksmith had a bit of work, though the inn and stables cared for few travelers. Villagers often sat idle and glum.

No workhouse had been built, however, in Lord Holmeshire's domain. The elderly and destitute were cared for in a suitable almshouse of old. A small school opened for the young to attend once crops were in.

On Sundays, come what may, the bells of the grand

medieval church just outside the village rang the day in and out. People streamed in its direction, and the Holmeshires came down the hill in a shining leather carriage.

"Thank you, ma'am, for allowing me to continue to worship in the chapel," Emma said, leaning close to be heard. "I so love going to the chapel. I've never been comfortable in that huge church." She appreciated the goodness of the countess toward her, which built an unbreakable loyalty and a desire to please. She pulled her gloves over her long fingers as they passed through the imposing gate of the centuries-old stone fence surrounding the castle.

"As you say, dear girl, worship must come from the heart," Winnie replied. Love for the abandoned chapel was a lifelong peculiarity of Emma's. She had been allowed by Squire Carrington at the bidding of his merciful wife to go off alone to the thirteenth century slate sanctuary on the far side of the village. "Perhaps there is a reason why you so love that little place," Winnie said.

Upon arriving at the huge Supplicant's Church with its Gothic spires, Emma left the landau and curtsied her goodbyes. The sky-high towers of the chantry were the source of disquieting legends, and winds passed between them making daunting howls. Emma shuddered. Gravestones filled the garden on every side and caused her concern for her unknown parents.

Emma was eager to leave it behind, and she hurried across a mossy stone bridge over the River Baird. She worked her way against the flow of a receiving line of villagers as they flocked to the eerie scene she had abandoned. They were accustomed to her different ways, and most had stopped coaxing her to join them. She occasionally reminded some a bit firmly that Jesus preached on a hillside. Surely she could pray in a chapel?

The clanging bells joined in with many cheery voices that greeted her along the way. "Emma, come have tea with us soon. Can you? Are you allowed?" "Emma, hello, hello." She smiled as she passed the beloved villagers and old familiar buildings—the stone blacksmith's shop, a dilapidated pottery barn, and the half-timbered bakery with pastries in the window. The bakery would open for one hour after church to sell the week's remaining goods at half price.

Emma peeked into various windows and even tried a door. Memories flooded her mind as she passed the girls' entry to the schoolhouse—how she had stood and giggled there with the neighbor's daughters. She had been teased by a lad when her braid fell down and had picked flowers for the sickly Mrs. Carrington from a planter near the door. She remembered feeding a stray cat fish she had bought for the Carrington family, which had caused her more than a bit of trouble.

"Emma, beautiful child. Look at you," a familiar voice said, bringing her back to the present, and she shook off the memories.

"Hello, Mrs. Amberton," Emma replied. "I have not had the pleasure of seeing you since I returned. It is lovely to see you again, and so delightful to have Anne at the hall with us." Emma covered her ruby with her gloved hand but could not hide her elegant beaded coat.

"Ah, it was hard to give her up, you know. She did hemming for me, and seams. Good she is with stitches, that one. You can be sure of quality work. But the little girls are taking it up to help me now." Mrs. Amberton hid her words behind a rough hand—"They must quickly improve. Do not worry, for I shall make experts of them all. You look a princess, Miss Emma.

Let me take a look at you." She pulled the anxious girl's hand down and smiled with content at the ruby. "Stand still, girl, and I see you've been taught to stand properly, not like us village poor folk, always bent over our work."

Pangs of guilt discomforted Emma. Poor Mrs. Amberton was indeed a bit bent over. "There is hope for my girls, I see," she went on. "Someone may take to them in this way. Perhaps you shall marry, and my Elizabeth will take your place." The matron sighed, "Oh, it could never be. At least my daughters are not stitching on dresses all day and night like their old Mama." She paused, then in horror at her words her eyes widened, and she threw her reddened hands over her mouth. "Oh, sure the Lord Holmeshire has set his eyes on you. Of course he has. You are, after all, a squire's daughter."

"No, ma'am, I am not the squire's daughter. I was only his ward and no daughter. I am certain you must recall. As to marriage, I have promised Lady Holmeshire I will remain her companion, ma'am, and the lord is engaged to a woman of his class."

"Of course, of course he is." Embarrassed, the aging seamstress turned to leave.

Emma reached to comfort her and whispered, "I confess to finding him terribly handsome."

Mrs. Amberton turned back, shifted her feet nervously and appealed, "Emma, I do dearly need more work and better-paying customers. We eat rather poorly, and with the days so short I must buy many candles. Do put in a good word for me upstairs there, Emma. I can fit a bodice like nobody can. Milady could come here, or I could come to her for fittings, that would be proper, and...and you could bring fine fabrics from London, and I could be seamstress to milady.

Course, I do not know the styles in London, but...." Frustrated with hardship, Mrs. Amberton sighed, "Emma, do remember us down here. Please do." A nod, a smile and a thrown kiss were Emma's reply.

More buildings, more familiar trees and the village square had awaited Emma's return. Seeing them ever the same gave her a feeling of stability. At last alone, with the townsfolk gone beyond the bridge, she held her hands out and slowly turned, reliving a dance of a circle of girls on the square. How she loved the memories of camaraderie and the feeling of the breeze through her hair. Most of those girls had never traveled from Holmeshire, and would spend their lives working long days, but she had been to London and returned by the age of two and twenty to live a contented life.

She sat upon a bench and traced the initials she had once seen a boy carve on its arm. She shook her head at him after all these years. She shook it again, closing her eyes to integrate the new realities of her life. A cawing crow reminded her to wake and be on her way, and she looked up defiantly, treasuring times from years past and wonderment over the present.

As she approached the old chapel, cradled in aged oaks at the southern entrance to the town, she sighed, amused at its appearance. Centuries of pushing winds and crumbling of the slate had left the place slumping. She hoped aloud that no one would bump it over upon her, and she laughed.

A ledge outside a receded window held a potted plant—someone had paid tribute to the ancient site. The solid door, which struggled to keep the structure upright, was stressed by the pressure of its incline. It was more difficult to open than in the past, and she did not dare shut it behind her. Her breath caught from the musty air inside.

Light from the doorway was dappled by leaves from the trees outside. The shifting windows were covered. Sunshine peeked in where shutters no longer fit the openings straight. Two familiar benches faced what had been a small altar—now a pile of toppled, decaying lumber. Strange—it had not been taken for fuel.

Emma felt alone with her God there and could take the time to think of the past and of what lay ahead. On this occasion, Emma studied the gray and brown of the ancient slate walls and thought of the times she had sat within them, a mere servant. Was she yet the same girl in this shimmering moiré gown and beaded coat?

Thoughts of good fortune and comfort played in her mind, and she nodded a peaceful smile. But questions crept in. She set her Bible aside and laid her hands on her lap. She lifted one to run a finger across a seam of her glove. She removed the silken fabric and looked wistfully at the simple ring on her finger.

Where did it come from, she wondered, *this thin circle of gold*? Winnie had given it to her before sending her to Miss Wathem's, but had told her it was her own ring, not the lady's. That was it, with no explanation. Could it have been from her mother? Who were her parents? Were they dead or alive? Why did they abandon her? Where had she come from, she wondered. "From the squire's doorstep," was all she'd been told.

The squire's doorstep. She closed her eyes, mystified, fingering the ring, and picturing herself—the infant in the basket with the white cotton blanket that Mrs. Carrington kept for her. She held her breath. The ring...the doorstep...what sense did it make? Someone must know, but who would tell? She'd questioned Winnie, but the countess had turned away and not replied. Emma opened her eyes, and they searched the dusty spaces in the slate thoughtfully.

A chilly wind rushed in. It restored the present, and she remembered her purpose for the morning. She sighed away the mysteries of the past and opened her Bible.

She read softly, "In the mountain of the height of Israel will I plant it; and it shall bring forth boughs, and bear fruit, and be a goodly cedar: and under it shall dwell all fowl of every wing; in the shadow of the branches thereof shall they dwell. And all the trees of the field shall know that I the LORD have brought down the high tree, have exalted the low tree, have dried up the green tree, and have made the dry tree to flourish: I the LORD have spoken and have done it."

She saw in it a comparison to her life. *Dear Ezekiel,* she thought, *were you watching for my rise above my station? I was, to be sure, a most lowly tree, and I have been commended above myself.*

She spent time praying and reading, comparing scriptures to scriptures, searching for understanding. She could not accept that "mystery" was the answer to her lifelong questions. What might God's tidings reveal to her, for why were they written if not to be understood? She read on.

Time whispered upon occasion in case she cared to recall that it was soon to have passed. She finished reading and made notes in her mind, etching in the fruits of her efforts, and then closed her guidebook.

She had often extended her stay beyond the duration of the preaching and praying at the church across town, but in this new life she must return before the stamping horses and impatient carriage would take their leave.

Strengthened, she gathered her things and went out,

51

pulling with her might to shut the door that bore up the chapel. She walked around it, absorbed in its antiquity. A gentle rain had begun, and the wind was whipping it into a mist.

She had an eerie feeling of being watched. Looking around, she saw something move in the shadows, and fear gripped her. A tall ragged man staggered out from the trees toward her, looked intently at her and scowled, but then stood still. He was intoxicated and would have approached her but for having had a sip too many.

Emma was frightened. She turned and wove her way through the village apace, back toward the security of the sound of people's choral voices. She paused across the bridge from the church to look behind her. He had not followed.

A shivering boy, six years old, approached her. "Milady," he said. "Do you need candles?"

"Why are you not at church, little man?"

"I must work, ma'am. I work in the candle shop." She noticed the store whitened and the window glass replaced. The building was surrounded by lovely plants, but this little boy was worn.

"On Sunday morning?" she asked.

"Every day, ma'am. Then I can have supper." He looked up with hopeful eyes.

"Thank you, child. I do not need candles. Take this. This money is just for you." Emma gave the boy a florin and told him to have Mrs. Amberton make him a warm jacket. "Do not tell anyone you have some money, now, just give it to her. Tell her to make the coat big enough for two winters. She will use good thick wool. And you wear the coat. You wear it so you do not catch your death. And go indoors, where you are safe." He smiled broadly, slipped the coin into his pocket and pushed a candle into her hand. Then, unsure of this display of manners, he ran away.

The singing had stopped, and the churchyard would soon be filled with the living. Emma crossed the bridge. As she neared the church, she looked sadly over the old, mossy gravestones in the place where Mrs. Carrington now peacefully slept. Some stones were large and notable. Others were mere nameplates. Some chiseled names were blurred with age, and others were sharp and clear—"Richard James," "Hilda Prichert," "A Young Traveler."

People ambled out of the church, shaking the hand of the priest and chatting about cold breezes and the appearance of daffodils. She had known and loved these people all her life. Elderly Mr. and Mrs. Teak, with him leaning on a stick, came out and smiled. The missus had once made a warm blanket for Emma's childhood bed. Lovely Lydia Jansby, the schoolmistress, waved proudly at her Emma.

The tavern keeper, Mr. Bealle, bowed his head to her. On his arm was the shroud maker, the widow, Mrs. Perry. "Emma, you do have your burial society subscription, do you not?" the widow inquired. "But why would you need that now? The countess will gladly bury you, and no doubt in style."

Following behind her, a hand on her shoulder, was Violet Benton, her sister, maker of mourning wear. "We never miss church, Miss Emma, and you should be here, too, I do say." Business was good should they keep themselves close to the church.

Mr. Seely, his Sunday best giving out, approached Emma. "There was a man looking for you, asking everyone about you. A tall lanky man with a jutting jaw. His clothes had holes—his shoes were no better than mine. Would not give me his name."

Emma was puzzled. That man had indeed meant to approach her. "I saw him myself," she replied. "I do not know who he would be. I cannot imagine." She put her fingertips over her lips and reflected anxiously.

"I told him you do not come here. I did not tell him where you were. I did not like the look of him. Here he was, drunk on a Sunday morn."

"Thank you, sir. I am sure you did the right thing."

Emma was uneasy. Had someone in this trusting village told him where she was? Who was he? What did he want? She dwelt on the matter till the time came to leave. It was not someone she knew, she thought, nor did Mr. Seely know him. He was clearly not from Holmeshire. How strange, for she did not know anyone from afar but for Miss Wathem and a few tutors. She mentioned it to Winnie, expecting to be comforted and admonished not to worry, but Winnie's expression showed startled alarm.

"You must not go to the chapel alone any longer," Winnie insisted, grasping her arm. "You must stay with us."

The footman's presence informed Winifred of the arrival of the carriage. The bishop approached, and she told him that she had concerns to tend to and must decline an invitation. "But do send notice and we will be happy to schedule a visit to your lovely manor," she said.

The family mounted their carriage after the appropriate waving and accepting of homage. The horses lifted their heads, responding to the reins to return the family home. "Take it slowly," Wills yelled to the driver, "I want to see the grounds on the way. I think I may go off to play this afternoon." He raised his eyebrows at the tyke beside him to entice him along.

"Are you hungry, Emma?" Winnie asked, "Cook

will have left some good things for us, and Barreby will be fretting until he can serve it."

Sundays were hard on Barreby. Nothing was being polished. Most were visiting family or whiling the day away. A few would have followers in for a rewarmed supper. Barreby did not trust outsiders, but he had been told to allow friends and family of the servants on Sundays. "How is he taking to orders from you, Emma?"

"He could not be more pleased than to have another order."

"Lovely. That is just as I would have it."

Wills pointed out an ancient oak he had climbed as a youth. Emma recalled furtively, fondly watching him from a distance, and hoped the memory did not show on her face. Affection was as hopeless now as it had been then.

Boulders and primroses and a rainbow took their turns at being the focus of conversation, and the family beamed with adulation as they rounded the final bend. "And lastly, my ladder," Wills pointed out as they passed his forsaken tree house. "Soon, Nick, you will be man enough to climb to Kingdom Come yourself. I named it so as it seemed so very high when I was a boy."

Barreby had fled the church in a two-seated gig at the organ's last chord and, along with a footman, represented the members of the staff at the entrance, stiff and polished, chin in the air. Winnie spoke as she climbed the steps, "Come to me in the sitting room when you can, Barreby."

"All seems well, ma'am," he reported as she passed through the door. She had allowed him to think so for the sake of the morning's observance. However, besides Emma's pursuer there was another matter.

Once everyone was dismantled and their winter wraps gone, he went in to meet her.

"Barreby, do not become upset. I have something you must watch for. My emerald and sapphire bracelet is missing. It disappeared this morning. I cannot imagine what has become of it."

"Ma'am," he said, and he pinned his arms against his stomach. "I am sorry. It will be found quickly and the thief punished." To be sure, the poor man might not sleep till it was found.

"Do be careful, Barreby. I do not care to have anyone accused of taking it unproven. It could be accidental, after all." Her fears hid under a trusting face as they had all morning.

"Ma'am." He knew the truth of it. The jewelry was too well cared for to have but disappeared. Normally under lock and key, it had been set out for Winnie to wear to church. Elizabeth had climbed the stairs a few times. Winnie had meandered about her suite from room to room, leaving the bracelet untended, but it should have remained where it had been placed. When the time had arrived to put it on Winnie's arm, it was gone.

"I trust my staff. Elizabeth is impeccably honest, and she recommended her sister without reservation. The girl was never in any sort of trouble in the town. No housemaid entered the room during that time. And we both know it was not Emma. Why would she take it? Just be aware, and watch for any hint of the bracelet."

He bowed and started to leave the room, distressed. Winnie stopped him. "Nobody is to hear of this, at least not until I give leave." As he left, she looked out the window in despair.

~Chapter 4~

The London Season, A First For Emma

Sounds of London's clattering horses, the noxious smells of sewer and industry, and the yells of a broom boy rose into the shadows of a time-worn room in Bermondsey. Tallow candles flickered by day, their cost having spared generations in the home the expense of the window tax.

But what did the young woman care about the lack of a window? She was out working by day. The darkness of the room hid the tattered condition of stacked blankets and cracks in the washing bowl. She hung her husband's wet trousers across the living space, their one room in a moldering house, while he dealt himself a hand of solitaire under a candle on a scratched and burn-marked table. The cards were bright and new, a gift from his wife.

Up the stairs and into the room strode Benedict Scott, the gaunt, lantern-jawed man seen in Holmeshire, and their few weeks of privacy ended. "They are on their way into town," he reported to his son. "I went to 'er village and asked around about 'er, and it seems as though nobody knows about this. It was a long, expensive trip for nothin'. And now my money's gone. All of it. A waste of time. A waste of money. But if I asked more questions about 'er, they woulda told 'em."

"We'll just 'av ta bide our time, Papa. We can't do anything right now, like I told you from the start." Charles, twenty-five years of age, was always pleased to take things slowly.

"I just 'av ta figure out what we can do. I'm not wantin' to wait on it."

"We 'av plenty of time for it. Sit down and play me." He gathered up his cards and shuffled. "Lucy, get my papa some of that soup."

"I need to know more of the law," the older man grumbled. "I guess I'll 'av to find the money for a solicitor." Lucy quietly scraped her money off a sideboard into her apron pocket, and brought the potato stew.

***

A white, stuccoed, four-terraced home in Belgrave Square, the newest bit of architecture, was much desired as an aristocratic home. Just southwest of Buckingham Palace, it was in one of the wealthiest districts in the world. There was no evidence of concern for the window tax. Rather, sunlight poured into every room when clouds had passed along. Their Graces, The Duke of Trent and his Duchess, had moved in just a year earlier, and this would be Winnie's third visit. For Wills and Emma, it was the first. The columned porch was a welcome sight to the guests after languishing in a coach for such a distance.

The countess wanted to stretch, like a child out of church, upon disembarking. Instead, she reached up to wave and acknowledged Helena's excited welcome from the balcony above the portico. Footmen came out to assist the group, and the butler, Grantham, stood at the door.

"I will announce your arrival," he declared to the visitors despite the greetings from above. The Holmeshires entered, and he tended to their needs.

Footmen met Nanny Bowen and the lady's maids, who had arrived in a second carriage, outdoors and led them to the area. "Servants' quarters are on the top floor," one of them announced in a cool manner. "The nursery is on the second, and I will show you the back stairs." They disappeared through the servants' door, taking Nicholas along. Their trunks were carried in behind them.

Wills and Emma entered the elegant entrance hall, casting more glances at each other than the building's grand enticements. When caught, they looked away in haste, remembering all that was right and good. The carriage ride had kept them in close confines at length, stirring up feelings meant to be quelled. If only this attraction would be gone, but no—instead it grew. If only life would change, but no—it must go on as it would, they both thought.

The two followed Grantham and Winnie up a grand staircase to the waiting duchess. She led them, turning to chatter and laugh, down a stately, forest green hall under Corinthian pillars to the drawing room. There watercolors lined the walls, the signatures of famous artists lying along the borders. Ferns beautified and warmed the atmosphere sitting atop marble pedestals of various heights along the navy and white papered walls.

Over a fireplace hung a portrait of the reigning Queen Victoria, flanked neatly on each side by paintings of the uncrowned late Queen Caroline and her daughter, the nation's beloved Charlotte of Wales.

Charlotte's rule had been defeated forever, not by armies or uprisings, but by her death at the birth of her stillborn son.

Feelings of grief that the portraits brought the visitors were graciously wiped away by welcoming words from His Grace. The Duke, gray subduing his once flaming hair, stood at attention to receive his honors in a stylish long, brown frock coat over a high-collared shirt and low-cut vest.

"I have waited this day to kiss my dear sister-in-law," he related as she curtsied and then kissed her cheek, "and we shall have tea together, ere I must leave. Is that not a fine greeting? But politics, it seems, must be argued. Please sit. Do I know this lady?" He motioned toward the reticent Emma, still standing rumpled in her traveling dress, near the door.

"Sir," Wills replied, as he returned to escort her further inside. "This is my mother's companion, Miss Emma Carrington. I pray, my mother cannot live without her for a moment, and she must remain with us."

"Well, you have grown bold enough to inform me of that, have you, Wills? I am happy to learn of it. I am an old bear, but you will be grateful to know that I generally leave the matter of whom we receive to your Aunt Helena."

The duke turned and mumbled, gesturing fully to the bust of a former king in the corner. "She has impeccable taste. She often forgets to invite Lady Embry to tea. The old hag will be coming to dinner, I fear, because her esteemed husband is worth all the misery."

"Now," he went on, turning back to his guests, "where does Miss Carrington care to sit after so much time in a coach? This chair over here, I propose, as I have not yet seen it lurch, neither left nor right." His gruff airs had been mellowed by the passing of years, and his marriage to Helena had brought him such joy that in matters at home he had become more a grandfather than a general. Her opinion meant everything to him, and she upheld his position loyally.

The ladies chose comfortable Queen Anne chairs, and Winnie reported a wish that she could put her feet up and still please dear old Miss Wathem. Helena laughed and said there was no need to please her anymore. They had always gone behind her back anyway, and especially when it was just the family sitting together.

"But sister," she said, relaxed and teasing, "How will we explain our behavior to Miss Carrington? Now that concerns me the more, as she has heard the worst of it quite recently and will remember the admonitions better than we. She may just remind us of Miss Wathem's rules."

"So it is true that you have not had Embry to tea, for you would have had admonitions aplenty from her and be quite informed." Winnie smiled and maintained proper decorum as always in a royal drawing room.

Tea was served as Wills approached the duke and expressed surprise that he had allowed a portrait of the deceased queen to be hung in his home. She was the rejected wife of his brother and with a dreadful reputation.

"Well, she is dead now, for one thing," the duke remarked, turning to face the image. "One must show respect for the dead, and I have deep concern for a woman whose husband is cruel toward her, God rest his foolish soul. I have not yet spoken to one person who would swear to me of improper behavior. Perhaps they feared to inform me of it for not knowing how I might respond. The trials proved nothing but left much to be imagined."

He poured two brandies and gave one to Wills. "For another thing, His Majesty would never grace my doorstep when he was alive even to concern himself with my loyalties in the matter. But I must not mind— he was a pointlessly busy man." He stood back and looked again at the portraits. "My wife, you know, was a dear friend of the princess," he said, pointing to Charlotte, "and the princess loved her mother...whenever she found it possible. It was not always easy."

"Her mother was good to me," Helena sought to persuade Wills, "and to your mum."

"And to others we know," added Winnie.

"And that is all that matters, now," the duke shrugged, "it all being behind us. Few of us in the family supported the regent in his follies. Sadly, my father lived to see it and would have been driven mad, were he not already." He sipped at his brandy and chided Wills, "Good it is to see you now grown enough to discuss matters of such vast importance. Ladies, I know you are exhausted from your travels. There are things to accomplish yet today, so I will take my leave and let you have some rest. Holmeshire, should you be up to it, I would like to take you along to voice your opinions, so we can learn what they are. If you are to help run the Empire, I must correct your thinking."

Laughter resounded. Wills bid the ladies adieu. Helena followed them to the door of the room, saying goodbye to her Trent and holding Wills' shoulder. She implored him to stay and not be so very grown up. Wills laughed and declined the request, and he joined the duke in his exit. Off they went to a grand hotel to defeat the newest bill before it might be introduced and before Parliament had even been opened.

Helena looked back at the portraits and mused, "Ah, those days, so long ago. I have not talked of them in ages now. We did feel sorry for the problems of Caroline, living apart from her husband and little daughter." She picked up the teapot and refilled the cups. "Our mama was angered by it all, but held her tongue. For her good graces, we were allowed to visit and play with the princess."

Winnie reminisced, "Helena, more than I, spent time with her. The poor thing was given her own house and household though just a child. It was probably that her father was busy and...." she said with a shake of her head, "did not care to be caught at it. What sort of example would that be for the future queen?"

Helena walked about slowly while they spoke. She was, at forty-one, a bit younger than Winnie and had married a year later. Her gowns were rich, and her hair was filled with jewels. One always knew her from behind for her sparkling coiffure and the elegant design of the back of each dress.

"Yes," she went on, "there were many scandalous reports about her mother. But Charlotte and I, and sometimes Winnie, spent happy times together when her Papa would allow her guests. I would stay with her, and we would drive the servants mad with running down the halls. It was not to be done. There were treasures to preserve, you see, and the airs of a princess to be learnt. Such a situation it was—servants raising a princess and her parents off in all directions. Three households for one family of three. At times, we would go with her to see her mother."

Winnie lifted her chin from her folded hands. "Another lifestyle existed in Caroline's home, and she was required to adapt. There was even a boy there who

might have been Charlotte's little brother—whoever
knows? Her mother said she had adopted him. She did
adopt a number of children. You shall meet one of
them tonight, Emma—Mr. Gabriel Hughes is his
name—but this other child she kept at her side, poor
woman, and people thought it must be hers."

Helena stood in front of Caroline's portrait, staring
at it. "Charlotte was terribly distressed over it all. Many
times she was not allowed to see her mother. But as she
grew she knew she had to stand up for herself and to
make her own life. It was surprising—she became very
strong. She threw out William of Orange as her suitor.
William was her father's choice. He was right for the
politics of it, but Charlotte did not wish to live outside
England and preferred someone she had met only once.
Her father was forced to consent should he care to have
a son-in-law and an heir to his daughter's throne. He
sent for Leopold of Saxe-Coburg-Saalfeld and told him
the future queen wished to marry him. How could
either say no?"

Winifred laughed and shook her head, recalling
Charlotte's firm stance. "After that I knew she could
manage as queen. They married and were terribly
happy, though it was for but a short time. The nation
expected to see them on the throne and looked forward
to it greatly." She put her hand beside her mouth as if
to tell a secret. "We could barely sing 'God Save the
King.'" They all laughed. "Helena was prepared to
spend time at their cottage as Charlotte recovered from
the birth...but of course, she never did." A long pause
ensued.

"I had wished to be in attendance there for the
birth," Helena said at length, "and I have never decided
whether I am sad or grateful to not have been there. Her
doctor was distraught. He destroyed himself three

months later while attending the birth of another child."

"How dreadful for you all," Emma said. "It was of course, before my time, but how dreadful for the nation."

"Oh yes," the duchess replied, "There was great, great mourning. The nation was devastated. They had placed so much hope in Charlotte and Leopold after the uproar of her father's life. As Lord Byron later wrote, '...in the dust The Fair haired daughter of the Isle is laid, The love of millions, how we did entrust Futurity to her.' I was beside myself. I insisted Leopold come and spend time with us, and he was hopeless, just hopeless. 'In just a moment of time,' he said, 'it was over. It was as though the future had ended. Rather than see my wife play with our child, I had an empty house. Instead of a nation celebrating the birth of a future monarch, they faced a funeral for two.' After he went home, Trent and I left for Switzerland to suffer our grief. I could not stay here in an ocean of sorrow. It was as though pain kept pouring in, and I could not bail it out fast enough."

Winnie spoke up, "There arose a desperate cry from everywhere, for two heirs had passed and left no one at all. Who was to carry on the royal line? Of all the king's brothers, none had legitimate heirs. All were forced to abandon their mistresses and children and search out wives royal enough to beget the next king or queen."

"And youthful enough, and willing," interjected Helena, "despite the princes being aged."

"Helena, though, had consented and married the duke, so, with her being of noble blood and married with the king's permission, they were in fine stead. The other princes found there were few from which to choose, and none cared to see the marriage of

Charlotte's parents repeated."

"That is why I am still beloved to Trent, I am sure. I spared the poor man from conscripted matrimony. We had mercifully fallen in love, ourselves, and married to live happily." Helena paused, standing behind Winnie with her hands on her sister's shoulders. "Charlotte was with child when she attended our wedding. We were a royal bride and groom with the Hope of the Nation at our side. After she died, we thought we would perhaps carry on for her. We would have a son to sit in her place on the throne, though her dying was the last thing we could ever want. The dynasty could not be left in our hands alone for fear that we would not provide an heir, and so German princesses were sought for the others. William became king after George, but none of his legitimate children lived. We thought we might provide the first of several heirs."

"But they have never had a child," said Winnie.

"No, we never could have a child. I could not do that for my wishful husband or for Charlotte. Not even for the country, to save the Empire."

"But the Empire is safe with a beloved queen now," Emma replied in an attempt to proffer comfort, which the ladies curbed their emotions to accept.

"Yes, we have our dear Victoria," Winnie agreed. "We are happy, for she gives promise of being a good queen. She has concern for the people. She has asked for reports on their living conditions, something which fits well with our intentions and hopes. We pray for her safekeeping, as you surely do."

"I do fervently pray that she thrives in childbearing, for there is but one to carry on for her." Helena's worries presented on her face. Surely, in her mind, Victoria would soon breathe her last. Her blind cousin would ascend, and he would again be the last of the line.

Winnie proposed an ill-designed solution. "You must keep trying, Helena, there must be spares should she not succeed, and sons are quite hard won, it seems."

"That is the greatest grief in my life—I am sure by now, being barren still and growing old, it is impossible for me. What a joy it would have been bearing the next monarch. I often imagined playing with my little king, presenting him with lovely gifts, turning him on my lap to look on me while sternly teaching him to rule a great empire. He should now be one and twenty, or twenty at least. Please, do not entreat me again."

She sat down and Winnie touched her shoulder, rendering apology. Helena sighed and said, "I do realize how very serious the situation is." She toyed for a time with a pillow. The past at last extinguished by an abysmal breath, she smiled and raised her eyes. "But Emma, just who are you, and what nation will you rule?"

"Oh, dear, you see, I do not know who I am, to be perfectly forthcoming." Emma, relieved to have left the heirs behind, battled other feelings that commandeered her thoughts and altered her face. "Perhaps milady did not say? I was left an infant at the home of Squire Carrington and raised by his wife. She took the kindest care of me, along with their children, and I adored her, but it was clear that I was not deemed a Carrington by the squire, who greatly favored his daughters. That is as it should be. Nature does as it does. I became more a servant, being especially glad to care for Mrs. Carrington. But when she died, he was done with me. I had spent some of her priceless hours on our lovely discussions, wasted them, robbed him of them, you know, and he could not endure my company. Milady graciously offered me a place in her service to keep me from perishing of the rain. How I came to be so blessed as to be stationed where I am today I cannot surmise, but my gratitude will never end." Her words were finalized with a nod.

Winnie was ready for a change. "Dearest ladies, there must be something better to discuss after these months apart. Emma, pray tell Helena of your stay with dear Miss Wathem." The ladies' conversation diverged in a much-preferred direction.

***

Upstairs the nanny and maids had been curtly introduced to their quarters and had put away their clothing, brushes and favored trinkets. Nicky had been tucked into bed in the nursery that Helena had created, just for him, to sleep off the exhausting travels.

The three servants sat down together in the adjoining day nursery with its gay gingham curtains to have their tea, hoping that the staff of Belgrave Square would not mind their absence from the downstairs table. After all, Elizabeth pointed out, they had barely arrived, Nicky must be watched, and Anne had not met the staff as of yet. "Surely, though, someone will take offense. That is the way here," she sighed. "You saw the glare of the kitchen maid who brought up our tea. On my previous visits they were so antagonized by my existence that I was required to eat next to the kitchen maids rather than next to Helena's lady's maid."

"Perhaps they do not like servants from other houses?" Anne meekly suggested.

Lizzie's corrective voice appeared briefly. "Or perhaps they do not like servants from smaller houses, or servants who outrank the scullery maid. And if I understand things properly from what I observed they do not even like each other. I am inclined to say something particular to the lot of them."

"It does not matter. Let it be. I will tell them I do not care to take meals alone here when Nicholas is sleeping," the confident Gwyndolyn stated. "There is no other nursery staff, no nanny belonging to this house, no nursery maid. It will have to please them. I suggest that we give the girl the kindest thanks when she returns for the dishes. Perhaps she will like that."

"Yes, you are right, Nanny Bowen. We should just be ever so kindly as Lady Holmeshire and probably the Bible would say. But will you not have a nursery maid here?" Lizzy was shocked.

"I have not been told of one. The footman did not say, and there is no one here. I have not come with the family before. Nicky and I stayed at Holmeshire, you know. But I do know I cannot take proper care of Nicholas and do the floors and laundry as well, nor is it my obligation, so I suppose there will be someone. I shall ask about it. Girls, tell me please, did you think Mr. Barreby acted strangely for a time before we left?"

Elizabeth laughed. "You have been there long enough to know that he always acts strange." Anne and Gwyn smiled.

"Yes, Lizzy, but I mean...just recently. Have you noticed anything different?"

Anne replied, "I thought he was poking around oddly in the house. I found him in our room once. It seemed most unusual. I did not know whether I should mention it to anyone."

"Anyone? Who could you mention it to besides her ladyship, silly?" Lizzy corrected. "There is no one else over Mr. Barreby." Anne could never say or do things right. Never mind if she should—for Lizzy's powers needed exercise, and Anne needed keeping in her place.

Gwyn continued with her thoughts, "Yes, that is

what I mean exactly. He has gone intently through everything in the nursery, as though he is looking for something, when he was unaware of my presence. I do wish he would tell me what it is that he is devouring the house after. Or at least I wish he would stay out of the nursery. It just does not please me for Nicky to see him behaving so. It disturbs his rest time, and I do not know what to tell the lad when he asks me what is happening." She frowned. "I have never seen Mr. Barreby so sober. I think he suspects me of having pinched something."

"I think he suspects everyone of having pinched something," Anne said, "But, nevertheless, he keeps a pleasant household like my Papa. We laugh and jest at supper. I am far more in fear of this Belgrave staff. What shall we do at suppertime? Where must we eat?" Her fidgeting appeared, and Lizzy pressed her hands to her lap with a governing glare. Anne conceded and held them still.

Gwyn was the decisive one of the lot. "I shall demand that they bring your food up here. We will see how that pleases the butler. If it does not go well you girls shall be forced to eat downstairs, I suppose, so no one is angered. If necessary, I shall stay here alone with Nick. I am the only one required to eat here, anyway, unless I have a nursery maid, and I best have one."

The butler was pleased enough to allow them to eat upstairs for the first day, but it did not last. And the kitchen maid was unimpressed with the gracious thanks she received upon reclaiming the dishes from their tea. She even stood and checked them for chips.

***

"Buy myself a home in London? Please, I am trying to eat my dinner." Wills put down his hand a bit too firmly and was surprised at himself. "I have enough to care for, thank you. I want only one house to be bothered with for now while I am single and focusing on the needs of the country, and the Northumberland air is much more pleasant. Why should I care to have a house in the city? I do not wish to throw parties, should you have thoughts about that. I shall leave that to Helena. She is a divine hostess. Is her dining room not perfect?" He parted his upturned palms to draw attention to its burgundy and gold elegance. "Someone will always take me in when I come limping into town, as my doting grandmother did a few weeks past. And someday I shall be stuck with grandfather's house to refurbish. How many can I manage?"

"Why do you think I have brought these peers here to dine?" the duke leaned toward Wills. "I need support to take on your stubborn mind. You shall be required to have a city house and entertain should you sit in Parliament." He leaned back into his chair. "Everyone must agree if they are to have Cherries Jubilee!"

Jovial Lord August-Crane raised his glass, "A house for Lord Holmeshire to be sure. It does not have to be a Belgrave mansion, my lord, but you'll need a home here. I agree." He leaned closer to Miss Carrington, uncomfortably seated in a room full of peers, and whispered, "I do favor tinned cherries."

"Lady Genevieve will have a home for you here. When she marries she shall have Chenbury House with her settlement. You shall be able to entertain well from there. But I hear you are not in a hurry to marry," the duke scolded, shaking his fork.

"And now I know the purpose of this. I must entertain, so I must have a house. The need for a house shall make me marry. Do you suppose she would allow me to live in Chenbury on her expectations? Or would the young ladies advise her against it?" At that he rolled his eyes, but in keeping with etiquette, ever so slightly.

The room was stunning, the banquet table sparkling with the chandelier's reflections dancing on the crystal and silver. Floral bouquets of spring roses, lilies and ivy trailed down its middle over elaborate, lacy linens. Footmen moved silently in and out as though choreographed. Serving dishes were attractively filled and daintily emptied. Everything was beautiful, orderly and agreeable. It was only the conversation that was trying.

"The benefits of marriage are not to be downplayed, sir," Lord Embry offered, waving a bun at him. "That is why I am a father so many times over, you see. At any rate, I cannot understand why you delay the inevitable. It is not as though you must sit home and gossip once married, you know." He covered his mouth with his fingers, but then threw his hands upward. "Pardon my misinterpretation of tea time, ladies. I realize it is not only politics that must be bantered about. My wife is so very clear about that. What would London do should one hand not know what the other was doing, after all? But, Lord Holmeshire, tea tables would be happier places if you fulfilled your obligations to womankind."

"Is there a lack of balls and dinners?" Wills admirably kept himself from fuming. "Are people in want of reasons to wear white vests or diamonds, or is it that the Abbey sits empty without more weddings? I simply cannot fathom the rush everyone is in to have me married. Must one marry in their early twenties? Emma, what do you think of it?"

The poor girl was in horror. Her heart raced as she looked to Winnie, who replied with a sympathetic nod, and back at Wills. "My lord, I cannot dare to voice my thoughts over these noble people."

"At least she knows her place," muttered the matronly Lady Embry, reaching for her bread and glittering more than the crystal.

Wills ignored her and continued to address Emma. "Ah, so you do have thoughts on the subject. I am glad to hear it. I shall come to you for counsel when it will not dismay you so." Emma took a deep breath and tended to her plate. "The duke has voiced his delight in having Emma to dinner, my friends. Have you not, Your Grace?" Wills took after his mother in his disdain for the rigidity of society. "She was a squire's ward, you know."

"A squire's ward—I am sure she is proud of that." Lady Embry snorted. "And just how many squires does England have?"

"I pray, madam, allow me my guests," the duke retorted. "Emma, will you join us tomorrow again?"

"Your Grace, thank you, I shall hope to," she sighed.

"I should not inquire, then, being a squire's ward, who her parents are, or pardon me, who they were, should I? Or when she was presented at court?" The lady stabbed her partridge.

"Lady Embry, you are the first to remind people of their social graces. Can you not practice yours?" the duchess countered. "You must consider your example. Eminence is enhanced by civility and charm."

The dashing Mr. Gabriel Hughes, having observed Emma thoughtfully through the meal and having admired her greatly, spoke up from several seats down the table. "How I wish I were to visit tomorrow myself. Alas, I cannot dine with Miss Carrington. I shall be fighting for the Crown in court and then be elsewhere." Mr. Hughes had been introduced to Emma earlier as the most successful and impressive barrister in the land.

"The Crown is very much in need of you, my learned friend. Here we can make do with just the few of us and enjoy your company another night," replied His Grace, his admiration for the barrister evident.

"I fear there will be very few of us indeed, my dear, as we and our guests are to dine at Handerton House," Helena said. "It will be the servants alone here tomorrow."

"And which party will Miss Carrington be with?" Lady Embry oh-so-sweetly inquired. Her query was ignored while the poor, mortified Emma longed to melt off her chair and down beneath the table, never to resurface. Could she bear any more of this dinner? Wills considered raising a toast to her for courage in the face of adversity, but feared that it would distress her for not being well-received in certain seats.

"We shan't be having such conversations at Holmeshire Hall," he commented pleasantly, hinting at who might and who might not receive invitations under his jurisdiction, "nor at my London home, should I be forced to produce one as a single fellow."

"I understand that Lady Genevieve is well acquainted with the proper ways of society," intimated the glistening, overly perfumed personage, taking advantage of Wills' nearly having brought up the subject himself.

"I understand that Lady Genevieve someday will have a husband to acquaint her with the more benevolent ways of humanity," countered the handsome young man. "I see that not a few people remain quite concerned about His Majesty, King George the Fourth, and his marital meddlings." Wills then emphatically announced, "And now we shall honor the peace of His Grace's home and his gracious hospitality."

"Perhaps, then, we should change the subject of our conversation," the dear Lady Embry announced. "Lord Holmeshire, are you looking forward to some time alone with Lady Genevieve tomorrow, perhaps on your knee in the garden?" The room fell silent with the ultimate in painful toleration. It was left for the portraits, the statues and the stately columns to demonstrate nobility—and hope that the occupants would perhaps learn the art of it.

Mr. Hughes made a particular effort to talk with Emma later in the evening, making sure she was quite comfortable at all times and uninjured by Lady Embry's attacks. He gave her a rosebud from the table for her "beautiful black and shining hair."

~Chapter 5~
A Visit to Handerton House

Elizabeth and Anne sprawled comfortably over the scrolled arms of a sofa upholstered in a dark classical print for the nursery. The afternoon visit to the suite meant light-hearted chat with Gwyndolyn and a warm and friendly woman, Adelina Darivela, who had stepped in to greet them.

Adelina spoke pleasantly with an appealing foreign accent. Outside the house she kept to herself. She wore lacy brown veils and could not be recognized from a distance. But she had Helena's confidence and took tea alone with the duchess upon occasion. Adelina was a servant of sorts, the creator of floral bouquets in huge crystal vases that beautified the great house from one end to the other. Though she lived alone elsewhere, supported by the duke and duchess, she was often to be seen in the mansion with baskets full of long-stemmed roses and seasonal flora.

Though five and twenty years of age spread between the women in the nursery, they enjoyed each other's company. They entertained Nicky and conversed, while he napped, about books they had read.

Anne styled Gwyn's hair for the evening at Handerton, as she would accompany the boy. They dressed her in a beautiful, pale-yellow gown loaned by Helena for the occasion, and she acted the lady, ordering them about.

Along with Adelina had come a housemaid, Hattie, who had not the friendly attitude. Assigned under Gwyn as the nursery maid for the Season, she was required to be present and take orders. Due to her continual scowl she was much ignored after an attempt by the three to earn her friendship. It was as Adelina signaled—she could not be won over.

Hattie was angered that she would eat upstairs with Gwyn and Nicky for the summer. It would ruin her life, she said, and she would have but one life as far as she knew. Anne and her sister were glad to leave Hattie behind to dress their ladies for the evening.

***

Emma descended richly carpeted stairs to meet the waiting Winnie and Helena on a vast landing. A silk settee of floral embroidery had been placed for those who cared to watch Belgravia through a red-velvet-draped window. The ladies were very much enjoying the show while awaiting the others for their outing to dinner at Handerton.

Outside the window, carriages bore smartly dressed gentlemen home for the evening and couples off to their engagements. Uniformed nannies led children home from late outings and greeted others who pushed perambulators across the streets.

Hearing Emma approach, Helena rose and turned away from London's happy proceedings. Winnie had chosen for Emma the most angelic dress she had ever worn—a sheer, white gown over a multitude of petticoats, off the shoulders and with billowing sleeves. The sun shone through the top layers of her dress, giving it a heavenly glow as she stood before a dark wood newel in its golden beams. Sadly, she felt worse for the distinguishing gown. "Shall I go, ma'am, truly, is it worth the fray?"

Winifred looked up from admiring the embroidery on her newly made gloves and turned. "I am sorry, my dear, that you have so much to endure on this foray into the Season. Wills does wish to make it clear how life will be in Holmeshire Hall for anyone who should care to perch themselves there. You will be part of our life there. Better that it is understood and agreed upon now than trying to change it later with no prior understanding." She paused and acknowledged Emma's position. "How can I make it more bearable for you?"

Emma supposed that avoiding the visit was out of the question, but she would attempt it once more. "Ma'am, are you sure we must press the matter? It is not regular for a servant to come to be a dinner guest at a noble's home dressed as her betters. I fear my gown may be more exquisite than that of the lady there who should wish to enchant her gentleman. I am most honored to wait upon you when you would be lonely in your home, but in society you have others to converse with. I could be content to sit at home and spare you ever so many comments and complaints."

"Emma, it is you needing to be spared. But I have my reasons. Please trust me," Winnie replied.

Helena wished to content Emma with some of those reasons. "There are numerous things to be dealt with in this society. I have seen frivolous, ostentatious, blaring waste of resources under the Regency and ever since. The peers and peeresses under George IV followed his lead, and to this day they pour out money on gambling tables and all sorts of debauchery. While I love the exquisite things our parents and His Grace have provided me, I cannot bear to watch wasteful, callous increasing of debts on useless vices. In the meantime, the streets are full of scourings, and the living conditions of the poor are wretched. Some of them work day and night and are then taxed for the air they breathe in their miserable houses—which air, I am led to believe, smells of sewage and dead animals. If Parliament will not, someone must begin to stand up for the lower classes. Her Majesty, the Queen herself wishes it. We must set the example for the wealthy to invest their riches into improving the deplorable conditions. I implore you to do your part by introducing yourself into the homes of the peers alongside your mistress. They must be introduced to someone of a lower class, to have to be seen with and made to talk to someone to become conscious of them all, to come to recognize them as worthy humans in need. You are an excelling example of lower class goodness to them, at least when we can get you in their doors. We do have some great standing and in most homes, our persuasion prevails. Few will create trouble. When someone does, we will fight for you, if you will just endure their malevolence."

Emma became thoughtful, staring off into the high spaces of the entry below. "I see," she mused. "I see. So it is for dear Mr. Seely I am here. And little Robin and Kate in the orphanage, and Polly Kensby, who went into debtor's prison with her papa. I see. Indeed…indeed, I can bear it. I can. I will." A determined smile appeared on her face, and she became proud of displaying the ruby on her neck.

Handsome Wills made his way down the stairs to meet the women.

"Good evening, Wills," greeted the duchess. Wills

bowed.

"A very good evening, Your Grace and Mama. And this astonishing creature here, Miss Emma Carrington, whose curtsies are a work of art. Look at her, Mama; see what you have created? Off we must go. The time has come for me to face the loyal opposition." Wills made a sweeping gesture toward the lower flight of stairs. "Is the nursery division ready? Have we yet heard?"

Down the last flight of stairs they went to investigate. They found the nanny and her charge waiting on a divan near the exit with Master Nicholas practicing his Visiting Manners. He was to be brought along to confront the future Mistress of Holmeshire Hall. Nanny Bowen would spend the evening walking Nicky through a visit in a most civil and gentlemanly way. They would remain with the boy's family and their hosts for some time until dinner. At that time they would separate, dine alone in Handerton's garden and enjoy the evening in its spectacular game room.

Nicky had been briefed and trained on behavior as a guest at a great house and had been given an extra-long nap whether he liked it or not. There in the entry, with all parties ready to go, Wills elicited horrified gasps when he taught the lad to hop from one of the checkered tiles to another. "Black tiles only," he commanded.

***

John Brown, Solicitor. The sign hung smartly over the doorway of the finest brick building on the street. Uncombed, Mr. Scott pushed his way through the bell-rigged entrance into the orderly front room. The scent of the building's freshly wooded walls was replaced with the stink of ale and tobacco. The clerk looked up, alarmed, as the derelict stumbled through and blurted out his name.

"Benedict Scott, here, to see Mr. Brown."

"Do you have an appointment, sir?" The youth knew of none and scrambled to find Mr. Scott's name on a tidy page. Puzzled and flustered, he lifted the book searching for a possibly missed note.

"No, I don't need no appointment. Where is the man?" Benedict looked impatiently at a clock and dropped some coins on the desk, keeping others hopefully stored in his pocket for buying rounds.

"I shall see if he can meet with you, sir, but I cannot guarantee it." The clerk's chair screeched against the hardwood floor as he pushed it back to stand. As he turned and left for a back room, Benedict retrieved his coins. The young man soon returned with a bald, businesslike man wearing a dark gray summer coat. He looked sternly over the top of his polished spectacles.

"I am John Brown. Is there something I can do for you?"

"You can help me solve a huge problem, sir. Sure's you want the best for your family, I must take care o' mine. Let's take it up in your office." And off they went, with Mr. Scott demanding the utmost confidence in the matter, and possibly a scotch.

***

"Here we have appearing before us the grand Handerton House." Wills said, waving his upturned palm toward the mansion on the outskirts of London. "It once belonged to the Royal Family. It housed visiting diplomats and royals from around the world. I imagine there were many royal teas served at those tables near the rose gardens."

Leaning into the carriage window with her fan held up to block the setting sun, Emma was stunned at the beauty of the gardens.

"The house was awarded to the newly titled Lord Breyton just nineteen years past," Wills stated. "He has no brother or cousin to inherit the house. He will never have a son—doctors forbade it at Genny's birth. Thus, when His Majesty created Breyton's title it was created to pass through his daughter to her eldest son. Everything is for our son to claim when Breyton dies, or it will be mine first should he die young. He is terribly angry that he had no son of his own to take it all. He meant to build for himself a sort of dynasty. He once warned my father that I was to be certain to have a son for the title, if you please, and for the house. I am to give the child his name. I suppose I shall try very hard to please on some distant day, but I am in no hurry to fill my nursery with his children presently."

Emma gasped as they rounded the long, oak-lined drive. The trees alternated with baskets of purple and white petunias hanging on wrought iron poles over ivy-covered grounds. Their unique fragrance drifted sweetly into the carriage.

"You shall have this and Chenbury House?"

"Chenbury will be her settlement—ours to use as we wish and hers for life should she someday be widowed. And she is to have enough stacks of money to burn to heat the place in the winter."

"And suppose you are widowed?"

"Chenbury would go to our second son, or to someone of Genny's choosing."

"And your heir will also have Holmeshire Hall?"

"That, along with my father's houses," Winnie joined in, "due to the grand shortage of men. I have no brother nor uncle nor cousin."

"Nor do I," laughed Helena, nudging her sister.

"I had far too many," asserted the duke, "and

83

should have been happy to give some away. I have adequate houses, but no son. Your heir might just as well have some of my trinkets, too. Why not? It sounds like he will be in dire need. Or perhaps you shall have a third son more in need of a house than your firstborn, as mine will not be entailed to your heir. That is how I shall have it—a country house for your third son." He and the duchess exchanged a resigned glance.

As the horses ended their clop round the red brick drive, Emma glanced with nervous anticipation at the mansion. The huge door was all that was saving her now. She longed to see the renowned interior, and yet she dreaded it.

This life would be wonderful, she thought, if only she could be accepted. How she looked forward to returning to Holmeshire to fluff up downy divan cushions for Winnie's comfort. But the time had passed for hope of deliverance from the evening's ordeal.

Footmen came to open the carriage door for Wills to alight. He climbed out to give the women a hand. Winnie and Helena stepped out of the covered landau, laughing and smoothing their skirts. Wills motioned for Emma to come along.

A stack of gifts, strapped together, was pulled from the back end of the carriage. Emma must enter with the people and not the packages. Gathering up her courage, she put one foot in front of the other as the guests were admitted and announced by the butler.

Greetings and pleasantries abounded for a time. Tense and anxious, Emma received polite smiles from the women but uncomfortable stares from Lord Breyton. She breathed more easily after a reception free of rude comments, though she could not help feeling quite slighted. Should Breyton stay away all would be well, however, and she was relieved when his attention turned to the decor.

Emma followed behind the party as the marquess bragged about each and every trinket. He had brought his love of India home, splashing it everywhere, leaving behind only the elephants. Breyton would have India in England.

His wife, Grace, had few opinions of her own but for strictly abiding the etiquette books, and she was ever aspiring to please any equal, her husband above all. He was her world, and she hastened to add to his collections when traders brought more into Town. She had new hand-tufted rugs for every season of the year, painted scenes and boxes full of what could not be shown. There was no changing the architecture of the ancient house, but the trappings were altogether Eastern. Genevieve despised it.

"I tire of showing this house, Papa. They have seen it all, have you not, Your Grace? But that Papa has added statues and enameled boxes to it. It is much too bright in color for me, just too much. I wish you would do it in a soft, pale French design, Papa—moirés and damasks in blue and pistachio. Would Louis XV not be lovely in this grand house? Then I would enjoy presenting it to these dear guests." Though allowed to speak her mind, Genevieve lived an orchestrated life and had tired of it. She longed to become mistress of a house on her own.

"I shall have it this way, my dear girl," said her papa, "for as long as I live. Perhaps my grandson will make the changes you request."

"I love old-fashioned rococo," Genny said. "I have purchased tapestries and paintings for my house in Holmeshire. Someday. But look at the veiled ceilings here and the dark colors on the floors and walls. One is at pains to even walk through the myriad wood carvings, palm trees and handiwork. I am oppressed and cannot bear to live in it any longer. Mama is happy enough with it all, though, are you not, Mama?" she sighed and looked at Wills. "I have sent my monkey away. I could not endure the horrid creature. It will be kittens and rococo for me."

Wills decided it best to inform her of the discord in their plans for the castle. She had presented the opportunity—it might not come again. Contention not being something he feared, he took her aside, not far nor out of view. They stepped under the fronds of a tall Kent palm near a brown-framed map, which covered much of a wall.

"I have been traveling, you know," he began. "I stayed quite some time in Italy and shipped home two and thirty crates full of lovely things for Holmeshire Hall. You will adore it, as how could one not? It is all marble in light colors—you shall love the light colors. It is very classical, very Italian."

Perhaps she could come to care for that? Or perhaps not. It seemed not. Wills took pains not to add detail for fear of worsening things. Should she recover, he might receive much opinion or an offer of assistance.

She stared at him, incredulous. Stunned, she could not talk. "Do tell?" she at last acceded. "What sort of things did you buy? I am breathless to see." Breathless, she hoped, to get ahead of it, breathless to come between Holmeshire and Italian. The futility of protest dawned on her, though, for the investment had been made. Holmeshire would be Italian, and the rococo would go to Chenbury.

Perhaps some of it would appeal. Or at least she could do her own chambers her way? And, she hoped, she could visit Holmeshire soon to use his supplies and recreate the home.

"Oh, no, do not concern yourself. It is all sitting in crates. Marble this, marble that, vases, paintings, materials to restore the house. And soon comes an Italian designer. He'll be there and gone quickly." She feared that very thing. She supposed that if she was ever to have things her way, she must live alone. The thought appealed.

And what was it he was saying now? "I would so like you to become acquainted with Miss Carrington tonight. You shall be great friends, I am sure." She cast a brief look at Emma, his mother's over-dressed servant. Perhaps the two of them would enjoy the Dower House?

"Miss Carrington?" Genny said with a wavering smile. "I am pleased to have met your mother's maid, but I have no wish to distract her from her obligations. I do have dear friends of my own, as you know. We have become quite occupied with Shakespeare, performing his works amongst ourselves, and hoping to perform it for our friends. It will be far too time consuming for Miss Carrington."

She paused, nervously realizing she had just invited her friends to Holmeshire Hall for lengthy visits, not something that would move matters in the right direction. She paused to regret it, resigned herself and then spoke on a third disagreeable matter.

"Wills, should I be allowed to address you so as your betrothed, I have a question to ask of you. This Nicholas," she nodded toward the tot under restraint of his well-bedecked guardian. "I fear to ask, since no one has heard much of him before, from where did this child come, my lord?" She hardly breathed awaiting his reply.

"I have no desire to hurt or deceive you in any way,

ma'am—"

"I cannot bear that you call me ma'am. Please call me by my name. And the boy?"

"Yes, my dear Genny, should I be allowed to call you that, I shall." He turned his back to Nicky and spoke quietly. "As to the child, he is not my son. Be assured of that. My sons and heirs will be your sons, too. I can promise you my allegiance in marital matters. My parents have taken great pains to teach me the dangers of infidelity—the trauma and the state of crisis that it can yield. The disease it brings on. It is my intention to provide you with the most pleasant home, the most comfortable life and the greatest confidence in your husband. You shall sleep in peace when I am gone knowing that I am a man of integrity to my nuptial vows. There, you are aware of my views on that. As to Nicholas, he is the child of a man of the utmost importance to me for whom I would do anything. I have taken responsibility for permanent guardianship of the child. Until we have a son, Nicholas has been entered into my will as my heir, as I must have one. I ask that you will give him the same security and happiness I intend to give you in our home."

"And so I must raise this child?"

"Please, Genevieve, with my providing all the help you should care to have in the matter, do accept Nicky as part of the family."

She studied the picturesque rug on which she stood, traced a design with the toe of her white-buttoned shoe and then looked back up at Wills. "I shall do as you say, my lord. May I ask, then, when we will begin this family life that we have discussed?"

Wills hesitated, not meaning to have created this adversity, and responded, "I will provide you with a proposal, someday, a far more appropriate proposal of marriage than the conversation we just had could possibly have been deemed."

Genevieve closed her eyes briefly. Irritated, she clenched her jaw. "I did not deem it, my lord, an appropriate proposal, but there has never been another. To be or not to be—that is the question," she flashed back at him. He patiently offered his arm as he turned to the group which was now examining a huge portrait of the great First Marquess of Breyton.

***

A dinner of rice and spicy curry was served around a long table decorated with bouquets of flowers and peacock feathers. Emma felt Breyton look across the table at her. He quickly turned his face when she looked his way.

She felt unwanted, but was determined to stake her place in the group and fulfill her purpose. She squirmed in her seat. If only something would be brought up to admit her to the conversation.

"Peacock feathers are widely used in fashionable Indian weddings," volunteered the marchioness, the Lady Breyton. "We have learned so much about the culture, weddings and all, you know." She realized belatedly that she sounded forward. Still, she was most decisively informed of it.

"I am not planning a wedding yet, Mother, and when I do it will not involve Indian culture," asserted her daughter, who had deeper dimensions of self-confidence. "I will thank you to remember that my interests lie elsewhere."

"Oh, indeed, I surely know of your admirable theatrical interests, my dear," conceded the panicking woman as she attempted to leave behind a bitter subject.

"Not just any theater and surely not your opera,

Mama, but Shakespeare and Shakespeare alone. I would like to announce that since there is nothing important happening this summer, Mama and I wish to throw a huge ball with the theme 'Midsummer Night's Dream.' I am sure Papa will allow us? A lady must have something to banish idleness and...and...wasted days." She clearly referred to the ebbing away of her life as a twenty-one-year-old maid. Certainly everyone at the table reproached her for it.

Lord Breyton replied, "I should think it would be a fine thing, my dear. You make your plans. I am surprised you have nothing else intended for this summer, though?" He looked straight at Wills who he had long presumed would marry his daughter, making her a countess and mistress over their houses at age seventeen. Wills smiled and nodded politely, not at all pleased to enjoy another evening at this discussion but enduring as the topic would surely burn itself out.

"We must find a larger ballroom than what we have here. This must outdo all balls ever thrown," Genevieve emphatically declared, drowned in exasperation. "I shall do nothing else whatsoever the rest of the Season but throw myself into this ball. We shall form a committee of some of Mama's friends and mine."

"We must talk more about that, my dear," replied the marquess. "We have ample space here and plenty to show off. And with such a late start, you will not find another place."

"Perhaps I prefer not to show this house off. I pray we will discuss it later." A short delay preceded her addendum, "This above all—to thine own self be true. No one else is."

Her father's voice raised a degree, "We shall discuss it together, your mother and I, Genevieve. Young ladies do not throw their own balls."

The discussion ended, ere the lord turn a bit too angry. He looked at Wills in a new and discomfiting way. Genevieve struggled mightily with the impulse to run from the room but was thankfully restrained by the acutely disturbed but well-disciplined lady within.

Wills would have preferred dinner at Belgrave Square. He decided, however, to push matters to the limit since he was, in fact, at Handerton House. Things were hopelessly miserable by now, and it might as well be done.

"I would also like to give a ball. I would like to invite some of those who do not often have the opportunity."

"Oh, who has been regrettably left out?" asked a guest, a sweet lady, innocent and with deep concern.

"Our dear Miss Wathem, my mother's governess, has not been to a ball in quite some time. We would especially like to honor her. She is growing old and may never again have the opportunity," Wills replied, knowing well that he would be assailed for it in this company. "She recently did us a great service by taking in Miss Carrington and assisting her to learn the ways of society."

Genevieve struggled to carry on as a member of the party. "To be sure," she said, "that will be most useful for Miss Carrington when spending time with her ladyship." She nodded toward Winnie. "I am very happy for you both." There was no strength for a smile. She could barely muster stiff toleration which attempted a masquerade as graciousness.

"And," Wills continued, "there are a number of middle class persons who have used their time and resources to assist those beneath them. It is time they received acknowledgement and honors, and I believe that a modest banquet and ball would be just the venue for such a ceremony. They deserve the best. Do you have any suggestions for such a ball, my dear Genevieve?"

Genevieve froze with her knife and fork, which she had at last raised, hovering above her plate. She looked at him blankly and blinked a few times, unsure she could believe he had involved her in this. A few seconds passed before she repossessed herself, set down her silver and composed a reply.

"I am sorry, my lord," she breathed, "living here so near London, I do not know how I could assist in this concept." Barely coping, she had hope upon hope the affair would take place after the Season in the Holmeshire mud and moors. After all, she was not his wife and was not required to attend.

"It is more than a concept, my dear. You see, just this morning I found a merchant and ordered silver medals made for the persons on my list of names. But I do fear leaving out someone deserving. Does anyone wish to name a person or perhaps a couple who has contributed in some kind way to the welfare of those less fortunate?"

Quiet ensued, and Helena sensed the need for support from high places. "His Grace and I could discuss providing a venue here in London for this ball. How would you feel about that, my darling?"

Wills interjected before the duke could speak, "That would be splendid, Aunt Helena. I wish to be able to invite Her Majesty. She has spoken kindly of the efforts of such persons." Perhaps this would convince His Grace and shock the Breytons?

The Duke of Trent wiped his mouth with an elegant linen, perhaps in excess giving him time to think, and stammered, "I, I, I have no problem with providing accommodations for a fine work such as this, though I was told last night that you prefer not to entertain? Would it perhaps be more appropriate to hold, say, a ceremony with some diversion? Musicians, perhaps? We have a spacious room with seating for such an event."

Emma saw her opportunity. With responsibility to the poor giving her new-found bravery, and with a quick prayer, she cleared her throat and threw herself in, come what may. "I can say, having felt the sentiments of common people, that many of the lower classes would welcome the good fortune of enjoying a banquet and ball." She held her breath. The duke raised his eyebrows and nodded, amused. Winnie and Helena smiled.

Wills did not allow time for the dropped Breyton jaws to snap shut. "I can manage a more elaborate event for this cause," he responded, "or are banquets and balls too much extravagance? Should that be the case, and some feel it is, there should be No More Balls."

"But my lord," Genevieve said meekly while touching the top of his sleeve, "it is the situation. I am sure you are perfectly aware of how this fits, or does not fit, the socially accepted customs. A small dance, perhaps?"

This opened the occasion for a convenient declaration. "Balls are unacceptable? Then we shall attend no balls in the future. Nor shall we throw any. I praise your perceptive views, my dear." Genevieve, eyes suddenly closed, pulled her hand back to pat her chest. Her breath came hard and fast.

Grace jumped up to her defense, "Oh, no, Genny did not mean that at all." She caught herself and floated down to her chair with all dignity, hoping to reclaim some good will. "Oh dear, Miss... Miss... is it

Carrington? Would you care for more of the Rhine?"

"No, milady, no, I am very satisfied. Thank you very kindly." Ah! She had been invited into the conversation. The evening was a success.

***

The coats and wraps and carriages appeared, timed impeccably with the midnight goodbyes. The mood had mellowed considerably, with the advantage going to the Holmeshires and on Breyton property. No middle class ball was settled on—no invitations were going out. The queen could stay home, and the medals would be given out with pomp in some setting or other. To Wills, it was just the principle. But Genevieve was on notice about the tone of life at Holmeshire.

Nicholas had behaved admirably all evening for those spending time with him, which alleviated huge concerns, but it did not garner him any gracious reception.

Winifred chatted warmly with Lady Breyton, and the marquess offered his arm to another lady for the stroll to her carriage. Wilfred took Emma on his, with Genevieve vexed, and expressed delight in the charming mix of perfect weather, India and Shakespeare that night. He even managed a quote himself as they neared Belgravia in the carriage.

"I will speak daggers to her, but use none."

"Hamlet, Wills?" Winnie inquired.

"Act III."

***

Elizabeth had done Anne no favor in talking of the servants' hall downstairs and its snarling occupants. The ultimate conclusion, Gwyndolyn had said in whispers to exclude Hattie, was they ought to be thankful for the obsessive Barreby and the order he maintained, as well as his insistence on friendliness and an abundance of forgiveness downstairs.

After all, how many times had he brought a bouquet of flowers down for their table when the maids had put new ones upstairs? And he had named each of the girls after one of the blossoms—Poppy, Honeysuckle, Tiger Lily. The Housekeeper and Cook had declined their names—Snake's-head Fritillary and Round-headed Rampion. Mr. Barreby had received interesting fodder on his dinner plate that night. He was a great sport, though, and ate the flavorless soup made just for him and burnt meat while everyone else laughed their way through the good cooking.

***

Dinner at Belgrave was early for the servants with the family being out that evening. Though the lady's maids had spent a full night and day upstairs, they now descended into what Elizabeth termed the Inferno. Was the duchess aware of the situation downstairs? Anne insisted that Elizabeth go first and used her as a shield. How glad she was to be just a bit of a thing behind Lizzy, who was built of a heartier appetite.

Maids were yet carrying food to the table when the girls arrived, and they received no greeting. They waited before sitting to see where it would be deemed appropriate. Heaven forbid they take the wrong seat, Lizzy whispered to Anne. Somehow the servants spread themselves out to cover the benches, and Elizabeth had to speak up for space. A man barked for "someone over there" to move and make room. The wrong people moved, and it was done over again. There were neither flowers nor Flowers at this table, but oh my, the good silver had been brought down, and Nobody was to say a word about it—Nobody being the girls from Holmeshire.

Anne was terrified to eat for fear of her elbow

touching the goddess next to her, but was expected to manage. After all, there was nothing wrong with the food, and did she think she was the queen? And how could Madam Elizabeth have gotten her napkin so soiled already? It is a bit of work to get them clean—did she know? And must Anne tap her feet so relentlessly? There was no orchestra to which to keep time, and they did not intend to hire one for her, at least not this week.

And then, yes, it happened. The poor girl, in trying to push the butter across to a kitchen maid, knocked over a pitcher of milk that was, after all, not just for her but for all those at her end of the table. And now, besides the huge mess, some of which had splashed into other peoples' dinners and even their frocks and hair, good people were going to do without milk. Anne covered her face with her hands, which it was pointed out was of no assistance whatsoever. Did she not know where the rags were kept? No, she did not.

She was just about to break down in tears when the building above them parted. All clouds graciously moved aside to permit warm rays of the sun to shine down upon the poor girl in the form of a handsome young footman who stood and shouted for some decent manners in that place. He stepped over the bench and got Anne some rags. "There," he said, "it is not so terrible, you see. Deidre (the goddess) did the same thing last week."

Harp chords and nightingales sounded and rendered everyone silent, or Anne deaf. She glanced up at the young man's face for a second with thankful eyes, but such a face it was, and it filled her capacity for memory completely. What happened during the rest of that meal she could not recall, not whether she cleaned up the milk or ate another bite or if anyone had commented on those subjects. In fact, she did not any longer fear the next mealtime but greatly looked forward to it. She often peered down halls in coming days to see whether any handsome being was carrying tea in the wrong part of the house.

That evening Elizabeth lost Anne entirely, and she mumbled to herself on the long climb back from the kitchen to the ladies' rooms. She did not mean the questions for herself but formulated a reply to them for lack of anyone conscious dwelling inside Anne's dazed little body who ought to have answered her superior.

***

Wills, upon returning from Handerton and parting from his family in the entrance hall, with careful timing nodded Emma in the direction of some sizable windows overlooking the gardens. She was tired from the long and tense day but accompanied him. Surely no one would object to their standing and talking there where anyone might pass? Nevertheless, she shifted her weight anxiously, for what of Genevieve? She would not stand there for long.

Emma made an effort to suppress her sentiments, though they willfully rose to make trouble. Wills remained happy through the conflict, not yet seeing that his path had forked. Emma was near, and that mattered more to him with each passing day—and what had that to do with Genny? Was Emma not but a very special friend?

"Is it not lovely?" Wills asked, staring into eerily moon-lit trees. "I suppose they will put a statue of me in there someday. What do you think? It is my fate, is it not?"

"Sir, you must first distinguish yourself. Do you suppose they will put it there simply to outshine the orbs and flowers and charm the ladies that amble

97

through?"

He laughed at her remark. "I suppose they will, will they not? They put up portraits and busts of the least of us in family houses. Surely my comely jaw line recommends me in the garden of a household duke?" he asked as he raised his chin and traced the edge of his face with a finger.

Emma glared at him in playful irritation, but made strict efforts not to flirt with this engaged and noble man. She indeed cared for his jawline, but determined to mind the conversation, for Wills was too free. "You must prevent it, my lord, ere it cause women to swoon as they pass or ladies to go home grieving that it is but a cold stone likeness. You suppose that you will afflict womankind for centuries in that garden, do you not? Tomorrow I shall report your designs to the master."

"My being his favorite nephew will stand me well in the situation."

"Your being the only nephew on his dear wife's side will surely get you a statue on that merit alone. However, I shall strongly protest for the sake of the ladies of generations to come. Now, I am sure Anne awaits in my room. She did not sleep well last night for the changes. I must allow the poor girl to finish with me and be off to bed."

"Suppose I had something important to say?" he retorted in jest, his eyebrows raised and his head tipped to the side.

"Why have you not then said it, my lord?" she replied. "I believe Narcissus stepped into your path."

"I believe you brought up my charming features."

"Did I, then?" she shook her head. "Should that be anywhere near truth it was to send you off glowing so the lack of candles in the halls would not be your death with your tripping over statues of charming nephews."

Emma guarded herself, stepping back for feeling very much like stepping nearer. "What, then, was so important?"

"Important? Ah, yes. It was about my statue. Where do you think it ought to be placed?"

"My lord, should they promise you a statue, I shall be the first to nominate a position for it." She looked around at the grounds below. "Do you perhaps care for cherry blossoms falling on you throughout the spring, possibly in hopes that you might attract more attention in pink petals? If so, should you have a statue, I will recommend that little nook," she said, pointing as if to issue a command. "Good night, my lord."

***

The darkness of Bermondsey shadows left navigating difficult for an aging drunk, but Benedict found some way to arrive in one piece. He leaned his full weight against a dirty wall to facilitate ascending the stairs. Lucy heard him come and rose in her nightdress to unbolt the door. He fell inward, regained his footing and hollered at his son.

"Charles." Charles rolled over on the straw mat.

"Eh?"

"Git my boots off, lad. I'd better not bend over, you know? It could cause a bigger than Buckingham Palace problem. Lucy gets to snarlin', you know?"

"Paw," Charles complained and covered his head with a ragged blanket.

"I got news for you, son." There was a long delay.

"Tell me in the morning." Another long delay.

"Lucy, git my boots off." She grimaced. "Lucy, do it. I'm gonna make us rich, you know."

"I don't see how. It can't happen. There is no way. I don't need no lawyer to tell you that." She sunk to the floor to unlace the second-hand Oxonians.

"Well, I got us a lawyer. And we have a plan."

"Tell us in the morning," came an angry voice from under the blanket.

"We're awake now, the lot of us," Benedict sloshed. "And it is a good plan."

Charles sat up, half awake, and complained loudly. "Give the man some tea, Lucy, before he wakes up the whole house." Lucy rose, threw Benedict's boots into a corner and returned her kettle to the fire. The irate but resigned Charles shuffled the cards on the floor beside his mat.

"Here's the thing, Charles. There's no law to get no money for us. None at all. None. What do you make of that? We shoulda kept that solicitor put when he came till he got something for us. But no, off 'e goes." He slammed down a foot. No reply was required. "But here's the thing. This man, John Brown, is a genius. He's come up with a plan. This is good. We gotta work our way into the household. Not all of us. One of us. Just one. And I think it should be me." Benedict grabbed one of the blankets from Charles.

"Oh, Papa. That will never happen. There's no way they're going to let any of us in the door."

"That's the thing, Charles. That's the thing. They owe us. They owe us a lot. They know it. They'll let us in."

The thought fully woke Charles. "Yes. It might be they would." Lucy brought the tea, and they sat down to deal cards and mull it over.

~Chapter 6~
The Worlds Fall Apart

Seven o'clock breakfast was decidedly painless for Anne, who exchanged several facial expressions with her adored one, exposing her captivating dimples. It was worse than the night before for her sister, who now had to deal with all the rudeness and insults alone while Anne was lost in a state of bliss. Lizzy was unaccustomed to her sister doing as she pleased, and it made things worse for her.

The Belgrave staff had noticed the clock striking Love at dinner and had attacked poor Simon before the table was half cleared. He was in service, they pointed out—there was no place for canoodling or distraction from duty. Their attitude worsened at breakfast when they saw him sit close to the enchantress, throwing smiles and tender glances in her direction.

Holmeshire became a word of derision, which mattered only to Elizabeth. Belgrave was an opposing clan on the offense. Though few words were spoken between Romeo and Juliet, they were not needed, and everyone knew that a feud must be declared to break up the bond.

101

Anne was sprightly at dressing Emma for the day. Beauty had never appeared so quickly. Elizabeth, on the other hand, could do nothing right. Several apologies into the morning, she let out a huge sigh and dropped into a chair, defeated.

Winnie waited. Becoming fearful that only half her hair would go up that day, she asked what was so terribly wrong.

The poor girl poured out her pain all in one sentence with a profusion of tears—how it was dreadful downstairs, which included the backload of insults from previous visits. Why didn't Grantham and the housekeeper take more control? And she had lost Anne, who she was sure would jump off the coach at the last moment and stay in London, probably under a tree, and her mother would never see her again. How horrid it is, she deplored, to be the only Capulet conscious at the breakfast table, so could they please eat with poor lonely Nanny Bowen? Winnie consoled her maid, promising to tend to the crisis.

Helena's maid, normally eager to please her mistress, muttered angrily under her breath through the morning routine hearing hardly a word that the duchess said about her painfully pulled hair.

***

Helena, Winnie and Emma met for breakfast. They were quite dazed by the moods of their lady's maids and tried to make sense of it. Only Winnie knew of recent events downstairs, and she kept it to herself for the moment, not wishing to disturb Helena's household further. However, at her request, Helena gave permission for the Amberton girls to eat in the nursery should it not interfere with Nanny's efforts with Nicholas. Would that, perhaps, solve the problem?

Winnie wondered, though feeling unsure of how to handle Anne's position. The girl did, after all, have feelings.

She informed the girls, adding that she hoped they would be happier having their meals away from less amicable persons downstairs. Lizzy stated that she could even more happily tear Grantham from limb to limb, but retracted it.

Anne sunk into a chair, her shoulders dropped, her smile gone. Mealtime was the best time of the day if held in the midst of the ferocious Montagues. She received counsel from Winnie that one cannot know a young man at one or two meetings, and she should think carefully. Did she not care to stay in service and have some expectation of a comfortable life around a table of good food? Few ate as well as servants in a grand house, did they? But Anne knew what she wanted. She would happily starve for an opportunity to know the young man better.

***

Emma arrived in the drawing room with her sheet music for the afternoon's entertainment to find the smiling Adelina waiting to meet her alongside the ladies. "Adelina Darivela," Helena said, "meet Miss Emma Carrington." Both curtsied politely, and Adelina stepped forward, radiating affection. She caught herself, hesitated, and curtsied again. She seemed unable to speak, and uncomfortable with the silence, Emma began.

"I am pleased to meet you, Miss Darivela. Are you a lady of London?"

"I live here in London, yes, Miss Carrington." Emma's brows raised at her accent. "I am most pleased to meet you. As for being a lady, well, I spent the afternoon with Nanny Bown, Elizabeth and Anne yesterday. They were charming company and made me quite eager to meet you."

"Ah, then, I am pleased to meet one of my peers."

"I do believe you are above me, Miss Carrington, dining at Handerton with lords and ladies," Adelina said with a smile. "Did you have a pleasant evening?"

Emma responded to Adelina's warmth and relaxed. "I made the best of it, thank you. I am more comfortable here with dukes and duchesses, I fear, owing to the kindness shown me despite my humble start."

"I know them to be gracious and considerate persons myself. I must take my leave, Miss Carrington. It was my pleasure."

Again, both curtsied, and Adelina departed.

The post was brought up and delivered to the ladies. Helena and Winnie discussed their letters. Invitations arrived, and they compared their diaries. How was Winnie to finish the year's shopping with parties to attend? This or that person had politely declined the request to include Emma at tea the next week, for the room was so small or the list so long. Perhaps the next opportunity elsewhere would allow.

Emma attempted to wait politely through their discussion. The butler had brought a note from Mr. Gabriel Hughes, and she considered how she might approach his request. She was ultimately obliged to interrupt. "Please excuse me, I offer sincere apologies. Mr. Hughes arrived, and has asked me to walk out. He would like me to present myself in the entry hall, should it be acceptable."

Winnie and Helena cast anxious looks toward each other. "Please, ma'am," Emma said, "I would like to go. He is a charming man, but do not worry—I wish to let him know kindly that my future is my life with you.

I do not intend to walk out again or especially to marry him, as I am sure you must realize, however likable he may be."

Emma's words relieved the ladies. Winnie replied, "Yes, Emma, you may go, but please ring for Anne and take her along. We cannot attend you at this time, and it is best not to go alone. It may give the wrong impression."

Grantham sent for Emma's wrap and for Anne, who arrived in a state very near tears. She came reluctantly, well supplied with handkerchiefs. Grantham showed displeasure escorting the women to the door, it not being meant for servants. Indeed, scullery maids downstairs questioned Emma's status, but there was Mr. Hughes, Barrister to the Crown, waiting at the front entry, and so it must be. Grantham handed him a note from Her Grace, which he read at once and nodded agreement to the butler.

The lawyer offered Emma his arm. They stepped out followed by Anne, who began whimpering at the sight of a couple arm in arm. Certainly she would never be allowed to touch her dear one's arm or even see his face again, what with meals in the nursery.

Her fussing was not heard at first. Mr. Hughes thanked Miss Carrington for meeting him at short notice. It was so seemingly thoughtless of him, he said, but the fact was he was free from work engagements unexpectedly and had been looking for another chance to talk with her after their first meeting a few evenings since. He would love to have heard her express great gladness he had come, but before that opportunity arose nothing could be heard above the lamentation behind them. Anne was bent over her first handkerchief, crying as she trudged along, so bent that she could not see where she was going, and ran right into the back of Mr.

Gabriel Hughes. She did not apologize, not having even noticed plowing into him, knocking him into a pillar and nearly into the area below stairs. She raised her voice to her mistress.

"Oh, ma'am, I am such a case of devastation."

"So I see, Anne, dear girl, let's find a bench and have a sit down. Come over here." Emma wrapped her arm about the poor girl's shoulder and led her to a seat. The astonished Gabriel regained his balance. He hastened to their sides to comfort little Anne as best he could, but stopped short to contemplate how it might best be done. The ladies sat down. The gentleman was yet some feet away and got to be beside himself, as gentlemen often are when a woman is in tears. He hastened to pick her the beginnings of a lilac from a nearby bush, as nothing nearby was yet in full bloom, in hopes that what existed of it could dispel some of her grief. But for all her sobbing to Emma, it was never noticed.

"Please, tell me what to do," she wailed. "I shall never see him again. The lovely footman, who helped me so downstairs—he...I...he may not ever appear near the nursery, you know, or in the hall near your room, and I may never know if he should care for me."

"Anne, you have found someone you care for? I see. No wonder you were so delighted this morning."

Poor Emma was lost for what to do. Her mind went back and forth, considering whether she should discourage this romance as propriety required, or whether she should help Anne in some way with it. Her puzzled look went from Anne to Gabe and back again. Could not Mr. Gabriel Hughes, this renowned orator, handle the case with some aplomb?

The gallant Gabriel took out his handkerchief and put it into Emma's hands for her consideration. He then stood back, hoping he had pleased her. He nervously awaited the outcome and admired Emma for her selfless efforts and the humble friendship she extended toward her maid. He was ever so grateful to have a woman present to handle this grievous feminine emergency.

Anne could no longer contain her thoughts and blurted everything out to the abandonment of reason and sense. "I was delighted, ma'am, yes, I am sorry, for I know I am in service, and I never intended to consider deviating from it being so privileged, but how was I to know? And now her ladyship has said we are to eat upstairs."

Gabriel was terribly confused by her comments, but she was a woman, after all, and how could she be understood? He looked to Emma for the gynecic wisdom that surely would, by now, have solved the puzzle, but to his dismay, Emma yet appeared perplexed. Someone must have some understanding of the situation and how to repair it, for it must be repaired that he not be required to endure more weeping while appearing to completely understand.

He, with chivalrous intent, suggested Emma obtain more information from the girl while he stood guard, or assisted with the belongings she had dropped, or best of all, located a more private place for women to sob and confuse him. Off he went to search, but felt most inconsiderate for it. He had abandoned them to passersby, and he promptly returned. Perhaps things would make more sense quite soon, he hoped with all his heart.

Emma's comforting touch and words had indeed calmed Anne. She was at least able to hear the words Emma spoke rather than her own wails.

"Anne, should you wish to leave service, I will

never stand in your way. But is there someone that has shown interest in you? What has he done? Or what is this about?"

"Oh ma'am, I just saw him. I was being teased and pushed on and treated badly, and he stood up for me." *Ah*, thought Gabriel, *no wonder, for he was Her Rescuer*. "And he looked at me, too, ma'am. He looked at me."

"He looked at you, Anne, and you are thinking of leaving service?" Emma replied.

"Well, what I mean is, well, you know, he was, oh I do not know, ma'am, we looked at each other." Gabriel and Emma both understood perfectly the meaning of this sort of captivity, now that it had been sufficiently explained, as well as the enormity of such an occurrence in one's life.

"I see, and you spoke to him, too?" Emma asked.

"No, no. I did not speak to him."

"No?"

"No. I did not."

"I see. Well, what can I do to help?"

"I do not know."

Emma looked up to Gabriel for the answer, but he was dazed. He managed to pick the lilac up from the ground where it had fallen, and he handed it to Emma. "Does she know his name?" he asked, avoiding consultation directly with the woman, who might, once again, become the source of a waterfall.

She turned to Anne. "Do you know his name?"

"No."

She looked up to Gabe. "She does not." He nodded his head, displaying clear comprehension of the fact.

"I shall surely talk to Her Grace and Lady Holmeshire on your behalf," Emma promised little Anne.

They spent the next half hour walking her, one on each side of her, as Gabriel's confidence in the situation had improved. They comforted her, pointing out puppies, a historical plaque, and a fountain. Gabe was so relieved to see the progress that he did not attempt to be walking with Emma and a chaperone, but instead was walking to compose and revitalize Anne. He was, however, even more impressed by the kind, humble Emma than before.

The time came, too quickly to please him, for him to return whence he came. He delivered the girls to the house and bade them farewell, with a promise to return.

***

"Genevieve, darling, it is 9 A.M. Are you dressing to come down?" Silence. "Genny," her anxious mother said, "I'm coming in." She stepped into the room and walked to the plump, silk-canopied bed where her daughter was hiding from the world for the second day.

"Mama," Genny said without the energy for expression and without turning to face her. "How can you engage a small child to another small child without waiting to see what kind of people they come to be when they are grown?"

Taken aback, her mother considered her reply. "Genny, dear girl, Wills is a wonderful man. We knew the family, and we knew he would turn out well. Your Papa said it was important to settle matters early on. Wills was the heir of the Holmeshires, and there were others wishing to make marriage contracts with him for the title—and all he stands to inherit. You must remember what Lord Holmeshire will have from his grandpapa and the rest of his family besides Holmeshire Hall and the properties that he now has. Remember the realm over which you will be mistress. We will be so proud of you. This creates a close tie to

109

the royal family, as King George the IV wished, and there are benefits to the lot of us that you, most of all, will enjoy. Lady Embry said we were terribly fortunate to make the match when we did. It may even be that you would not have gotten another good marriage. Some never do, you know."

"I could not get another good marriage, Mama? I am undoubtedly far too plain and quite unpleasant in company. Thank you." Genny turned her back. "And you think I need a good marriage. For what? A word? Countess is just a word, a word that comes with a lot of expectations and rules. Many a woman has become a countess or even a duchess or a princess only to become terribly unhappy. So for what? Another house or two? I'll have Chenbury should I never marry. Papa has given it over to me, and it is all I would ever need, is it not? You do not even have a son for Handerton. It will go to whomever I marry, and so I will have two in London alone. Do I want to leave London and live in the moorlands in a mossy stone fortress? No. For another house or two, of whatever description, I must live with a man who does not wish to throw balls? I will not need houses if there are to be no balls. Enough about houses; money? Do I need more money than I can ever spend? No. I do not."

"You need a fortune to pass on to care for the houses, darling."

"I could sell one house and live forever off it."

"But there is much more to it. Many things were involved in the decision. You know that. Papa and I could see your distress last night, though, and we talked about it."

"Yes?" She turned and looked at her Mama with a twinge of hope in her reddened eyes.

"Papa has mixed feelings, and he seemed torn, but

there is much good about Lord Holmeshire. You will be in excellent circumstances should anything happen to us. You must be protected from those strange men that endlessly follow after you. Wills will protect you."

Genevieve turned away, face down, and pulled a thin red throw blanket over her head. "But I have servants to protect me," she argued. "And Wills will be away often."

Grace hesitated. "That is true. He will be. Wills is involved in government now. Papa says he will go far in the political world."

Genny threw the blanket off. "But lords in Parliament have a life in their homes, as well. And that is the life that their wives share."

Her hope for a reprieve gone, she buried her head again. "This man…some important man's misbehavior landed him a child that he could not bring home, so Wills brought him home, and now I must raise him? It makes me look a fool. And I cannot even know whose son he is? Should not a man who is going far in the political world have a happy wife as well as a distinguished life?" She let out an angry wail. "All that, and it seems that we will be devoting our lives to feeding the poor, does it not, Mama?"

Lady Breyton sat down on the bed. She played with some blankets and pushed up a pillow. Her daughter had been focused on this marriage for years. She had worked to learn what a woman was to learn and could skillfully manage the role of a countess and an aristocratic household by now. She had avoided involvement with other men, had waited longer in life than most girls to marry…and now was turning against it all.

This would not work for the Breytons. They had arranged their matters neatly, and their daughter was to do just so. She was to look impossibly lovely at her Westminster Abbey wedding. Wills was to rise in Parliament with her Papa's help, and she would be on his arm at the most elite events. She was to be the perfect picture of a titled lady and never to dirty her hands with anything beneath her.

Grace tried to warm her to her commitments. "There are worse things in life. He could be a selfish, ignoble man, but he is not. That will work to your benefit, as well as to that of the poor. Let him help the poor—just do not get much involved yourself. Papa never allows me to dirty my hands with such things. I've been happy doing as your father says. Give money to your steward and have him handle it. You can well afford to give some to the poor, and it will bring you praise."

"But can I afford the behavior of such a man? Not at all. People will be astonished at him at every turn. I shall have to hide behind my parasol at every garden party." Her anger now prevented her from taking it lying down, and she bounded out of bed. She ran to her vanity and pulled a brush roughly through her hair. "Mama, must we think about destitution all the time? At least we should forget about it when we are together at our dinners. Let Parliament handle it away from the dining table. Let those who do have good food enjoy it."

"I dined at Buckingham Palace not long ago, Genny. The smell of London's sewage in the drains under that palace is most unpleasant. It is hard to leave the problems of London outside of even the home of the Queen. Now, Wills must be promoted. This is what he is passionate about, and so Papa shall support him on it and push through his reforms. Papa is altering his own viewpoint to support Wills, which will bring him much other support. Perhaps, then, Parliament will improve the situation. Wills will have the credit for it, and you shall be his wife, the Countess of Holmeshire. You shall be hailed everywhere as the wife of a great man, and later as the mother of the Second Marquess of Breyton. We shall be so proud of you."

"Mother, it is not me you will be proud of. It is you yourselves. You will be proud that you taught me to do just what Lady Embry thinks I should do. You will be able to breathe easily at tea, knowing you will not be scolded for my indelicacy, and you will be admired as the glowing mother of the Countess of Holmeshire. Surely, if there were a marriageable prince, Wills would have been left behind." Lady Breyton caught and held her breath as Genevieve went on. "These opinions that you express to me belong to my father and to Lady Embry. All of them. You do not think for yourself—not ever. I simply do not want that for myself. I do not want to submit my wishes under someone else constantly as you do, Mama, until I do not even know what my feelings are anymore. And I do not wish to be an ornament on an earl's arm. I want my life to be meaningful, fulfilling, and worthwhile. I want to do something grand myself."

Grace shook her head and replied, "It is the way of society, Genny. It is how things are done. I am a marchioness, and surely you understand that I cannot be disapproved for your conduct." She straightened the bedding as Genevieve stood, eyes closed and hands on her hips. "Darling," Grace said, "we are to have tea at Belgrave Square soon, in a few weeks. Or likely we will see Lady Holmeshire somewhere sooner yet. We can prepare for more pleasant conversation than what we had at dinner and ask Lady Holmeshire to talk to her son about these things. Please, now, prepare yourself for the day. Be my pretty little lady again."

"No doubt we are to have tea with Miss Carrington. Perhaps they will invite the scullery maid, as well."

"I agree, my dear, that we must preserve proper social graces. I will discuss this, too, with Lady Holmeshire. Lady Embry is utterly horrified, and I have never seen your Papa so upset about social order. He is sorely distressed."

"No, Mama, please. Allow me to discuss it with Lord Holmeshire at my next opportunity, for I fear there is much at stake."

Genevieve found that the opportunity would not arrive soon, for Wilfred was too busy himself with Parliamentary matters, hotel meetings with assemblies of deliberating gentlemen and a week out of town to tend to his castle's redesign.

***

Anne's mood had been very low since meals downstairs were no longer on her diary. Several days had gone by. How was she to know if her dear one was thinking of her?

The kitchen maid surely did not let on when she brought meals to the nursery. She seemed to represent the Montagues with a smug smile. They were very pleased to have won the war without ever a fight.

Footmen rarely came up to the area of the nursery, and if they should, they were at the far end of the hall and then gone. But Anne also had to deal with the Capulets of the nursery who were greatly opposed to her romance and with Lizzy trying to regain her position as commander of her sister.

"Lizzy. What have you done to me?" Anne moaned. "How could you tell on me when I had found such happiness and destroy me?"

"You were perfectly happy all your life before you

went down those stairs. You can be happy again," was the reply. "This could cost you and him—what's his name? Do you even know his name? It could cost the both of you your situations."

"I do not want my situation—I want him."

"Stop this, Anne. You do not even know him. He might be a despicable rake. If you were with him, you could not go home. How would you see Mama again, or Papa, or the girls, or Freddy?"

"I could write them."

Elizabeth glared at her sister and stamped her foot, but gave up for the moment. She turned her attentions to hurling a paper ball at Nicky, who dodged it with a look of fear on his face.

Anne was alone with her problems. Only Emma and Gabriel, of all persons in the universe, seemed to care, and they had no authority in the matter. However, Emma might try to help her—would the ladies do her bidding? Things could not be left to chance. Anne must find a way to see Romeo. She wandered about the day nursery, contemplating the matter. As she passed by a window, she saw someone look up toward her—a footman. Yes, she believed it was him—her footman! He was there, carrying the post and looking with concern up at the nursery. When she appeared through the glass, his apprehensive expression became one of delight. He cared!

***

The door to the drawing room swung open for Grantham to announce a guest. "Mr. Gabriel Hughes," he said. The gentleman had been overtaken by a cloudburst, and the butler had taken great pains to somewhat dry him off. He took a few steps in and stood just inside the door with the look of a guilt-ridden intruder. Helena enjoyed his company and warmly greeted him.

"Mr. Hughes, do come in. Join us. We have been whiling away the time and are delighted to have you call. Have you arrived to complain of your excursion with Emma and Anne, or is there a happier reason for your visit?"

"Your Grace, Your Ladyship, Miss Carrington, I thank you for receiving me. Should I complain, it would be for the rain, which just a few moments ago caught me having left my umbrella in lieu of my cane. It is good to see you all and be allowed to step in. Surely I should have washed away in that downpour. I had in mind entreating Miss Carrington to walk out with me again, should her chaperone be of better constitution this day, but how inconsiderate it would be to escort a pair of ladies out to be drenched alongside me."

Helena spoke up. "Then you shall stay and have tea. One must keep etiquette in its place, for it does not consider that a gentleman might have been drenched within an inch of his life. We must charitably overlook that you are not a lady come to tea in the appropriate gown and save you from certain washing away. Tea is soon to be served, and it has been some time now since we have had the opportunity to enjoy your company."

"I shall be most grateful to stay indoors in such good society if only you will find me a chair cushion not wrapped in silk, for I should hate to ruin the hard work of so many industrious worms."

Emma enjoyed his winsome conversation, and she hoped she should not have to break his heart. She felt the sooner they could talk the better it would be for him. She hoped there would be no more delays, but apparently this afternoon would be spent in company with the ladies. "How very kind of you to visit, Mr.

Hughes," she said. "I am grateful for your assistance with Anne's unhappy afternoon."

Gabriel ascertained that Anne had survived to this day and stated he hoped ever so much that her problem could be solved in a way suitable to everyone. Helena assured him the matter was being discussed amongst the family, and that all aspects of the situation were under consideration. To be sure, she said, they wished everyone high and low to be happy, but such things take time, and there would almost certainly be no pleasing the Belgrave staff should there be any allowance for Anne's feelings.

Footmen arrived with a wooden chair along with tea, cream cheese-watercress sandwiches and a few pastry selections. The ladies and Gabe all wondered if Anne's beloved rescuer might be among them. Simon was indeed there, forgetting himself and his duties. He seemed to wish to speak, looking directly at Helena despite the rules in great houses.

Helena asked if he had something to say. He opened his mouth but then looked around, for the first time conscious of the fact that the room was occupied with guests. He was out of place entirely in taking this matter to Her Grace at tea, nor was he allowed to go to anyone other than Grantham with his concerns at any time. "No, ma'am," was his disconcerted reply, and he looked to the wall.

The other footmen were quite perturbed that he had nearly overstepped this boundary, that he might attempt to talk to the duchess on another occasion and that it could result in his perpetual happiness. They later reported to Grantham, informing him that Simon's behavior was thoroughly inappropriate. He was quickly replaced by another footman for future teas, and was given duties that did not put him in direct contact with the mistress of the house, who was, as the butler well knew, a sympathetic woman.

Helena filled gold-trimmed porcelain cups as all took their seats at the table. There was some talk of the case Gabriel was arguing in court for the Crown. Helena spoke to the women about a case he had won, how he had overcome huge obstacles and proven what was needed for justice in the matter. Mr. Hughes had, in fact, had some involvement in ending the death sentence for minor crimes. The queen was particularly fond of him, having learned of that great work, according to Helena.

Gabe was happy to see a delighted expression appear on the face of the woman he favored, and whom these praises had apparently impressed. There was also some parley about upcoming social events, coordinating together as to which they would attend, with Gabe making a mental note of what parties Emma, in particular, might be allowed to grace. And, of course, some great surprise was declared about the heaviness of the early summer rain shower.

"And now," Gabriel asked Emma, "may I inquire about your life and your dear family? I do recall you were raised by a squire as his ward."

Emma gave a half smile and thought for a few seconds. "There is not much to tell, I fear. I was dropped on the doorstep of Squire Carrington as an infant some two and twenty years ago with no calling card, and it seemed they had to find a name for me." Gabriel's concern was validated.

"Oh, my dear lady, that is sad to tell."

"I do not know, sir—it could be I would have had a difficult life elsewhere, but I was raised as a squire's ward and taken in by the Countess of Holmeshire. I was educated for two years by a governess and tutors. I have come to live as a spoiled guest at Holmeshire Hall rather than serve and am sitting today in the drawing room of the Duchess of Trent drinking a very fine tea. They are terribly good to me. It seems a very blessed life to me, and I intend always to show loyalty and appreciation for it."

"Indeed. I am glad of it," Gabriel said. "They could not have chosen a lovelier, more worthy girl to favor in this way." Emma blushed, but she made the effort not to look away, as young women must learn to accept such praise.

Winnie joined in, "Mr. Hughes had a sad start to life, but has made a fine gentleman of himself."

"I have had every advantage," he replied, "at least after a short time as a bit of a stray kitten in the streets of London. But it made me willing to work hard to never fall back into such sad straits, and to do what I can for those who are so unfortunate."

"The streets," Emma gasped before he had finished. "At what age were you on the streets?" She leaned forward to receive her answer the sooner.

"I only remember being there, sitting on the side of the road with other dirty children not far from me. I recall being taken into a fine carriage by a well-dressed lady and given a wonderful bit of food from her basket. I remember my amazement at her shining carriage, her thick, embroidered jacket and the delicious confection. Oh, yes, and she gave me a neatly cut little sandwich as well. I was taken to a grand house such as I had never seen and scrubbed like I never had been. They tell me I was about four years old."

"Four," Emma choked. "You were alone on the streets at four? Who fed you? What did you eat?"

"Apparently I was there for some time before that day. I do not remember anything before the carriage ride, but the street people knew of me and explained everything to the princess."

"A princess? It was a princess that took you in?"

Helena joined in, sharing her memory of that day. "I was with Princess Charlotte that day. We had gone for an outing with Caroline, Princess of Wales. We were riding in a lovely park watching people walk in the sunshine, and then we traveled farther into an area in which I had never been. The farther we went, the sadder I felt. There were people calling out to us desperately to buy things from them. One had buttons he had dug from the mud of the filthy Thames. He had tried to clean them, but we did not dare even touch them. We gave him a coin for his trouble. A woman begged a doctor's help for her injured child. We gave her money for a doctor. And then we saw beautiful little Gabe. We asked some women where his parents were. They had been near when his mother had died, they said, and he had no one but them, though they could not much help him. The Princess of Wales took him into the carriage and brought him home."

Helena leaned toward Emma, lowered her voice and went on, "This must be kept a strict secret. Very few people know he came from the streets or they might shun him, you know. She adopted him as she had other children. She did not keep him in her house but found a genteel couple who would raise and care for him. She paid his expenses and made sure he received a start in life to become a man who could care well for himself. He has proven to be a man who certainly deserved the help, for he, in turn, looks after others."

"That was the day Helena came home and told me how she wished to help the poor," Winnie mused. "She was very persuasive with our parents and was, at times, in tears. It made me realize how difficult life can be for others. So you see it turned out for the good, for Mr. Hughes and for us."

"And for me," Emma replied. "Perhaps that is why I am here."

"Then I am the gladder for having lived it," Gabe declared.

***

Time had gone by slowly for poor Anne, who paced about, trapped between the ladies' rooms and the nursery. She would see her loved one below the window when he returned with the post a few times daily, and he would look up hoping to see her, but neither could find a way to communicate with the other. Waving would have been noticed, and she could not throw open the window of Nanny Bowen's nursery and go undiscovered.

Anne had determined that should much more time pass in this way, she would take matters into her own hands...and the day had arrived. Anne knew what times of day her darling was to be seen looking up at her window, but the doors of the building were guarded by Montagues, and she did not know if any had defected to Simon's side. She could not step foot near the main door which he passed on any pretense. And she surely could not saunter through the kitchen and out the servant's door.

So she conspired, her scheme requiring the assistance of a hapless geranium from the nursery. Nanny Bowen was preoccupied when Anne abducted the plant.

Next she devised that she might be admitted to the drawing room above Mr. Grantham's sacred entry door. She approached Grantham, curtsied politely, and asked to enter the room. This puzzled him, but he assumed it related to a lady's plant, and she was

121

granted access.

Inside the room she curtsied again and asked Her Grace whether she could please put her precious flower out on the balcony for just one afternoon to receive a dose of extra daylight. It was, she said, her very own living thing, and she thought of it as her baby.

Helena was confused, as lady's maids did not step in this way, but for the sake of the poor bit of botany it was logical enough, and she gave permission. The timing was perfect. Juliet stepped out on the balcony and dropped a note just as her Romeo passed beneath. He had been dismayed not to see his dear one standing at her window post, but he was now aware of the reason. He caught the note, smiled widely and passed by as proficiently as ever.

***

Genevieve and her mother moved ahead with plans for the Midsummer Night's Dream Ball. Several times they had in their committee for tea and planning.

Eventually invitations went out to all the best people. Everyone called in their seamstresses asking for wispy, sparkling gowns in pale color, cut with pixie hems, trimmed with flowers and vines, some with wings, all with garlands or crowns, all full of mystery and intrigue.

The group made plans for decor that would turn Handerton's ballroom into a nocturnal forest. They called in craftsmen, searching for those who could create the needed items. Genevieve nearly forgot her problems for fitting all the planning and work into her unrelenting schedule.

Other than for his trip to Holmeshire, Wills never missed a day at the Palace of Westminster, paying rapt attention to the speeches and deliberations of the gentlemen. He held back as a junior member, but was given an opportunity to speak once through Lord Breyton, and he rose to the occasion. His words were greeted heartily—it was apparent that he would be a highly respected Lord in the chamber. A few even suggested to him that he set his sights on the role of Prime Minister within a decade or so.

Unexpectedly one day, Wills arrived at Handerton House to call on Genevieve. She had been planning and working with the young Lady Katherine Embry and Miss Samantha Highmore, her closest friends, and her mother. All were surprised and delighted when Wills was announced at the door of the glassed-in palm room where they had gone to induce woodland thoughts in the tropical atmosphere. Even the butler could not help but exult at his arrival.

"Please, have a seat, my lord," beamed Grace, The Lady Breyton. He bowed his head and stood as the women moved themselves from a table to grasscloth divans near a proliferation of palm leaves hovering over ferns and orchids. He took a seat after they again sat.

"Good day, milady," he replied, "and Lady Genevieve, Lady Katherine, Miss Highmore." He paused. "Is this perhaps the committee for your ball, Lady Breyton?" She nodded and said that yes, it was in part the committee. He continued, "I am terribly sorry to have been so long away. Although I have been in Town for the most part, I have been working very hard, and I was, in fact, away for a short time."

"We heard you were away," Katherine expressed sincerely, relieved and respecting that Wills was at last here and had not yet committed any faux pas. "Did you have success with your project at Holmeshire?"

"I should love to share my story of the matter with you very much, but I am terribly short of time today.

I'm afraid you will all find me to be very rude. I came to ask whether Genevieve would be permitted to leave you all to accompany me on an outing? We shall be in a public place and will not need a chaperone." Smiles brightened despite his abruptness. Grace winked at her daughter's friends and then stood to ring a bell for Genevieve's wrap. She turned, though, to Wills with a warning.

"Please, Lord Holmeshire, do keep Genny at your side. There have been strange men watching her for some time—more and more recently, and we are frightened."

"I will be at her side, Your Ladyship. Do not concern yourself. It can be only a brief outing, so should you ladies care to wait, I promise to return her to you quite safely within the hour." All nodded in agreement, and Genevieve stood up to prepare. It seemed a short bit of time he had set aside for this outing and likely proposal, but Genny had decided to accept that her future husband would be a very busy man.

Wills waited rather impatiently for her cloak and then requested, "Genny, dearest, would you please remove your jewelry?" Puzzled expressions replaced every smile, Genny's most of all. She removed her necklace and rings and gave them to her mother, took her gloves and parasol and went out the door, bewildered by this perplexing man.

The coachman knew where to go after helping them to their seats. Wills sat uncommonly near Genevieve, but she felt comforted and protected. Her sense of safety and Wills' silence moved her to talk to him of her troubles.

"Mama mentioned that I am followed. You should be aware that it is true. I know of no reason for it and am frightened."

"You are a lovely young lady. Someone is, perhaps, wishing for an introduction. Is the gentleman alone?"

"The horrid man is alone when watching me but not alone in the practice. It has happened several times, and with two or three individuals separately. I never leave the house now without at least two guardians as well as my chaperone.

"I see. And what has been done to discover the intent? Has your Papa searched the matter out?"

"He has simply ordered the steward to be sure I am protected and has forbidden me to go alone. I must have the two largest footmen with me. But he behaved strangely. My impression is he knows something, and it worries him."

As Wills thought the matter over, puzzled and concerned, Genny noticed a change in the scenery. The carriage took a few turns, and she was compelled to ask, "Please, Wills, tell me where we are going?"

She realized they were leaving her privileged existence and heading for a different world. The smiles and laughter that had surrounded them near Handerton faded to expressionless faces in dirty, narrow streets. People stood still against the walls with no place to go and nothing to do. Most stared and followed the carriage with their eyes. Many held out their hands for something, anything.

They arrived at a street corner where Genny was surprised to see a number of well-dressed men among the ragged, forlorn people. The carriage stopped. Wills dismounted and held out a hand. Genevieve accepted the assistance with hesitation, with fear on her face and thoroughly puzzled. She looked to him for an answer.

"Here, my dear," Wills said, "is the world that I am

fighting to heal. My friends, these peers, have come to walk with us to provide you with protection and to learn more regarding my concerns."

None of the men had the spirit to greet her or speak, and simply nodded their heads for they were already disconsolate. They all began to walk together. They passed dirty children huddled together, a few dangerously asleep on the road's edge. They saw children carrying small, tangled loads—all that they owned. They passed tearful children, but for most, what was the point? They were beyond crying.

Genny closed her eyes for a moment, hoping to relieve her heart of a new kind of ache. There were women and men, and there were families. Many had collected scrap to sell, or picked a few flowers from some park that they offered. Some were half-dressed for the cool weather. Bigger, stronger men had more belongings and warmer clothes. Three children lived inside one large coat and were watched over by their father, who was missing an arm. She asked for his name, but what could she do?

People asked for money or food. Wills and the gentlemen handed out coins. One man thanked them but asked in desperation what he was to do when the money was gone.

They passed a brick building with no door on the opening. Inside, without furnishings, were huddled twenty-some people in family groups, some peeking, frightened, around the walls. One woman sang, soft and low, a nonsensical, melancholy song. Genevieve sympathetically nodded to her but felt like a hypocrite. What good was a nod?

A few drunkards passed through the area alarming people. A loud preacher exhorted any who passed to fear for their salvation, and boys were chased down

126

some stairs by an angry woman. A lad swept horse dung from their path and held out an open palm.

A man saw the cluster of gentlemen and hurried his family across the street between rolling carriages to ask for work, promising honesty and hard work should there be a situation for him. One of the gentlemen stopped to speak with him, and Genny watched as they walked by, hoping with all her heart the man would be given a position. He looked strong enough, clear minded, and was certainly more than willing to work.

What could she do? Could she help these people, or was a lady to keep her hands clean of it, as Mama had said?

A woman sitting in a grassy lot cried out as the group passed by, "Milady, ma'am." Genevieve, startled and concerned, looked in her direction. "My…my baby was born today here in the wind and rain," she cried out, "and I cannot warm him enough. He'll die, ma'am. Please, what can I do?"

Genny's concern became horror. She altered her course and walked toward the woman, her mandated refinement faltering and losing its hold. She drew near to the newly delivered, shivering woman with pleading eyes. Would the woman even live, she wondered? Genny looked, dismayed, at the infant. She froze in astonishment, so dazed she could not act. Then, recovering her senses, she took off her lush cloak and wrapped it around them to trap the mother's lifesaving warmth about her child.

"If only I could be sure you would be safe with it," Genny said, "that nobody would take it from you." The expensive cloak would bring someone good money. How could she protect her?

"I'll care for her, ma'am," said a teenage boy standing nearby, "She is my mum, and I'll watch over them." He was a thin boy, but spoke with such conviction that Genny, at first hesitant, felt reassured. This young man was intent. He would surely do his best. She reached out a hand and pulled him nearer his mother.

Genny obtained a few coins from Wills and gave them to the youth. She told him his mama would need plenty of good food to care for the baby. Still, she felt their help to be so short lived it was all but in vain. What would become of this family?

The woman burst into tears and expressed thanks to both her and Wills. "I'll work again soon, ma'am, as soon as I have my strength back," she vowed. "I really will. I'll find us a little place. I'll work hard." Genevieve prayed from a bleeding heart that the woman would live that long and turned away. She wished to forget.

"It is enough, Wills, I've seen enough. My presumption is broken. Take me away," she asked. She took the lead back toward the carriage.

As they walked, her strength built and her mind began to churn. She gradually developed a new look, a new bearing. Lord Holmeshire saw a true lady emerging from a paradigm being shed. He waved, and his carriage came to meet them. He nodded his thanks to the army of men that had surrounded them, and the two rode away. Genevieve sat looking straight ahead, deeply in thought in her seat.

"I'm sorry, my dearest," Wills said. "I needed to bring you here to see what I am working for." He hoped for a positive reply as he coaxed her forward to put his coat around her shoulders.

"I do now understand what you are working for. And I will be doing what you are doing with my whole heart." Wills heaved a sigh of relief. What he had surmised from her expression was true—she said it herself. Would this unity last?

He expressed appreciation that they could concur on this effort. This would truly bring them together. She spoke, though haltingly, absently, of nothing but the mother and child until they approached Handerton House. She became silent as they rode up the majestic drive. Wills then spoke.

"How would you have me dress for your ball, my faerie queen?"

Her concern and thoughtful state was momentarily overthrown. She looked up at him. "Oh, Wills, I did not think you would care to attend."

"Let us agree—when we marry we shall work very hard always to help these people," he said, "And then, with a clear conscience, we will go to a lovely party and forget these dismal things for the night."

She smiled broadly. "We shall thus maintain our connections to those who can assist."

As he walked her to the ivy-covered entrance, he said, "I will not have you depressed by it but empowered to help that your spirits are lifted, and you can enjoy dancing and eating and drinking with your friends. We will send out what is left for the poor and hungry."

"We surely will," she agreed. As he delivered her to the humid palm room and her curious workmates, she could hardly turn her mind back to Midsummer Night's Dream, but had thoughts of baskets of food and piles of blankets for the poor. She failed to hear his next words.

"I have met with the designer and unpacked boxes of supplies. The designer heard my needs and has come to London to work on a variety of arrangements." He leaned toward her, trying to get her attention. "I had hoped, by now, to have drawings to share with you, Genevieve, and see which plans you preferred. However, it is taking more time than I expected. I shall send a message when they arrive, and we will arrange a date to sit with him and consider the choices. I shall certainly wish to have your impressions." This assured the marchioness, wrongly, that there had been a proposal.

"My impressions on what?" Genevieve returned to the present.

"On the designing of Holmeshire Hall," Wills declared. "Someone please tell her what I said. I am late to return to a meeting. Goodbye to all, and please make plans to receive me frequently."

She sunk into a chair at the table as he bowed and left, appearing thoroughly lost to them all. Curiosity devoured her mother and friends. They watched her, waiting to hear something that made sense. "Genny," said Lady Breyton from her seat, taking her daughter by the chin. "Please inform us of this outing. Has Lord Holmeshire set a wedding date?"

"No, Mama," she replied. She turned her face away to break her mother's grasp, and then back. "There are more important things to care for."

More important? Could there be something more important, Grace wondered? Was something wrong with Genny? Katherine and Samantha looked at each other for answers and then back at Genevieve, leaning closer to read her expression.

"You see," she began, her face flushed with emotion while pushing away rock crystal stars and a silver-plated moon they had spent hours designing, "There are real problems in the world, quite unlike whom we ought to invite to tea, or whether someone has pleased us with their manner."

They remained confused. She pulled her weight up in the chair to clarify. She must be strong, must she not, for the task ahead? "There are cold, wet, hungry people, people that simply desire to work for an income," she said. "They ask but to have a home and food for their families, but they have no means, such as we do." Her friends sat up straighter. A look of understanding dawned on their faces, and fear and horror on Grace's.

"Where did he take you that you could not wear your jewelry, Genny?" asked Lady Breyton in a fairly sharp tone, with the first of her own opinions teetering on configuration.

"He took me to the real world, Mama. We stepped out into the world where that necklace could have fed a family for a year." Grace gasped in alarm. "We were safe, Mama," Genny continued. "We were accompanied by ten men. You ought to have been there, too. Why have we not been there before, Mama? Were you hiding this from me? Hiding, perhaps, the most important thing in life—living people in want of food? You should have been there. You all should have been there."

"What was it, Gen? What did you see?" Samantha asked, fear on her face.

"People, Sam. I saw people with problems, children with little clothing in the cold wind. People hiding in a little room, afraid of us when we looked in. Why are they afraid? What is it we do to them? And there were...." She covered her face at the memories.

Suddenly she sprung up, looked about the room and cried, "What are we doing living in this...this huge jewel box, this gilded and draped goliath of a house, when there are people with little even to wear on their backs?"

She ran to the door and looked out at the hall and up at the ceiling. "Gold overlay on the borders?" she cried. "Why did we paint gold on the borders when people are starving?" She walked down the hall, taking long steps. "Golden picture frames." She ran into a footman bringing tea. "Silver tea sets," she yelled at the terrified man, "Food that will be thrown to the dogs for not being eaten. Servants have spent hours just decorating these candies." She picked some up and threw them over a railing to the floor below. "How could we?"

She ran down the long hallway, up a flight of stairs and into her room, where she dashed India off her tables and threw herself onto her bed. The women followed after her, the girls terribly concerned and her mother furious.

~Chapter 7~

This and That Effort and Everyone Tries

The weather cooperated perfectly for Anne the next morning. Gwyn, upon approving Anne's suggestion regarding his health, had asked to take Nicky out in the sun to a park accompanied by the lady's maids. They were given permission to go and even a carriage to use along with a footman for an escort.

Anne had hoped Simon would be given the responsibility, but that was foolish thinking. Mr. Grantham was in charge, and it could never be. She had planned, though, for either eventuality. While not on the rear of the carriage, Simon would simply become lost while out for the post and find himself in the park. The ladies must arrive at the right time, for Simon could not stay long—his duties called loudly, and he would be missed.

However, Nicky was having a bad morning. His stomach hurt, and Nanny had to find a solution. Though her nursery back home was well stocked, she was now in London. She could only hope that charcoal bits she had brought in her small medicine bag would work for the pains. Getting them down little Nick's throat was the worst of it, but Anne managed with her sweet, gentle ways when Gwyn could not with a firm stance. Once down, the small black lumps were declared to be successful at their endeavor.

Hattie, pointing the way down the long hall, commented that perhaps Anne should stay in her own area in the mornings. How was she to scrub and mop with everyone in London in her nursery? Anne, who had found cause to develop some stamina, pointed out they would soon be gone for the morning. Hattie could re-mop, but what have we here? There was no mud. It seems that lady's maids did not track mud about.

Dressing Winnie took Elizabeth longer than usual, but Anne came to the rescue. She knocked and stepped into Winnie's suite to see how she could help, and she proved quite useful. Winnie's hair needed but another twist and a few flowers. The buttons were stubborn— covered with fabric, so move over Lizzy, and Anne would do it for her. Anne was graciously thanked by Lizzy's mistress. It did have Lizzy a bit piqued, but Anne no longer cowed to her every whim. Life was at a critical turning point—she would pull the horses in the right direction and get them there on time.

On this particular day, they arrived at the park on schedule. Anne fell in love with flowers like never before, causing her to lag behind the other girls. Chatting with each other and playing with Nicky, the women became oblivious. Once they adjusted to Anne's being so slow, she slipped around a large Memorial statue. There were flowers there, too, but she did not think of them for a second.

She found Romeo sitting on the artistically twisted wooden bench she had praised in her note. He jumped to his feet, all smiles, and bowed to her as she curtsied. He gave her a bouquet he had purchased, for his grandmother should anyone ask, but there she was and Grandmother was not. These flowers, this ribbon—could she ever put them down? She would keep them near to her always—they were as precious as life itself. But time was short, and she must admire her bouquet later.

The two sat down together, all too aware of the need for brevity, and at last learned each other's names. They had many questions but spoke hastily, desperately, and asked only a few, knowing they would soon be discovered by angered nannies and maids.

"Anne Amberton, such a lovely name." He thanked God for having learned it at last. "Miss Anne, then. I shall never forget. Is Holmeshire far from here?"

"Aye, terribly far, and 'tis a very rough ride. Did you always live in London?"

"I did live near London, and my grandfather and father were groomsmen for the royal family. I was fortunate—we had a cottage on the grounds. Was your family in service?"

"No, they live down in the village. My sister and I are in service. Do you like lollipops?"

"I do—I love them. I am afraid I must go very soon."

She gave him a lollipop she had bought for him and wrapped with loving care. "I do hope we shall be able to talk again."

"I am sure we will find a way. Do you read and write?"

She nodded yes, and laughed. "Recall the note I scribbled and dropped to you from the balcony."

"Ah, yes—brilliant. I have written down places I can be at certain times, and I shall watch for you there.

135

Come only when safe, and should you not arrive, I shall wait for the next go." He gave her the list on a piece of old paper. She slipped it into her pocket. "And be sure," he continued, "to be at that window every opportunity to reassure me that you still care to see me, should we not meet otherwise."

"That desire will never change, sir," she promised, "but I do not know how I will bear it when we leave for Holmeshire again."

"Write me notes," he said as he tried to pull away, "and leave them for me behind the general's portrait near the duke's bedroom door. It is at the far end of the hall, down from the nursery. You can slide them behind the linen on the bottom of the frame. No one walks in that area from their breakfast till they dress for dinner but for the valet. He will not mind. The housemaids— watch out for the housemaids. I have excuses to go there and shall retrieve the messages and leave some for you."

"How wonderful this will be after so much time," she whispered. "I must go now. I shall soon be hunted down."

"We must be together. We must find a way. I do so wish to know you better."

"I shall write long letters to leave you. I will tell you all about myself, and you do the same."

"I shall. I shall."

Anne reappeared around the statue, this time so happy that her mates knew exactly what had happened. She poked a rose bud into her bouquet as they approached, but they knew better.

"Where did the white lilies come from, Anne? None grow here." She had no reply. "Where were you? Is it that footman? Where is he?" No reply. This was truly Shakespearean. They were Romeo and Juliet alone, with no support, no help and no one to understand. But they were impervious and happy now. They had found a way.

***

Holmeshire Hall gardens bloomed. Caged linnets could be heard indoors and skylarks filled the air without.

"I 'eard that Lord Wilfred has arrived 'ome from London," announced lanky Mr. Scott, "and I 'ave come 'ere to talk to him."

Barreby stared at the unkempt man with hat in hand. "And should he be here, who would I say was calling? Do you have a visiting card, sir?"

"Card? I don't 'ave any sort of card. I do not need one. But I know the lord will want to see me." He nodded his head firmly. His conviction was surprising.

"Your name?"

"Mr. Benedict Scott. Father of Alexander Scott." He rose up on his toes and thrust out his chest.

Barreby's eyebrows went up in interested surprise. "Mr. Scott," he said, and nodded his head. "It is kind of you to call, but Lord Holmeshire has returned to London."

A sudden burst of anger on the part of the caller sent Barreby backward a step. "Gone back to London? It took everything I 'ad in the world to get us transport from London to 'olmeshire to see 'im. And...." Mr. Scott tried to calm himself, "you say he's gone back to London." His voice became sweeter with every word. "And 'e'll be back when?"

"He'll return with the end of the Season," the butler replied, "when hunting begins, and possibly later."

Benedict, nourished with a quart of ale, wove about on the porch. At length he spoke. "Then 'ere we are in want of a place to stay. There's three of us." He plunked down the tip of his walking stick.

Barreby managed not to cough and sputter. "I am afraid, sir, without a card or a letter from the Lord Holmeshire, I would not be able to offer you hospitality. You will find an inn in the village near the road." He shut the door without apology, preventing the miscreant from falling in.

***

"'e's gone," Benedict shouted at his son. "Back to London. We're lost. What are we to do now? You said 'e was 'ere to build on his 'ouse."

"He was, Paw, I know he was. I checked it out good."

"Well, you checked it out wrong. He is not here now." Benedict was as loud as could be, but the couple had waited for him down the road, so no one in the house heard the complaints. "We cannot make it back to London. We'll starve 'ere is what we'll do."

"Come on down to town, Paw. We can find stuff. Village folk are good. They'll help us. We can look for work should we 'ave to. They'll 'ave work you can do somewhere."

***

Anne's responsibilities were limited that night with the ladies staying home. She found herself free from the time they arrived home till she was to dress Emma for dinner. She told Gwyn and Elizabeth that she was going to prepare clothing and jewelry, but they pointed out, Lizzy being quite firm, that she had about six hours for that. She may as well relax for a time now they were home. No, she said, she believed she had buttons to resew and a stubborn spot to remove. "'Twas a good thing Mama trained us well," she pointed out to her sister with far too much cheer.

Off she went, knowing she was under suspicion at

all times. Once down the pillared hall and into Emma's regal quarters, Anne quickly ran past the bed to the dressing room and threw stockings onto the proper table. She tossed some sewing tools near the dress she hung out for the evening. She had a bit of a mess, but at least it looked as if she was in the middle of her work.

She hurried to Emma's desk for fine, perfumed paper, the new sort made from wood, a steel dip pen and ink. She closed her eyes and bit her lip, feeling guilty for taking these expensive materials, but where would she find common ones in a house such as this? She could rarely get to the shops, and these felt exquisite in her hands, a perfect medium to express herself.

Anne wondered where to sit for this labor of desperate love. Should she stay here and risk being found by Emma? Would her sister perhaps appear to check on her? Aye, she thought, she had best go elsewhere. Her own room was too far away, so…could she perhaps go into a vacant guest room? Aye. She would not be expected to dare hide in there.

She put the supplies in a woven sewing bag. She walked in the most casual way to the next door and looked up and down the hall. Entering, shoulders hunched, she closed the door behind her. She made herself comfortable at a desk in a low-ceiling nook where no one would see her who might open the door, giving her a chance to hide behind a nearby wardrobe should anyone walk in. Relax, she told herself, and breathe.

And now, what might she write? Pure adoration? How would he take to that? She could not wait for him to write first and set the tone, or she would surely burst. Then they could never be together.

Each word must be done well the first time—she

had no blotter. She kept watching the door, hoping not to be found at this, which made thinking all the more difficult. What could she say? She wished to propose immediate marriage and swear to never let go of his arm for any reason, but that was far from acceptable.

She contented herself with writing how utterly lovely it was to have talked with him that day—how she had grown up in Holmeshire Village in a family of eight, and had been well trained in the ways of womanhood and seamstressing; so very well trained that here she was a lady's maid, and she would very much like to meet with him again.

All went well for her—not a blotch nor a smear, not a crease and not a sister or nanny bursting into the room, though they had in fact looked for her in Emma's rooms. This all encouraged her very much, and she made her way through the second story halls to the duke's area. There she inserted the document behind the framed picture on the wall, which, incidentally, did not prevent the perfume from filling the air.

***

Lucy obtained a job at John's Favorite Inn serving in the kitchen. Her industrious ways saved the situation for her little family. They had a warm room to share right above the cook stove. A willow outside the room's window provided shade and a roost for migrating songbirds, delighting her as she dressed for work at the break of dawn each day. Charles was overjoyed at the plump, stuffed bed and vowed to remain in it for the rest of his life. In the following days, though, he was forced to search for work at least a bit as Benedict sat in the pub. His first beer on the third day enlightened his mind, and he decided to try a new approach at the castle on the hill.

"Mr. Benedict Scott again, sir, father of Alexander

Scott." Winnie's growling dog did not much help his case.

"I recognize you fully well, sir, though you have combed your hair."

"Yes. I am sure, sir, that you are quite well aware of the need of a good family for a proper income. Now, my daughter-in-law 'as found lodging for 'erself and my second son Charles in the village and 'as a small income. My son is looking for honorable work amongst the farm 'ands, as he is well experienced at that," he lied, "to take proper care of his lady. It is only myself, now, in want of employment from Lord Holmeshire so I am not a useless old burden on a young couple who should be planning an 'appy little family. I am sure you 'av the authority to do as you know the lord would do if he were 'ere and grant me a situation in the 'ousehold. I would require a position that does not involve strenuous activity, being a few years older than some. I'm just the man to supervise some of the stable 'ands or to manage the lads who work in the gardens."

"Many of our workers are as old as you, sir, or older. I have the authority to hire servants who arrive with good characters whether the lord is in residence or not. I am the steward of the house and choose to serve as butler as well. But I do—"

"Then there you 'av it. I can take your situation as butler, allowing you a reprieve as you are gaining in years as well. The income should, besides, go to two gentlemen, sir, in a cruel world where many are not employed. But, ah, why are we discussing it out 'ere in the cold?" Benedict looked his sweetest, and then fully as pompous as a butler ought, though his stick failed to support him well when he swayed.

"Sir, there is nothing to discuss. I have want of no help other than skilled builders next fall. I will ask you to knock at the servants' door should you have a question in the future. Good day." He closed the door. Benedict stood outside and yelled that the lord would 'ear of what was done to Mr. Alexander Scott's own father at the lord's 'ome.

***

Simon made his way to the hallowed picture frame early next morning with a note he had composed the night before in the privacy of his room, having sent his roommates on a wild chase. They did need to know around 11 P.M., did they not, whether all the horses were healthy for the next day's service? Or at least whether the stable hands had gotten off to sleep and would not complain about early hours? The men were glad for the opportunity to pour themselves a mug of ale with the kitchen unattended and then care for these matters.

Simon had not all the concern Anne had for the aesthetics of his letter, but with sincere feelings to express, did so beautifully. His opening words were a nearly poetic tribute to Anne's comeliness, followed by expressions of desire to find a way to keep her near him always. He wrote how he would surely become depressed should she return to Holmeshire, and might she stay? He elaborated on the dreadful treatment she had received at the hands of Grantham and everyone under him at the downstairs table. He quoted them, railed against such ill manners, and praised her gracious treatment of them in return. He apologized that he could not continue writing but would surely write again the next night should he find the privacy. And finally, here he was at the hiding place, receiving a perfumed note from his angel and replacing it with his hastily composed profession of love.

***

142

The following Tuesday, the ladies were in the duchess' rose and cream-colored sitting room when a message was brought in for Winifred on parchment from Holmeshire Hall. Forgetting caution, she read aloud:

"*'Dear Most Honorable Lady Holmeshire, I have thoroughly but discreetly searched every drawer and pocket in the castle and have not turned up your missing bracelet. Perhaps it has been sold, I am sorry to suggest.'*"

Emma interrupted in a near whisper, "A bracelet?"

Winnie sighed, "Yes, actually, a bracelet did go missing. It was the sapphire and emerald bracelet that Charlotte of Wales once gave me from her collection." She winced. Helena and Emma looked at each other and gasped.

"When did this horrid thing, this…ah…misfortune befall you, ma'am, do you know?" asked Emma, tapping her heels and looking back and forth between the ladies.

"It was the Sunday after Wills returned from Italy, before church. It had been laid out for me to wear. Emma, I well know that you did not take the bracelet," Winnie said, nodding her head to reassure the girl. "Why would you? You had never stolen before and have had more than adequate opportunity. You are shy to wear even the small ruby necklace. And where could you don such a bracelet but for dressing to go out with me? Now, how could you be suspected?" Emma sighed and relaxed, but the bracelet was yet missing. "Let me go on," Winnie said.

"*'However, I am happy to relate that as of this moment, all silver and any jewelry left behind is safely accounted for and locked up.'*"

She looked at Helena and smiled, "I am, of course,

not concerned about my silver, but you know Barreby and that he must report."

"'Yesterday and a few days before, I had visits from a man claiming to be the father of Alexander Scott.'"

Winnie looked up, startled, and Emma covered her mouth. Her ladyship continued reading,

"'He desires a situation as butler in the house, or any supervisory position where he should not labor. I've turned him away as he had no character and presented evidence on both occasions of being drunk. However, he and his second son and daughter-in-law have arrived to live in the village below. Yours most sincerely, Mr. Daniel Barreby.'"

Winnie's hands with the note dropped to her lap, and Emma rose to her feet.

"Ma'am, Alexander never spoke well of his family. This is a matter of serious concern. I am greatly afraid."

"Thank you, Emma, for your opinion. I received the same impression from Barreby's message. I shall instruct him to alert the staff to be wary of any situation that may arise."

The sitting room door opened for Mr. Gabriel Hughes to be announced. He received the usual warm welcome, though Emma deplored the conversation that might arise. She took her seat again, and he sat. The party cheered a good deal, and they spoke of journeys, great ships and the ever warm sun of the Caribbean islands.

After time had passed, enough for Gabriel to have been gracious, he said, "Although the company of you ladies, all three, is a great pleasure, I do wish to talk alone with Miss Carrington. Having burst in and intruded so already on your time, I am ashamed to ask, is there a place where she and I could talk together, with the young lady's permission?" Emma nodded her willingness, though she slipped down in her chair as her heart leapt to her throat.

Helena thought and then rose to her feet. "My sister and I will leave this room. We have a matter of importance to discuss and arrangements we must make. You may visit here together for as long as you might wish. The footman will remain." The two ladies gave Gabe their kindest regards, glanced with half-smiles at Emma and left the room.

Gabe assisted Emma to rise, and they moved from their stiff dining chairs to a down-stuffed, white sofa. Gabriel stared off into space as he transferred himself, nearly speaking twice once they sat. Emma sorted her prepared expressions of regret, searching for one to mercifully stop him before words appeared that could not be unsaid. She raised a finger to signal her wish to talk just as he cleared his throat and spoke.

"Miss Carrington, you have but recently met me, I am quite well aware." Having at last raised the courage, he went on to make his case, grateful to have spoken in time to stop her preventing it. "I am horrified at myself for being forward in this matter," he said, "but you see, I am more troubled that someone else may appear, someone who does not love you as well nor would treat you as well, before I feel it more appropriate to take the opportunity. Therefore, you see, I must declare my feelings today and hope you will understand my haste in the matter. I have seen for myself and have heard that you are an admirable woman. You are certainly beautiful in every way—in face and form and outstandingly in manner. In the few weeks I have known you, I can barely eat unless I am fortunate to be with you, or hardly sleep at night for visions of your smile. I am a barrister—therefore I am well able to support you in comfort on my earnings alone. Besides,

I have been left a truly charming country cottage and some considerable income to manage the house through the estate of Her Late Majesty the Queen Caroline of Brunswick. My foster parents, as well, have left me a pleasant home here in Town, which is where I dwell for much of the year. It is not so grand as this Belgrave mansion, but I can entertain comfortably in it; that is, when a hostess may be found." He fumbled with his pocket watch, not wanting to forget any vital part of his preamble or fail to pour it out before she could decline. The remaining words, if said, might prove a great temptation to her. "As a barrister, my wife would attend the royal court; therefore, you would spend as much time as you wish with your friends during the Season. All other wishes of yours would be given the greatest consideration. I should dislike, very much, to ever decline your request. I wonder, then, dear Miss Carrington, if you would make me ever so happy and become my wife?"

He put up a finger to stop her from replying and added, "I felt great urgency, indecorously, in making this request, but I shall give you as much time as you wish to reply. I shall assume that until you give a reply you are considering the matter. Please be assured of my lasting faithfulness and love, and do consider my words."

Emma could have been easily swayed, kind-hearted as she was and not wanting to hurt him. She had listened intently, watching his face and how it gradually raised as he gained confidence. His eyes had lifted from overseeing the wringing of his hands and had settled with a hopeful gaze into hers. He surveyed every motion of her face, the direction of any turn of the corners of her mouth and the leaning of her body to ascertain her thoughts.

How touching, she thought, *that a great barrister who could fight in court for the Crown and win each case should first be so hesitant to speak and then appear nearly desperate*. His eyes remained fixed on her, his speech concluded. She could not escape his hopes to hide and take a moment to think, for though her mind had already been settled, her heart was battered. He was soft-spoken and charming. His promises appealed. The country cottage...how she would love to see it. And especially because of the feelings she did not wish to bruise, she sought to find an excuse to assent. But no, there was much involved that had been thought out many times. Winnie had not encouraged her in the match, and she did not want to leave Holmeshire Hall. There was too much at Holmeshire to leave behind. She did not wish to say what she must, but summoned up her strength and spoke with finality.

"Sir, I am honored for all my days beyond words. I have, though, committed my life to the companionship of a countess. Therefore I must, with deep regret, turn down your kind proposal."

Gabriel looked about for solutions to this obstacle in the line of a candle, the silhouette of an orchid, the fringe of a pillow. There were none to be found, and he could not speak.

He rose and walked to the window, where he stood, his elbow in his hand. Emma looked down at the floor. At length, Gabe returned to sit at her side, and after clearing his throat, he professed, "Miss Carrington, I shall wait for you. I can do nothing else. I wish her ladyship a long life, but it seems that mine will be a lonely one. Please tell me that should the time ever come when you are free from this obligation, you would be able to love me?"

"Oh, sir, I most possibly could, but I cannot promise to ever marry you."

"Could you tell me, then, that you will keep my particular request in your mind these many years? That perhaps you will continue to see me as a friend of the family?"

"Sir," she paused and then said, "I do not wish to much encourage you. What can I say? You are kind, patient and good. I could not ask for a better husband, I say with abundant conviction. But I have words to speak that will dissuade you from this proposal. I must share with you a secret of mine which will, indeed, greatly dishearten you. No one must know."

He nodded agreement to his silence on the matter.

She leaned over hesitantly and paused to build up her courage. She glanced at the footman and covered her whisper to Gabe.

His eyes widened as he looked at her in disbelief, but she maintained a steadfast gaze. He paused and thought, then shook his head and waved his hand as if to say it did not affect his request.

She looked down at the floor and back to his eyes and went on, "You must, then, promise me one thing." He sat up the more straight, that his word would be seen as gold. "Should you find another during these years, you will not wait for me but marry," she said. "And you should seek another, sir. You will need a wife, and…and you will need sons. You have wonderful things to pass on, and I cannot promise I could ever marry you. Should I become able someday, I do not know that I could give you sons as an older woman though we should marry. And, as I am most sadly aware, you have no family to take your abundant possessions at all."

He considered her words and rose to his feet. She

did the same. He bowed his head at length and then answered.

"Miss Carrington, I can promise that should ever any eyes look at me as yours have, and reach out and pull me into a soul the way yours have, I shall marry. I will notify you by letter and marry. But I have looked at a million eyes in my life, and they do not have the dominion over me that yours have." Gabriel looked toward the door as he contained his grief. "I shall take my leave now. God be with you." He nodded his head toward Emma and walked out. Her eyes filled with tears.

~Chapter 8~

Misery, Difficulties…and What Is This, Now?

"Emma, you have not told us anything of your conversation with Mr. Hughes. Indeed, you have not said much about even the weather for the past few days. Tell us your secret. What are you so deeply pondering?" Helena asked, setting down her stitching to compel a reply.

Sympathetic expressions had often shown on Emma's face and short spells of gloom followed by a lifting of the chin. At the moment her eyes betrayed faraway thoughts. "Did he indicate a desire to court you?" Winnie pried, hoping her friendly manner would excuse it.

Emma turned her gaze from the strolling of persons in the great outdoors and looked at Helena. "He indicated a desire to marry me, ma'am," she said, "but I gave the proper reply and have let it go."

"The proper reply?" Winnie tipped her head and rendered a hopeful smile. "Does that mean he does not interest you?"

"Ma'am, he is a kind gentleman," Emma replied to

her mistress. She straightened her posture as responsibility displaced her sentiments. "I have the utmost respect for him, though I do not intend to marry him. I have been shown both undeserved generosity and the greatest kindness by you. Along with that has come duty to you and to the orphans Robin and Kate, as you are aware. I take my duties seriously and shall never sway from them. Besides all that, you know I could never leave Holmeshire Hall." She was sweet, but steadfast. "I thank you again for my privileges which come at great social cost to you—to the both of you." She rose to leave the room, but Winnie gently pulled her back to her seat.

"Emma. You are a most serious and dependable girl. I commend you greatly," Winnie said. "I am pleased with the way you have responded to this situation, and urge you to remain of this mind. I wish very much to see you live in happiness—I trust you believe that."

"Ma'am, please do not concern yourself with it. Mr. Hughes has asked me to continue to look upon him as a family friend. I told him I would most certainly do so. In response, he has promised he would marry should another woman enter his life. I shall continue to encourage him to do so, since I am to remain at your side."

"And no doubt he has promised to call upon you the very day I die. Is it true, Emma? For I would not want that." Winnie's concern surprised Emma. She had delayed discussing the matter, having expected Winnie to encourage her to marry Gabe—a suitable gentleman. But here instead, Winnie was opposed.

"Mr. Hughes has wished you a long life, ma'am. He fully respects my wishes." Winnie nodded, but her expression did not change. Helena, too, held back sentimental expression and picked up her embroidery while nodding agreement to Winnie's undisclosed concerns.

***

The lavish Empirelands Hotel, its majestic candelabra accented against rich, dark-wood walls, harbored some small difficulty at a round corner table where five men sat on a balmy afternoon. Some had never met—they were introduced as drinks were poured and sandwiches set out.

"Lord Holmeshire," said the Marquess of Breyton. "I have asked you to meet with me and these gentlemen to discuss some of the policies you are introducing in Parliament. Some of your ideas are insightful to a striking degree. You have earned much respect. However, there are matters you are not yet aware of, I fear. One in particular bothers the House. You have spoken up a few years late, for this matter has been settled," Breyton declared. He was not to be crossed. "Let me read to you what Patrick Colquhoun wrote some time ago." He pulled out a printed paper and read,

" 'Poverty…is a most necessary and indispensable ingredient in society, without which nations and communities could not exist in a state of civilization. It is the lot of man—it is the source of wealth, since without poverty there would be no labour, and without labour there could be no riches, no refinement, no comfort, and no benefit to those who may be possessed of wealth.'

"In my opinion," Breyton continued, "poverty is a necessary part of God's plan to show how rich his blessings can be upon those whom he has placed in higher positions. It is God's right to bless one and curse another, which is why the poor will always be with us. Now, of course, the poor must eat and have shelter.

That is only right and quite undisputed. Governing a country, such duty as you and I have, means, in part, caring for the people on its land. A few years ago, but a very few years, older men than you, and wiser, with keen concern for the people, rich and poor, took up this matter at great length. Much debate was carried on— much work was done. The decisions were made. Parliament required that the poor be helped in a specific way. It is important to give this method an opportunity to show its benefits; but here you are, a mere youth in Parliament, trying to throw out what was at long last established through the work of erstwhile lords while you were yet at school or taking your first Grand Tour."

"My Lord Breyton," Wills replied. "I am sure you are referring to the workhouses—the *only* legal means of the government to provide for the poor these last years? Where the people therein must work hard, not earning enough to move out on their own? Where the food is unpalatable and the living conditions miserable? Where family members are separated, never to see each other again?"

The marquess took a moment to think in his padded, leather chair. His eyes on the wall, he lit a cigar. "It is the workhouses I am referring to, yes," he said, "to be sure. The workhouses were never meant as a welcoming place with fine cuisine and feather beds. People must prefer not to live there. Should the workhouses be pleasant places, we could never build enough of them. Men and women would fall back on them rather than work. The point is for the people to make their livings outside these places, to search hard for work, to accept offers of employment, to find more pleasant and profitable ways to provide for their families. They must teach their young to carry on family businesses. Thus they do not burden others and bring down those around them. That is what makes a society work."

"They must work while we do not? We inherit more than we can spend in our lifetimes. Money comes into our coffers from rents charged on the working class, from the sale of trees we did not plant, from sheep others tend. We are handed multiple grand houses and land and furnishings, and precious stones and metals everywhere. Look at your own houses, my lord. And the poor have no means to make a living."

"Are you suggesting I tear down my house and dole out the pieces to the poor? A gold lamp to one and carpet to another?" Breyton looked at his minions for support. "As I said, God blesses whom he will."

"Of course not, my lord. But I cannot accept that God made any man to suffer," replied Wills. "I suggest the poor have not the advantage that you or I have to provide for ourselves. Do not consider them lazy, sir. I have seen men...and women and children...digging in the sewage that was the Thames for bits of things to sell—or pleading for work when there was none. I cannot hire them all, but I intend to hire many to work the charity houses I intend to build."

"And who would oversee their work? Who would watch to make sure your fine managers do not steal the resources, sir...my daughter?" He checked that the other men yet nodded agreement.

"Sir, I intend to find honorable and honest men to oversee these homes. I intend to pay them well enough that they wish to continue in their situations. These would be men who have lived the conditions they will help to improve, men that have seen misery and sorrow and who care to help others escape it, or at least have their urgent needs met." Wills' goodness brightened the sarcasm-permeated dark of the corner.

"Then you intend to sell Handerton and Chenbury to buy charity houses once you have your hands on them?"

"No, my lord, I intend to run a charity financed by the efforts of individuals interested in the welfare of the people. There are many respectable ways to raise funds. I would have preferred the queen's government as well find more humane ways of caring for its own citizens, people who have expressed their wish for gainful work to do. I am sure you are quite aware that Her Majesty the Queen has expressed a desire to improve the living conditions of the poor." Wills frustration mounted, and he said, "You well know Handerton will go to our son, and Chenbury to your daughter alone."

"Have you nothing more to say than what you have expressed from your seat at Westminster?" Breyton jerked his head about as he spoke, and his nostrils flared. "I have heard it all before. Please remember, you and Her Majesty are young—you are new at this business of running the world. Take counsel. Time will mellow your idealism, sir, and help you to find your way without endangering the foundations of our country. You would have the lower classes confident enough to rise up against us." Breyton shoved his plate across the table. He blew smoke into Wills' face and chose a new fight. "Your mother's effort to bring abandoned orphans into our homes and social functions is despicable. Soon she would have our sons dancing with filthy women in tatters. Watch—they will seduce our sons and bear children to take our money and ruin the happiness of our son's marriages. It has happened before."

"Sir, my mother is trying to do no such thing. She introduced one suitable woman into society, but as her favored companion. I cannot say I understand it myself since society objects, but my mother wishes it, and it is entirely harmless. The girl is both civilized and charming."

"It certainly is not harmless, sir," Breyton contended. He paused to barely compose himself and leaned forward on the table. "I hear tell, Holmeshire, this young woman turned down marriage to a suitable commoner. You know as well as I do she has set her sights higher. She wants a title."

"Please, sir, that is not the case. She is merely loyal to her situation as the companion of my mother. I know her well to be a person of integrity."

Breyton heard none of what Wills had to say. "She is not to be brought into society again. I demand it. Lord Holmeshire, just why have you waited so long to set a date with my daughter? Do you find her…less attractive perhaps?"

"Not at all, sir. She is a beautiful young woman who has made me proud, and we intend to marry soon. I was simply busy with other matters for some time."

"Other matters—like traveling? Visiting mistresses? Bringing home children for my confused daughter to raise? Refurbishing her home without her opinion? You intend to marry only now that you have destroyed her pleasant view of life and won her over to sobbing philanthropy."

Wills spoke slowly and firmly, maintaining his respectful bearing. "You can fully trust, sir, that Lady Genevieve is the only woman whose bed I will ever have visited." Breyton scoffed, but Wills continued. "Nicholas is the son of a deserving man who is unable to raise him. I will not bring home more children, and Genevieve will not take on more care of Master Nicholas than what she so chooses. He is fully my

157

responsibility, and I am quite able to care for him with the help of my staff."

"And he has been made your heir, I have heard?"

"Only till Genevieve has a son, sir. He will then continue last as my heir after our sons."

"But he will remain in line as an heir. And I am to believe he is not yours? It does not work that way, sir." Breyton leaned down on the table, bringing his face nearer Wills. "My grandsons might then be murdered for my money—quite a fine way to run a family."

Lord Breyton put down his cigar. He turned, as he was not long to remain in his seat. "I am most unhappy, sir, that I have no son of my own. Should I leave everything to you, I would surely care to know where it would go after you. Therefore, I did some investigation to find out who this Nicholas is whom you brought into your home, as well as to visit my daughter in my home. As it turns out, sir, there is no record whatsoever of this Nicholas in Chancery. You have simply taken a child from who knows where to raise as your son, if he indeed is not your son. I shall further investigate this for the sake of law and order. And, sir, Genevieve has told her mother that the two of you should never have been matched—that you are too different, and we were foolish to pair you so young. I can see she is right, as ashamed as I am of my own naivety. Holmeshire, you have taken a refined and sensitive young lady into the worst of humanity, exposing her to danger, taking her clothing for another woman and bringing her face to face with a dying baby. My daughter is above this sort of 'outing,' and she is above this sort of future. Mr. Bernard Spencer, here, whom you have just met, is my solicitor." Spencer nodded with a wavering smile, and Breyton continued. "George the Fourth is dead and gone, rest his soul, and Spencer has begun work to dissolve the engagement between you and my daughter and subsequent bequeathal of my properties to you before Handerton should become a charity house. You may send your solicitor to visit him, if you will." Spencer handed Wills a card. "I hope Spencer does not require the services of a barrister in court, although he will likely be hiring one at least in the matter of the bastard Nicholas."

At that the four men rose and left the hotel, leaving Wills to sit alone with his brandy, smoke trails from Breyton's cigar and a life full of troubles.

***

The nanny and maids sat together in the day nursery waiting for their lunch. Nicholas was out on a pony with Helena. Gwyn and Lizzy belabored the fact that Anne spent far too much time on Emma's clothing these days, and they did not care for it. What was she really doing, they asked, and where was her mind these days? Surely she had something up her sleeve, but they could not tend her to the point of exhaustion.

Anne, now with her bouquet ribbon about her wrist forever, took the verbal beating as a matter of course, knowing she could find no way to pass messages to her beloved without enduring at least that much punishment. She was thankful the girls enjoyed each other's company and did not follow her every move. Meetings with Simon were impossible with him also watched, but oh, how she loved the letters her Romeo left. She could not sleep for thinking of things she would next write to him. If not for sharing a bed with Lizzy, she would write letters all night.

Suddenly, the nursery door opened, and who should enter but the caustic Mr. Grantham and two towering footmen. The girls were struck with fear and jumped to their feet. They ought to say something respectful, or perhaps defensive, but not one could utter a word. What was awash? Had they come to accuse them of something? To order them about? To give them a lashing? Surely it was to be severe, for it required three men to accomplish it.

Mr. Grantham strutted across the room to Anne and held out his arm. "I shall escort you to lunch," he remarked with finality, and then looked at the door, prepared to head in its direction. She looked at him for a moment, her eyes wide and mouth opened. Was this a joke? Some sort of a test? Was she to be taken to a dungeon and chained to a wall? Perhaps her letters had been discovered! What could she do? What should she do? She looked at the girls. Their white faces offered no explanation or suggestion, just repressed alarm. She walked to his side and, trembling, put her hand through his arm.

As they stepped toward the door together, the footmen came further in and offered their arms to the nanny and maid, which arms were also accepted with anxious, shallow breath. Out the door went the three pairs, and to the top of the stairs.

Silence reigned as they descended to the ground floor, past the statues that surely knew what this meant but would not tell, and down more flights to the dungeon. The servant's hall. There the long table was set with the servant's flatware, and the maids, footmen and stable hands were lined against the wall in silence.

The three women were stood at their respective seats, according to their rank, by their escorts, and Grantham ordered Simon, who was equally bewildered, to leave his position and stand next to Anne. He followed orders well and took his place, feeling nervous inwardly, but to all appearances remaining ever the savior Anne required at her side.

At that cue, the other servants went to their places and awaited Grantham, at the head of the table, to sit down. All servants would eat together today. Food was served, drinks were poured and polite remarks were made when speaking was required. Actual discussion was impossible, as this new sort of behavior was rehearsed. At the conclusion of the perplexing experience, Grantham informed the women of the hour of the next meal. He said they would not be escorted again, and would they please arrive on time.

Back to the nursery they went, exchanging astonished looks. Not one of them had a word to say once their release was granted. And Simon went to his duties just as stunned.

***

Charles crawled out of the Scott's downy bed fairly late each morning to perhaps look for employment. One morning, Benedict was somehow awake first and up with a cup of coffee in his hands from the kitchen below.

"What's your plan, son?" he demanded, trying to quench a headache.

"Well, Paw, should it warm a bit I might go out to the mills today. It seems the farms do not need anyone right now. Strange in the summer, I say. I'm 'oping Lucy can provide money enough to buy me an apprenticeship someday."

Benedict put down the cup and folded his arms. "Son, that means of making our fortune would take a million years. I have a better plan." Charles cocked his head to the side and smirked in doubt. His father continued, "It seems they do not appreciate my capabilities up there at the castle. What they are looking for is a strong young man who can dig up the ground," he sneered, "or muck out the stables. The only way I can see to get you inside the 'ouse is for you to work on the grounds for a while, watch the fine dandies and learn their ways and manners. That could take a while," he cackled, and slapped his knee. "Then you can request to be moved inside and become a footman. You can stand around and listen at dinner. You see what I mean?"

"I do, Paw."

"I mean, I would rather be inside there, myself, working things out, but it seems I cannot get in. You'll 'ave to do it."

"I understand, Paw. I do. Well, should it warm up a bit today, I'll go on up the 'ill and see what 'appens."

"Should it warm up, nothing, Charles. You cannot get in there with lazy ways. Now get to looking your best and go on up."

"All right, Paw, I will. Let me 'av some breakfast first, and settle down."

***

"Winifred, we have been the best of friends since we were girls, and I am always pleased to receive an invitation to tea when you are to be present. But I have something to tell you that I fear may cause discomfort between us."

The marchioness and her daughter had been seated in Helena's stately home and were served crumpets on regally patterned plates. Caught between factions and for once angry of her own accord, she faced away from her friends and fanned herself rapidly. How does one scold a friend who has done nothing wrong? *And yet it must be done, she thought.* How does one take sides on a matter of prominence and preserve the approval of the loser? How difficult this would be.

She bumped the table and sloshed the cups of bergamot tea quite improperly, but she did not notice.

"Are you aware of the excursion Lord Holmeshire took Genevieve on the other day?"

"No, I cannot say I have talked to Wills in a few days." Winifred smiled, unsure if she should. "He is terribly busy, I fear. But it is for the good of the people."

"I must inform you that he came unannounced to our home and took Genevieve from her friends, from our ball committee work, and he dragged her through the worst of London," exclaimed Grace, selecting her words exactly as required by the particular Lady Embry. "He even took her out of the carriage into the crowds, exposing her to great danger, and broke her heart over things she could not ever have helped. The world is the way it is, and a young girl should not be made to feel responsible for it. I believe he expects her to invest her future assets to changing the world, as he had her give her brocade cloak for a dirty woman to wear in the mud." Lady Breyton squirmed in her seat and added, "I surely expect an apology at the very least."

Winnie sat stunned, maintaining dignity though truly in shock. She looked for confirmation at Genevieve, who was somberly listening and nodding at times.

Grace went on, maintaining the firmness sufficient for her dismay. "Lord Breyton has decided that in harmony with Genevieve's declared wishes, her engagement to Lord Holmeshire is to end. We cannot have our daughter put in harm's way and our fortune threatened when she has the possibility of a bright future ahead of her. There are many eligible men of suitable position who will be able to give Genny the future she deserves as the daughter of a marquess. We are searching already."

Winnie was speechless, with both hands plastered to her mouth. Helena and Emma were astounded, but appeared to be in some doubt as to the way matters had transpired. Tea was in the saucers, and no one was concerned in the least.

Grace added, "Lady Embry and I realize Lord Holmeshire has hired men to follow my daughter, as if she were apt to misbehave in some way. This cannot be tolerated." There was a long pause with Winifred shaking her head. "Have you no reply? Are you not ashamed?" asked Lady Breyton.

Genevieve waited, but at length, having heard no comment from the astonished threesome, made a declaration. "Given that nobody seems to have anything more to say, and in view of the fact that my father ordered me not to marry Lord Holmeshire, the command being against my will, I would like to state my intentions."

Lady Breyton did not expect this rebuttal and swung around to face her daughter with her mouth improperly agape. Genny continued, "I grew up quite unaware of the harsh realities so many people must live with. Whether I should marry Lord Holmeshire or not, I shall involve myself in charity work. I shall spend any money I have, either way, to build houses to help the poor. Father has threatened to withhold income from me should I not cooperate, and so all I have to offer at this time is Chenbury, which he has put in my name. Therefore, should I not be allowed to see Wills in the future, I request you, Lady Holmeshire, to ask him to use his money to outfit the house for the use of the poor in any way that he wishes. Whether for offices or for shelter, Chenbury is available to him."

"Chenbury a shelter," Grace choked out, unable to believe her ears.

Genevieve ignored her mother's astounded expression and reached for a sugarloaf. Removing its wrap, she continued, "And please tell him for me, dear lady, that should he wish to elope, I shall watch for him outside my window. I do not expect it, however, as he would have troubles in his career from it."

Everyone sat in stunned silence, Grace processing her daughter's words in her mind as to whether they had actually been spoken. She wished to reach out and pull them from the air.

But Genny spoke again, "One last thing, Your Grace and milady—should I be thrown out of my father's house, I shall move into Chenbury and administer my charity while living in a small suite in the midst of it. Should I not have an income, I will starve there and shan't see my parents. Should he move to take Chenbury back, I shall come to Holmeshire, married or not, and throw myself upon your good will."

Lady Breyton was destroyed and utterly defeated. What could she do? No young lady behaved this way. Most were married by Genevieve's age and rearing their sons. This could mean no heir to her husband's title and fortune. Lord Holmeshire was to blame.

She could not bear a moment more of this tea party and stood up to leave, not yet having touched her cup. "Come with me, Genevieve, we have things to discuss," she said. Genevieve obediently stood and followed after her mother, but she stopped at the door, turned around and blew everyone a kiss. Helena solemnly returned the gesture, while the other women sat stunned.

***

Shortly before dusk, Charles knocked on the great oak door at Holmeshire Hall. Barreby appeared, and his eyebrows raised at the tall young man in shabby dress.

"Sir, my name is Charles Scott. I am the brother…"

"Of Alexander Scott," concluded Barreby, nodding his head and frowning.

"Yes sir. That is, I am the brother of Alexander Scott." He shuffled his feet, avoiding Barreby's eyes.

"Yes. I request you, Scott, to knock on the servants' door."

"Yes, sir, that I shall do most promptly." The door slammed shut. Charles drifted his way about the house searching for the service door, poking at ancient stonework and tugging down climbing vines, quite pleased with the marks they left on the wall. When he at last arrived in the entrance, a kitchen maid was waiting for him, displeasure having been passed her way from Barreby over the situation.

"Please step inside, sir. Barreby has given up the wait and is gone. I shall call him for you." Barreby chose to be slow to return, and the young man was found flirting with the maid who was trying, indignantly, to do her work.

"Pretty little curls there round your cap, miss."

"Mr. Scott," she replied. "I shan't have any of that."

"Mr. Scott," Barreby demanded as he walked in, "I believe you are a married man?"

"I am, sir, I did not mean any 'arm." He stood at attention.

"Flirting is not allowed amongst the staff."

"Amongst the staff, sir. I believe, then, that you are offering me a position 'ere in the 'ouse." His head bobbed in affirmation of the post he was about to accept. "Amongst the staff, you say."

"No, I am doing no such thing. We haven't any positions available. Is there some other matter that you have come asking about?"

"Oh no, I 'av arrived to offer my services, sir. I was told that you 'av want for stable 'ands or gardeners?"

"No, we do not."

"I would be 'appy, then, in that case, to work inside the 'ouse, perhaps as a footman."

"Oh, would you? Why is it you Scotts wish to establish yourselves here? I shall send a letter to your wife, should we require a replacement for a footman, and ask her to find me a man who is not married for the position. Much of the pay is food and accommodation, and you have a wife to care for." Barreby was tiring fast of these men.

"I see." Charles struggled to find some crack in the situation to pry apart. "You, all of you owe your positions to my brother, Alexander Scott, you know."

"What? Your brother?" exclaimed the maid, with widened eyes, "Oh, excuse me, sir," she conceded to Barreby, who then spoke quite firmly. The cook and kitchen maids stumbled by, carrying pots smelling of savory food and a stack of plates, staring at the invader.

"Though we owe him plenty, sir, our situations are entirely safe. We do not, despite any perceived obligation, have positions to fill. We are preparing to take our supper here, so I ask you to take your leave. I shall remember you if I can provide anything."

"You could provide a meal, sir, if you please, as it has been carried beneath my nose while it is at this time being set out."

"I shan't, Mr. Scott. Go to your wife for a meal. Good night." Barreby stood his ground, waiting for the finality to be accepted. Charles's mind yet worked slowly at finding a way to turn matters around. Barreby said again, "Good *night*." Charles at last understood the situation and gave up the attempt.

***

That night, the Trent and Holmeshire families ate a peaceful dinner. Shocks and trials of life were forgotten over table linen embroidered with golden thread, hand-painted china and sparkling goblets. Talk of shopping for stylish hats, a charming operetta, and the wonderful seafood medley pleased one and all. However, they concluded their conversation more quickly than was the custom, and retired all together to a sitting room. The duke refused a tray of candies to sweeten the discussion to come. The servants cleared the family's table and went down the stairs to dine at their own.

In the long, narrow servants' hall, Simon was nodded toward Anne's seat near the head of the table, and they all sat down to a repeat of a civil meal. This time, a few ventured benign comments, offered bread or gravy or mentioned the delights of a summery day.

The meal neared a peaceful end when some rose from their seats and stood at attention. Anne and Lizzy froze, not understanding the change. Others looked around with puzzled expression and were startled to see His Grace hovering over the seated staff, arms folded and lips pursed. Those remaining jumped to their feet.

"I see Grantham has made some improvements in the atmosphere at the dinner table here, and I'm glad to know of it," he began. "I tolerate few persons at my table who cause me trouble, while trying to swallow my food, with such rude and snobbish declarations as I have learned occur regularly at this one downstairs. I am quite surprised you can eat the agreeable food provided and mortified that my butler has not managed this better in the past."

He looked at Grantham, whose sheepish retreat showed only in a deep breath as he maintained a commanding stance.

"I have spies to inform me of the atmosphere in the

kitchen and household from the scullery and servants' hall to your attic chambers," the duke went on, "and I have discussed my unhappiness with what I learned in a meeting with my top staff. I chose to come down here tonight and make it clear to each and every one of you that should you not maintain order and efficiency in a tolerable sort of way, you will be dismissed. A glance at *The Times* has assured me there are an abundance of servants with characters seeking situations." The duke looked down the row of workers on one side of the table and up those on the other side. All held their breath in proper formation.

He continued, "Let us assume that when guests arrive from other houses, whether they are nobles or their servants, they are to be treated as guests and not as intruders." He cleared his throat. "Now, it is quite out of the ordinary for a duke to appear in the kitchen to address his household. And this one never shall again. Should the conditions be more than I expect my steward to handle one time more, I will simply replace the lot of you."

He turned and spoke in the direction of his top staff. "I am gravely disappointed to learn that my butler did not have better control, and he will be the first to go should I find him incapable of his position. The cook and housekeeper are also to maintain peaceable relations amongst their staff. Lest any of you should, subsequent to this discussion, lose respect for those in authority having seen them reprimanded and fail to obey them, you will go along with them."

The duke took a deep royal breath and everyone yet held theirs, hoping he was done. However, he shifted positions and softened his tone of voice. "As you know, I was one of several sons of King George III. Of the lot of us, perhaps you are aware that none fell in love with a bride suitable to our position early in life. Some fell in love, indeed, but due to their station were kept from marriage to the ones they cared for. I remained single, not having found someone I wished to share my life with and refusing to marry someone I disliked. Perhaps that was the best way as shown by the experience of my brother, King George IV, and his tumultuous, miserable life. In my later years, as you know, I found the perfect woman. How happy I was that she was agreeable to becoming my wife, she was acceptable to the King, and I was free to marry her. I have lived in the greatest happiness since. I know such intoxication does not befall every man, though it is not a favor meant for princes alone. Having seen the distress that develops from prying lovebirds apart, I refuse to be part of such an evil thing. The damage to persons is too great when rules become swords between hearts hopelessly entwined. I know the rules of great houses, albeit I do not always live by them. I know of the need for order and discipline and expect it here. But should ever a case of regard develop between a man and a woman in my service, they must be allowed to court away from this house and to make their decision regarding marriage. This arrangement cannot become a problem for the household, or the couple must find work elsewhere." The duke nodded his head in thought. "I expect the lot of you to keep this directive known within this house only, as it is not regular, and I do not wish to start some sort of blaze within another household."

He shifted his position to face the astounded couple. "I expect Mr. Jones, here," he said as he nodded toward Simon, "will need some fair amount of time off from service. He shall be allowed one hour each afternoon, arranged according to what is needed in this house, to walk out with his lady for the remainder of the Season." He addressed them personally. "You may continue your covert communications as before. The fragrance used is one of my favorites." He turned and left. Everyone was dazed. No one dared snicker but for a few of the footmen an hour later in Simon's room. That matter was merciless, though he slept it off with a happy heart.

***

In a state resembling shock, Simon and Anne had not spoken to make arrangements to walk out. They had picked up and cleared out of the servants' hall without breaking eye contact or ceasing to glow. But the next morning came, and they were the first of the servants to meet for breakfast. They were deemed early enough to carry plates for the maids, but hardly minded as they chatted cheerfully to the irritation of the others.

Simon was required to sit with the footmen again but took a spot down on the opposite side of the butcher block table from her where he could meet her sparkling eyes with his adoring pair. Her dimples never receded at meals from this time forth, which utterly enchanted him, and he found her regular spilling of beverages most endearing.

After breakfast on this first happy morning, he told her he would signal to her at the window when he was allowed to walk. Anne, therefore, saw to it her work was done early and went to her window more often than usual. During an afternoon watch, her darling appeared below bringing the post and signaled her with a huge smile to come downstairs. She rushed to a mirror for last minute touches and hurried down the stairs. Simon delivered letters to the butler, who reminded him somewhat politely he had but one hour and not a moment more, and they must leave through

171

the servants' door.

He then stood near the stairs, shifting from foot to foot while waiting for Anne. Dimples in good form, she arrived, and they made their way out. She took his arm promptly after leaving the house. Thrilled to be together and legitimately at that, they strolled in the sunshine toward the gardens of Buckingham Palace, heaven having smiled upon them.

Anne expressed quite some anguish, feeling certain the duke had read their notes, for what other girl had been so betrayed to the world? She was most embarrassed and had survived only because she must, as they might now walk out together. But Simon could comfort her. He had learned from the valet that the duke had read but one, the first written by Simon, which had exposed the details of the first dreadful meal downstairs. The paper had thoughtlessly slipped out from behind the supposedly capable, framed ancestor, had been picked up by the valet and handed to the duke. He had read and replaced the letter, and ordered an investigation into the allegations upon it. Simon had retrieved Anne's envelopes always sealed with Emma's stamp. None had been compromised. The duke was indeed a good man, and the valet had likely laughed it off.

Thus began the first of many happy walks about Belgravia in the early summer of the year for a far less tragic Romeo and Juliet.

***

Exactly one week after her visit by Mr. Hughes, Emma received a letter from him. After skimming it privately, she read it aloud to Winnie. It said:

"'My dear Miss Carrington. It is utterly wrong for me to write you, but I feel my loss more than I care for propriety. You may expose my misbehaviour as you see

best. It is a delight when I think of you, although I do not allow myself too much of that pleasure for fear I would begin to pressure you against your will. Indeed, I do not wish to make you unhappy in any way and pray that you do let me know if an occasional note would do so. I look forward to seeing you again at the next dinner or ball to which we are both kindly invited. I walked throughout a great house last night looking for you, but you were not there, although I was overjoyed to encounter Lady Holmeshire. I am grateful I have much hard work to otherwise occupy my mind. Please contact me immediately should you have any wish I can fulfill. My very best to you and your dear friends at Belgrave Square, Mr. Gabriel Hughes."

"Yes, Emma," Winnie smiled. "I did see him last night. I thought it better not to bring the matter up and plunge you into a romantic delirium." Both laughed at the phrase. Emma's laugh, though, did not free her of apprehension.

"I hope, ma'am, you understand that I do not intend to marry Mr. Hughes. I wonder if perhaps this might not be too difficult for him, chancing meetings with me at people's dinner parties."

"I think there may be some danger of that, my dear," Winnie replied, "but he will come to realize the sincerity of your decision over time. I hope you understand I seek your greatest happiness—and his— but I do wish to firmly dissuade you from any possible change of heart in the matter. Perhaps it should be made more clear to the gentleman."

Emma lay awake all night wondering about her words. What was it about Mr. Hughes that she ought to be sure to refuse him?

~Chapter 9~

The Onset of Happiness and Quite Some Bewilderment

Wilfred at last had a morning to stay in and rest. He did not hurry himself to get up for feelings of trepidation. It gave him the time to look about the room. The darkness was comforting. The ironed sheets were crumpled, but it would keep a girl in work and off the streets, he thought. He wondered whether Lady Genevieve was as shocked as he over Breyton's decision and whether she was yet thinking of the hungry and homeless.

Upon rising, he took his time lounging about the spacious room. He longed to stay in his quiet suite for the day. The navy and red, vertically striped drapes could remain closed—how well they blended with the dark—and he could take breakfast alone. Perhaps he might read a good book with the drapes drawn just a bit—nothing governmental or weighty, perhaps some poetry.

Yes, he told his valet, poetry—ah, tea and poetry. Coffee! Coffee and poetry. That would be perfect. No, wait. Mother. He had not spent time with Mama in ages, he sighed and told the valet. Perhaps he should dress and see what Mama had on her diary for the day. So, he thought, he must put on those stiff old clothes. She may be waiting at breakfast for him. He would go down. His mind was heavy with concerns, though, and Mama was the least of them. There was the question of Genny, the matter of Emma…and now there was Mr. Hughes playing on his mind.

He leaned against the wardrobe, nodded and confided his troubles. He stood absent-mindedly being dressed for the day, going over his thoughts again and again without resolution. At last he left his room and headed down august halls he had not yet taken time to admire. The smell of bacon began to reach him, and his mother was indeed waiting for him in the airy breakfast room when he arrived.

"Good morning, darling—is it not wonderful sitting in a house with such windows?" Winnie said with a warm smile. "I love the light. I do hope your room was dark for the morning, though. How nice that you had some extra sleep. You have been dragging yourself about so lately. I told them to leave the food here a bit longer."

"Yes, Mama, it was the slowest start to a day I have enjoyed since we arrived. I truly needed a morning in very much. Now I must decide what I am to do with an entire day off. I did not plan anything so I would not be forced to fulfill obligations. What is on your diary?"

Winnie smiled. She would not schedule herself out when Wilfred was to be home, and he knew it well.

"I could spend the morning in with you," Wills offered. "Or I could drive the curricle recklessly about in the park with you hanging on to your hat. We must, and I shall chain you down that you do not fly off into the roses." He shook his hand in the air and sucked on its side, deservedly pierced by an imaginary thorn.

He looked out the window at the manicured grounds with their stone walkways, gallant statues and morning shadows. "Perhaps I shall take Emma out for an afternoon walk in these gardens," he tossed out, expecting an adverse reaction. "But only should you be able to carry on with her missing from the sitting room for a spell. I require her assistance to look about down there."

The news of Mr. Hughes' proposal had distressed Wills, though he had meant not to be so affected when a gentleman would appear on the scene. He had presupposed someone would indeed propose to Emma. He desperately wished to speak to her and fortify her in her decision to refuse the gentleman, but it was not his place as an engaged man…or what now? Was he even that? Everything was now in a state of disastrous discord. He went back and forth, from Emma to Genevieve to Mr. Gabriel Hughes, from possibilities to probabilities and back, his once aligned and promising life in shreds. Through it all he was most disturbed at Emma's receiving the attentions of another man.

At the sideboard, he habitually dished up a large plate full of muffins, poached eggs and deviled kidneys, all atop pieces of bacon. He seated himself on a chair across from Winnie. Soon realizing he could not possibly eat, he pushed the plate away.

"You must not walk with Emma, dear son. You well know that. Perhaps with Master Nicholas?"

"I understand Emma intends to insist His Grace position a statue of me underneath a cherry tree. She says it must be done, as I am the most handsome of men on the face of the earth. Humble as I am, I simply wished to dissuade her before she proposes it."

But Wills was not hard to deter. He knew

circumstances were determinedly against him in the domain of romance. Mr. Hughes had spoken to Emma already, and Wills was happy to have heard of her refusal. Yet, he had doubts she would remain unwilling, at long last, to accept the attentions of a handsome and wealthy man. Nevertheless, Wills determined to behave properly in this situation, staying uninvolved till it was fully resolved. Could he? He must stave off his heart.

Genny remained. He would not abandon Genny and must find out what she felt. He had considered at great length how all of this might affect her. Would she feel torn, loving her parents, obeying her father, even marrying another, but live in anguish over the ended engagement? Or would she now simply turn from him and focus her attentions again on balls and a social life? She was, after all, at last free to accept attentions, consider proposals and perhaps even choose her own husband. Would she demand to marry Wills himself? If so, what would become of that demand? Lord Holmeshire would support her decisions, whatever they might be. But for him, life seemed for the first time to be agonizing and formidable. And they call this sort of thing, he thought, love?

"I have disturbing news, Mama," he declared, regarding the matter best brought to light anon, "I met with Lord Breyton yesterday at the hotel."

"And I had the pleasure of meeting with his poor, dear wife over tea. Well, we nearly had tea. I was made quite aware by my troubled friend of her husband's decision regarding Genevieve. *That man vexes me so.*"

Wills was surprised at her sharp hostility toward the marquess. These sentiments had never surfaced in his presence. But he was grateful to know the matter was out in the open; his mother had survived the initial shock and she apparently did not blame *him*.

"I do not know what do to now, Mama," he worried aloud. "I can hardly disappear from her life with her future dashed to bits. She may be in distress."

Winnie consoled him. "I do not know if this will make it easier for you or more difficult, but she was at tea, too. She looked well and content." Winnie hesitated and leaned forward to take Wills' hand. "She told me to tell you, right in front of her mother, that she intended to go forward with charity plans, and should you wish to elope she would be watching out her window for you. Now, of course—"

Many possibilities had tormented his mind, but this was a new notion, and his training failed him. "Oh my—that never occurred to me. Elopement!" He nearly shouted, "I never dreamed she would think of such a thing. What a disaster this has become. Elope?"

He gained some command over his reactions, but looked at his mummy for help. "I cannot do that—I would marry her against her parent's wishes, but not in that way. She must persuade them. I must win them over. I wish that day had never happened. Why did I not see what would come of it? I simply thought it might bring her and me closer, or at least make her aware of what our life would be. I don't know. What a foolish decision. I thought I was doing something wise and virtuous."

"I know, dear. But this sort of upset in life sometimes throws things up into the air, and they fall into place better afterward. Give it some time to settle."

Wills nodded skeptical agreement. "I do hope so, Mama."

"She appreciates having seen the situation in the streets. It made her think, and surely that is good. Going into marriage before examining what life will be like is never wise. She seems settled for herself, now, having seen in what battle you are contending. And she seemed to be content with what decisions you would make. I think it will turn out well in the end."

"So she wants me to decide?" he said, his eyes wide and his brow knit. "I just do not know what to do. I must know her wishes. Please, write her a letter asking for her thoughts."

"That is a brilliant idea, son. I shall send her off a note, and then you put your mind at rest while we go for a ride. Perhaps she will reply later today."

The butler entered the room with a post on a silver tray for Wilfred. His mother's words and Grantham's presence enabled him to brighten his frame of mind and recover his cheery ways. "Ah—now how did you find me in this huge house?" he questioned the man with a laugh.

"I knew where the food would be, sir," was the straight-faced reply as Grantham glanced at the hefty helping on his plate. The Holmeshires laughed. Wills took the letter from the tray and broke the seal.

"It is from Lady Genevieve," he said, skimming through it. He sighed happily. "Oh Mama, this is perfect—all is well."

"What does it say, tell me," she asked.

"Listen."

"*Dear Lord Holmeshire, I hear you are aware by now that my father has banned me from our marriage. I hope this does not cause you any great grief. Of course, a huge change in one's life is unsettling, and one must use all one's power to look ahead and find something new. Should you feel as I do, it will not be overwhelmingly distressing for you. An arranged marriage is different from one in which two persons fall hopelessly in love. Yet, we grew up with the expectation that we would wed. Should you wish to pursue our marriage, I will support your decision. Should you, however, be content to leave it as my father wishes, I am happy enough with that as well.*

'I threatened my parents with our eloping, with the result that my income shall continue from Father. You need have no concern for my future. My parents hope, then, I will not marry you for being in want of an income. Papa is opposed to your views of a sudden, and to your having taken in the little child.

'What I wish to extend to you more than anything is that I hope you will take an office in Chenbury House, any room that you choose. There, along with me, you could run a charity to benefit women like the one we saw on the grass in London with her cold and blue baby. I ask that you would find that woman and her sons, and bring them also to Chenbury, where we can provide them with work in setting up our project. As it turns out, I will have money with which to accomplish much. Please inform me of your desires in all these matters. Fondly, your dear friend, Lady Genevieve.'"

"That does it, then—now I know what I shall do with my day. I must go out and search for that woman. I have not been able to bear the thoughts of her and that poor baby in the cold. We must find her lodging till we have everything decided. What shall I do? She wishes to work—I can give her work at Chenbury when she is able, as we have Genny's permission. I have so much to think about now, and to do." Wills rose to his feet, his hands on his forehead with his eyes closed to think, leaving his breakfast untouched.

Winnie tried to slow him down. "Should you wish it, I will take Emma and search for a room for the woman," she said, setting down her newly poured cup of coffee. She stood up. "We had a quiet day planned with you being free, and so we have the time. But please take a moment and eat something?"

He took his chair and in haste, pushed it in. He spoke quickly as he turned, eager to leave. "Oh, do search for a room—that would be wonderful, Mama. It would save that baby. I do hope he has survived this long." Wills could not move fast enough. Helena entered the room, shocked at the apparent state of emergency existing there.

"Your Grace, Aunt Helena," Wills pleaded. "Please, send a letter to Genevieve telling her I am searching for the woman, and my mother is finding her a room. Do not delay. Oh please, please excuse me." He started out the door, but realizing how confusing and surprising his request must have been, he turned back and apologized. "I am sorry, Aunt, I am in such a hurry. Please do this for me?" Wills was out the door to have a coachman called before she replied. She nodded, though she was, indeed, bewildered.

Riding through the dismal area again, he became concerned when, after quite some time, he did not find the woman. Where could she have gone? Could she have gone into a workhouse where her sons would be taken from her? Perhaps she was convinced it would be the only way to save her child's life and had traded her scant remaining happiness for his life. He hoped she had not. With the child's loss of his loving mother, it was a deplorable solution. He jumped down from the carriage, dejected, and began to ask about her.

"Have you seen a woman wearing a brown silk cloak with purple designs? She would be with a young lad and a baby whom she would keep warm beneath her cape, or so I do hope. I am here to help her." At first there was no positive response, at least not as to her whereabouts, but Wills did not give up. He checked in old residential buildings, asked in shoddy business establishments and even inquired inside a rat-infested area workhouse. After a couple of hours searching on foot, a boy heard his query from a distance and called out, "I know where she is, sir." Wills turned, and the ragged child pointed to a metal staircase on the side of a building across the way. There she sat, she with her sons, wrapped in the cape. Wills broke into a grin, thanked the boy with a coin and hurried across a weed-infested plot to see the family.

She smiled at him and said, "Sir—it is you!"

"Do not get up. And the baby? How is the baby?"

"The baby is warm and doing quite well under this fine cloak. I have many times wondered, sir, your name? I wish to give the baby your name, for I know it was you who brought the kind lady here. I hoped you would return that I could learn it."

"My name is Wilfred, Lord Holmeshire. And I wondered about your current living arrangements?" The teenage boy stood up, came down off the stairs, and bowed.

"My mum sleeps on the grass, my lord," he said. "Though it is rocky, she is now warm. We are grateful for that."

"I have a better arrangement for you," Wills said. "My mama is searching for a room for you at this moment, if you please, and a bit of work will be provided should you be able to manage it." He addressed the woman. "Are you well enough to work when you recover from your laying in?"

"Or, I am afraid, sir, my laying out," she replied with a laugh.

"We are both quite well enough to work, my lord," the lad replied for her. "My mum should rest and care for the child, but I am strong and can work, should you allow it. Please, sir."

Wills smiled, impressed with the lad's ambition and desire to help his family. "Can you come now, the three of you?" he asked. "Are you free to leave the area?"

The woman, overwhelmed at the kind efforts on their behalf, spoke up. "Allow me to tell someone we are going." She shook her head in disbelief. "I thank you with all my heart, my lord." She signaled, and the little boy who had shown Wills the family ran to find his father. The woman told him they were fortunate to now have a room, and no one need worry about them. Wills informed the man, while the family was taken into the carriage, that they were working on a plan to provide what they could for more of the people. Time would unfortunately be needed, he bemoaned. He climbed the carriage steps, and off they went.

Wills ascertained the woman's name was Abby Smith, and the lad's, Henry. He asked what sort of work they had done in the past. Abby said she had been a washer woman in a laundry shop, but when she came to be with child, she could not carry the buckets of water, and so was replaced. Her dear husband had died soon thereafter from illness that had passed about in the area. Henry's job at the wash shop was not enough to rent their room and buy food, so they lost their dwelling. Homeless people were driven from the area by the businessmen, she said, and Henry could no longer get to work. Now they had nothing and nowhere to go.

Henry asked Lord Holmeshire if he was married. "No," he replied. His expression sobered, and he changed the subject. Should they not visit a seamstress for clothing? Surely they were in need. Abby said she knew of a used clothing shop that would be less expensive and allow them to have clothing immediately, should he not mind. She had nothing with them, she said, after all, and they needed to wash what they wore.

They stopped at the shop, spent a bit of time looking through the carefully cleaned and folded apparel, and all three came out clothed quite decently. They had extra in a bundle and nappies for the baby. Wills had chanced upon a lovely, fine dress for Abby that he carried out over his arm, and he suggested they tear up their old apparel for rags. There would be no need to dress so poorly, he told them, with the income they would soon earn.

The horses clopped along and drew them down a misty road to the elegant Belgrave Square, and Wills sent a footman inside to learn from his mother whether rooms had been found. Soon they followed Winnie, Emma and Nicky in a separate carriage.

"How very lovely," Wills said, as the group stopped before a white stone edifice and under modern lights. "They have the new gas lamps on the street. This should improve the safety of the area." He exclaimed he was also pleased with the quaintly trimmed building which was well maintained and attractive.

Winnie had found the family a pleasant suite of rooms in which they would be most comfortable. It was furnished pleasantly. The suffering mother and son stood in awe. The flat was the most wonderful, welcoming place on earth. How could so much good have come to them in these few days?

Winnie and Emma smiled as they talked with the two and helped them settle their few items in. Candles and a silver snuffer from Belgrave were unwrapped, and they found a teapot to make hot tea for the new mother. They had brought crusty bread and soup from the duke's kitchen. Wills hungrily assisted them in emptying the pot.

Nicholas was happy to be helping "a cute baby," and wished it to be his very own brother. Little Nick's determination amused the adults, who also laughed heartily as the baby made funny shapes with his mouth. Wills told Abby to rest for her confinement, and Winnie said they would send a servant to help until she was strong. Employment would be available for Henry at Chenbury very soon.

***

Wills sat down at his desk and read several letters from the lords of Parliament, some of which were discouraging indeed. He intended to write Genevieve, but before he could, he found another from her on his desk.

"I have such plans," she wrote, *"and can hardly think of anything else. First, I would like to use Chenbury's large banquet room for an auction hall where we can sell off donated items such as my tiresome trinkets. The banquet table can remain in place, as there is adequate room without moving it. We could, therefore, hold honorary dinners at any time. The dance room would make a wonderful theater with a bit of redoing. Perhaps we could take out a wall to make it larger, and we could put on Shakespearean productions, which would entertain many and produce funds for our project. What grand fun it would be.*

"I am sorry not to have awaited your reply before carrying my thoughts so firmly in this direction. I simply desire this too much to allow you to say no. It is what I care to do regardless of anything else, and I suppose I am quite independent at heart. I received a note from Her Grace saying you would search for our poor mother and child, and I do hope you will locate

them very soon. I pray the dear baby has survived. Fondly, Genevieve."

Wills had spent the most joyful day of his life, for giving does, indeed, bring the greatest happiness. Genny's note conformed nicely to the pleasant direction of things. If only Gabriel Hughes did not so frequently assail his sanity. He penned a reply to Genny's two notes—they were, after all, somewhat engaged.

"Dearest Genevieve,

"First let me comfort you in that I have located Mrs. Abby Smith and her two sons, Henry and little Wills. Henry will be a most zealous worker. The baby is healthy, and it appears he will do quite well thanks to your kind assistance to his mother. You have clearly saved his life. Your generosity will make it a happy one, I am sure. Thanks to your urgent request that I locate her, and thanks to the efforts of my mother, the family is warm and delighted in a suite of rooms within walking distance of Chenbury House.

"I plan to cut back my time at Parliament to do more for the poor. Since I have come under your father's disapproval, my support at Westminster seems to have pulled back. I do not have the influence I once did, and there is great support, again, for the workhouse arrangement. My ideas for the poor are simply not a subject that the lords are willing to discuss any longer at this time.

"If I am to accomplish anything much, it must be with my own money and whatever you and other generous souls wish to do. Your funding ideas are brilliant. The use of Chenbury for this project is an enormous help. It will enable us to begin building or buying houses for shelters the sooner. I hope to have many beds before autumn rains fall. I could appeal to

my uncle for support in Parliament, but I feel there will be greater peace and happiness should we turn to the good will of our friends. We should simply move ahead and not spend time and energy battling over it. This will mean housing, clothing and food for those in need quite soon. Once the benefits of our efforts are shown, perhaps the government will give our approach more consideration.

"As for the matter of marriage, I prefer to talk when we next see each other. Please inform me of when we can meet at Chenbury and begin work on our project. My Aunt Helena, my Mama, Emma and Nicholas all wish to join us in this happy project. They will be of great assistance. Sincerely yours, Wilfred, Lord Holmeshire"

His letter made it to her hands that evening, and they were both sleepless with joy.

***

Come the following Wednesday, Mrs. Amberton sauntered past the new brick telegraph office in Holmeshire village. *It is preposterous what they say they can do*, she thought, frowning as she hurried past the devil's very window furtively glancing in. A voice from inside called out to her, and she ran the other way. The door opened and banged shut as someone came out behind her, calling her name with a familiar voice. Puzzled, she turned around. It was young Mr. Wells, who had returned from training in London not long since. He stood beneath the handsome, new, swinging wooden sign over the shop, motioning her into the building with an astonished face, determinedly gesturing.

"Mrs. Amberton—our first telegram came through but a moment ago, aye, and it is for you." The men inside had no interest in the message itself, but were

188

thrilled the machine had actually worked. The office filled with noisy rejoicing, and a bottle of champagne was loudly uncorked.

As she stepped inside, they shouted, "How quickly it came from London!" "Have a bit of the bubbly, Mrs. Amberton." She heard none of this for all her disbelief. She disputed with somber piety that she or anyone could receive an untouched message from London.

"Where is the message, then?" she huffed. A young man shoved a glass of champagne into her hand. She feigned indignation, evil never having passed her lips, but being the center of attention and celebration, she was forced to drink it down. Mr. Wells handed her the paper.

She looked at it, and an expression of disbelief distorted her face. "I am to make two hundred woolen cloaks for The Lord Holmeshire and have them done by October?" she cried in disbelief. "I would have to hire folks to do that." She gave the machine a dirty look, as it had quite obviously concocted this message under the influence of the devil himself who was out to ruin her. The machine started clacking, and another message came to be. Mr. Wells rushed to pick it up.

"It is for Joseph Darby at the Woolhouse—he is to send fabric to Mrs. Amberton and put it to his lordship's account."

Everyone looked about in awe of the messages, excepting Mrs. Amberton. She clapped her empty glass down on the tabletop, threw down her message and went out the door, annoyed at the gullibility of the young and worried for their souls.

It was not until Darby arrived at her crowded little house with four large crates of fabric that it began to occur to her that this affair was something she should take into consideration. Could it be true, or had he been fooled by the possessed machine? Then along came Samuel Silverton with a good quantity of thread and said he had delivered materials elsewhere for two hundred men's and boy's warm winter hats in varying sizes.

Her eyes flew open as the six-year-old from the candle shop brought a basket of candles, and she began to, if not believe, at least earnestly wish to.

"Beeswax," she shouted to her startled children. "Perhaps this *is* from his lordship, as I've never had a beeswax candle in my life." The bees near Holmeshire were to be employed as well, it seemed.

Though the Amberton's thatched cottage was now overfilled, she pushed the necessities of life against a cracked plaster wall to make room for her pile of new materials. Without a doubt, these things had fallen from heaven. She determined that one way or another, with the help of her children and some friends, she was meant to make those cloaks.

The next day, any shred of doubt was at last dismissed when a horseman appeared at her door with a small bag of coins. It was payment in advance, he said, for a month's work. This good news was too much to bear, and Mrs. Amberton ran out to buy a bottle of champagne at the back door of the pub. The Chenbury charity was to benefit the struggling economy of Holmeshire quite nicely.

***

Back in London, Anne Amberton had been blissfully happy. One day, however, when she was about to meet her beau for their rain-or-shine walk, she found that her shawl, which had been hanging on a hook near the servant's door, had been cut into strips with a scissor. Anne burst into tears upon finding it so, feeling threatened and despised.

Simon came inside, puzzled at her not appearing outside the door, and found her weakened and collapsed in a chair. She had not wanted him to see her in such a state but felt great relief at his knightly reaction against the unknown villain.

He took the matter directly to the housekeeper. She, wanting to retain her position, called everyone in and lined them up for interrogation. Nobody claimed to know who had done it, though a few had faces that seemed to hide facts. The housekeeper was, however, satisfied with her accomplishment.

With that handled unsuccessfully, Simon returned to the damsel in distress and ascertained that she could not be looked upon with a reddened nose. His promise to look at only the scenery for a full ten minutes convinced the maid to rise to her feet to go walking out. At Simon's request, a kitchen maid loaned an adequate shawl for their stroll.

Anne's recent bliss was gravely hampered by the occurrence, and she became afraid, though of whom she did not know. Simon saw her fear and began to realize the great responsibility he must take on should he become lord of his own house and the protector and provider of a wife and children. Would it ever be possible?

The couple stopped walking, ten minutes having slipped away, under a weeping willow. Their boot tips nearly met on a brick walk that rounded up to a half wall covered with vines, backed by bushes attempting to put forth white flowers. All that beauty, the songs of a skylark and the buzzing of a number of hard-working bees went unnoticed.

Simon's poverty disturbed his mind, indeed, his very life, in his view. "Tomorrow, Miss Amberton, we shall buy you a new shawl, but I must apologize. This will mean I can purchase none of the confections we have enjoyed, nor a cup of tea out, for a week or two." His shoulders dropped, and his voice broke. "I would like very much to become your provider, your protector, your dearest loved one forever, yet I fear I could not properly succeed. The only benefit I could offer you, should we marry, is my deepest love and companionship on my Sundays off. I could not often see you. I could provide you with only the smallest home here, and with little to furnish it as did my uncle for my poor aunt. Should we have children, I fear that you and they would suffer hunger and want. I work long hours, and my work is in London. Your parents and family are in the north, and I fear you could not be without them. In a few weeks, you will be taken back to Holmeshire, and I will be left alone. As an aspiring gentleman, I cannot ask you to stay and give up your security, and surely I could not find sufficient work in your small village in this harsh economy."

Was this to be known forever as the worst day of Anne's life? "And yet," he continued, lifting his chin, "I am completely given over to you, and I cannot bear to face a life without you. I must do my best to change my situation." He paused and looked more deeply into her eyes. "If you please, I propose you give me a bit more of your sweet time. For who knows if, in the next months or year, with sufficient effort my circumstances might change, and I could offer you a more satisfactory home?"

She nodded agreement. He relaxed and went on to say, "I have taken great pains to educate myself, and I am capable of a responsible position. I search for one as I go about the duke's business in Town. One cannot apply for a position when dressed as the duke's representative, and there is never the opportunity for it on Sundays, especially as I intend to spend every minute of them with you. Yet with you as my undeserved and perfect reward, I am much inspired to find a way. Should I find no solution, no satisfactory position within a year's time, I shall free you to consider another husband with a better income and situation should you wish to leave service and marry. I would find my joy in giving you over to a better life."

Anne took his arm to walk along the bricks, and she expressed her concerns. "Although we have had the favor of the master, and he has offered us freedom to marry, it seems in truth it would not work well for servants. A servant's income is meant for one who lives in the master's house. We must search for another way. Surely there is a suitable position somewhere for you. I shall talk to my mistress." She paused walking and took both his hands. "But I am willing to wait far more than a year should it mean we can be together thereafter. I would never consider another husband as long as you live. As for leaving you behind in London, I do not know how I could. It would be leaving life itself behind. I shall seek to stay in service here, perhaps for the duke, and will see you as best I can."

***

Helena, Winnie and Emma sat, each with a lap desk, writing letters to friends when Grantham brought messages on a silver tray. Helena picked up an exquisite note stamped with the queen's seal.

"Oh my!" she exclaimed, "I have a message from Her Majesty." She opened it and read with a puzzled expression. She turned it over, contemplated the contents, and a look of understanding crossed her face. "Winifred. The queen has received a letter, she says, and has a request she does not understand. She spoke to her ladies, and one suggested we be called to the

Palace. She has asked that you and me and His Grace visit her on Friday next. Would you be able to accept?" She gave Winnie a look and nod meaning "you do wish to be there."

Winnie nodded agreement and said, "Oh yes, I would very much like to go. I shall cancel any other engagement."

"I am afraid this is one residence where we cannot bring you, Emma. How I wish we could."

"I understand perfectly, Your Grace, for there are only so many toes upon which I might step," Emma replied.

***

Abby was tearfully happy and enjoyed the days with her son. Her new little home was so very pleasant. Modern steam-power printed wallpapers had won the house hunters over, and the landlord had chosen a plum divan and golden beige chairs to match. Abby dreamed of the day that she could choose a vase to hold flowers and linens for the little round tea table. Winnie had assured her that should she choose to stay there, the cost would be within her means on the salary she would receive from Chenbury.

Her son would make enough, too, that they could eat and dress, and he would be able to save for the future. And would he like to improve his education, making him more valuable to his employer? There were tutors living on the very street. Having observed him at his efforts and deeming him worthy, Wills would pay to have him trained in the ways of business.

***

Thursday had at last arrived, the day the charity team was to meet. Though Abby was to stay home to care for and cuddle her little one, Henry was ready to go out the door well ahead of time. He was able, he told her, to bring in muffins from a bakery, and would she like fresh milk to drink? For a man brought milk into town each day. He pulled a footstool near her chair so she would not strain herself and went in search of the milk man. Life could be no better, she thought, but for big Henry to be with them to live it.

At the appointed time, the charity team met in the drive of the magnificent, if smaller than Handerton, house. Little Nicholas ran in circles round a splendorous labradorite fountain. The gardeners had kept the greenery perfect, and the indoor staff, though reduced with no one in residence, had kept the house clean.

Today Chenbury woke and opened its arms to the project at hand. At the stroke of ten, the chosen hour, the butler opened the wood-framed, beveled glass doors, and the small band entered the entry hall, rounded by faux walls. Champagne was opened and enjoyed by all but the excited Nicky, who had a pretty etched goblet of apple cider.

Lady Genevieve took them on a tour of the grand house and told them her thoughts for some of the rooms. All were to be adapted for executive and fundraising purposes but for a suite on the second floor that would, should it become necessary, become her home, and the downstairs servants' realm. Maintenance for much of the building would be in the hands of the charity, providing work for the poor. She turned the chairmanship over to his lordship.

"If you please, then," he began, pointing to a room off the entry, "I choose this room for my office to oversee the charity as a whole. I expect much of the year it will be occupied by a responsible assistant, my being far off in a country house. So, Genevieve, please choose your office, where you will organize productions. Each of you shall have an office. Please search one out near here. That includes you, Mr. Smith. I will choose one for your Mama, down the hall and out of the way, where her child can attend her. And the ladies should consider whom they might wish to have as an assistant to run their branch. Someone, perhaps, from the middle class and educated who would responsibly carry on the work while you are away from Town. Please choose with care, that we will have success."

Henry was shocked and replied, "My lord, you say I shall have an office?"

"I have seen your reading, your writing and your determination," said Wills. "It is apparent that you schooled yourself with intent. You will be given intensive training to oversee shelter homes—will you work hard at it? Should you continue your responsible manner, you will have a position for the rest of your life. We shall obtain a grand top hat, as you will be a gentleman, and you must look the part." Henry wore a broad smile for the remainder of the day.

"I wanna hav'a office," Nicholas chirped.

"You shall have a position right here," Wills replied, and lifted the young one to his shoulders.

The women were told of their positions in the charity and were left to stake their claims. They began to uncover furnishings and called to each other with excitement. Wills received Genevieve's permission and followed her to her office.

"This house is elegant," he remarked as they walked.

"It is, a bit, for charity administration," she said, "but I do not wish to spend money changing rugs and wallpaper. I prefer that our money go for the intended purpose."

Wills agreed, and they entered her chosen room. She excused herself to look over carved white borders along the pale blue ceiling of the room and examine other features. He gazed for a moment with deepened respect at the proficient young woman. As she took out and returned volumes to a bookcase and pulled open the drapes, he paced with his eyes to the ground, turning his top hat in circles in his hands.

When satisfied with the tour she had taken, she looked back to Wills. He asked her to sit for a moment. A soulful expression appeared, suggesting her sorrow for the conversation to come. She sat, tense, on the front edge of a silky, mint-green chair, and he just across from her on its plush footstool. "The matter of marriage—" he began.

She allowed no time to pass before she interrupted. "Wills," she said, "I do hope you are not intent upon our marrying. I know you did not choose me, and I did not choose you." Genny let out a sigh and her hands dropped to her lap. She looked away, and then back to him. "You are a remarkable man. You are bringing about remarkable changes. You are a wonderful earl over fortunate subjects."

She rose and turned, gesturing toward the city, and said, "My interests at this time relate to what I can do for this charity, for the people in want, for the future of this country. I want this work to be my life, and it is here in London."

Returning to Wills, she said, "While you and I are firmly and most happily united in the Chenbury project, we as individuals are different in many ways. I cannot imagine living in the country. I love the Town and I love French design. Perhaps I am selfish, but I am utterly tired of my parent's controlling my every move and making my every decision, and I do not wish to go and live the rest of my life subject to the control and decisions of another. I cannot envision caring for Nicholas or the two or three dozen children that might arrive in our nursery. To be perfectly honest, I cannot imagine dying in childbirth. I wish to live to a ripe old age, doing just what I care to do."

Wills nodded understanding of this unusually independent woman, but her brow furrowed. *How bad this must have sounded*, she thought, but she pressed on to bring this grievous discussion nearer its end. "What sort of wife could I be?" she said. "Surely not a proper countess whose life must be all those things. Do you see how different we are?"

Stepping closer to Wills, she clasped her hands in front of her heart. "My choice, if it should not hurt you deeply, is for us to not marry."

Wills waited as she looked downward in deep thought. Then she went on, "It would give me some peace with my father, who cannot endure opposition in Parliament. I do not know to whom his fortune and the Handerton estate will go; some good person I would hope, but my sustenance is provided. Whether I should choose to marry anyone ever, I do not know. They are trying to find a new match, but I prefer my independence. Should I not marry and have sons, Chenbury may go to whomever my father's properties go, but by then surely another place could be found for the charity."

Genny looked down at the floor. "I am sorry for Papa. He will not leave a legacy if I do not have a son. My mama has been angry, but she is adaptable. She will love me and be my dearest friend in the end regardless of my decisions. But I do very much wish for you to marry and have children with someone you rather especially love. That should mean more than a title, and I want you and your wife to have both. You see," she sighed, "my parents were long engaged by arrangement. My father told me but yesterday that he once fell for another woman, and it was very troublesome for him. It nearly cost him his marriage to my mother. He no longer wishes me to face such vexation. Suppose one of us…suppose you are in love with someone else, as I suspect you are. How could we ever be happy?"

Wills covered his lips with his fist, nodded his understanding, and said, "How very brave of you, Genevieve, to face a new life, not knowing what it will bring, not having someone to live it with you. You do seem able to control it and succeed, and I commend you." He turned away to the window. "Though it is true that I do care for someone, I do not think she will ever be my wife, so my future is uncertain like yours."

Quiet reigned as they struggled with emotion. Brushing her hand over the back of the chair as she passed, Genny walked to his side. Wills spoke again. "Neither of us has had this situation, this facing of life alone before—single, you know. But I shall enjoy, very much, working with you to help the poor. I would enjoy, so much, any visits you might care to pay to Holmeshire Hall, where you shall not, then, be expected to fill the nursery."

They both laughed. "To our union at Chenbury. To your wonderful balls and freedoms and happiness," Wills said, raising an invisible goblet.

"To our new queen, to Chenbury, to your happy future, to my mama's ball, and your Awards Night. There is much to live for," she replied, doing the same.

Will regained a serious, but sentimental bearing. "Genny, considering that you are not seriously involving yourself in the marriage mart, would you yet wear a ring designed for you by a very dear friend?" Wills reached into his coat. Having survived the conversation with a calm bearing, female courage and a dry handkerchief, Genevieve came to tears and disintegrated into sobs as the ring was produced.

***

The marquess was most displeased with his daughter's rebellious stand and her new outlook on life but took solace in that members of Parliament backed him zealously and abandoned their support of Lord Holmeshire. Perhaps Genevieve would mature beyond this, he thought, and life would return to normal— without Wills. The Breytons had begun the hunt for another "suitable husband" with lands and a title and hoped this time he would remain suitable.

Lady Breyton met with friends to discuss this, as everyone must know it was their choice to break the engagement and not his. Their opinions on how to proceed were welcomed. Lady Embry came to tea carrying a longhaired cat and a rather too large allotment of influence over the Marchioness of Breyton one day at Handerton House.

"We are looking to other countries, now," Lady Breyton said, attempting to hide her desperation over her spinster daughter. "With the Earl of Holmeshire out of our way, we might even make a royal match."

"It is indeed time to put royal blood into the family from one country or another, since you have none at all," Lady Embry advised with her nose in the air. "This is very fine. Meanwhile, the Holmeshires hie in the opposite direction, dragging that common girl along everywhere they go. What a shame." She leaned toward the ladies and hushed her tone. "She does not go to church in Holmeshire, I hear. It is merely a show, then," she said with her voice raising again, "that she condescends to go in London. And her abominable necklace is becoming a bore. She wears it simply everywhere."

"Perhaps his lordship will marry her now—can you imagine?" Grace said with a suitable scowl, shaking her fan in the air. "It would be quite convenient for the lot of them. If Lord Breyton had known how he was to turn out, romping with the peasantry and all—but everyone thought it a good match. His Majesty, George IV, was pleased to have it so indeed. And here Genevieve has passed up many a fine young man because of him. And they will soon bring their wives to our ball," she said, shaking her head.

"I hope Lady Genevieve did not invite that…foundling to your ball?"

"I am afraid that, against our wishes of course, she sent the girl a belated invitation. She simply does not listen to us anymore—a most strong-headed girl. It is a trait she acquired from her father's side. But," she hastened to add with a vigorous nod, "do be aware I expressly stated she should not."

"As you most certainly ought to have. But you must take control of your daughter. And you can have the staff refuse a paid companion entry, you know. I certainly would should I give a ball. The girl is a housemaid. If the Countess of Holmeshire could but see what she is doing—it is utterly shameless."

"It is our home and our ball, and I certainly shall refuse her entry."

***

"We need somebody inside that 'ouse," Mr. Scott complained. "We need to get them to trusting us. The only thing I can see, now, is for Lucy to take a position there."

"I have a position right here," she snapped. "I'm

not giving up a position and our room and board. I'm willing to work for my money.

"Yeah, Paw, I wish to stay right 'ere in this warm flat. Three meals a day, a soft bed—Lucy's doing fine for us, Paw. It's good enough for me." He shuffled his cards.

"You must get a position, Charles, and pay for your meals," Lucy warned, "or they'll throw you out." She picked up clothing after the both of them. "I shan't put in a good word for you." She shook their holey shoes at them. "And I'm not sleeping in the middle anymore. Help me shake up the bed."

"We'll never have any real money should we not get into that 'ouse," Benedict replied, climbing onto the bed to sleep off a few.

* * *

Morning brought breezes through windows in Emma's room, tossing long, wispy curtains about like flags. But morning was not the cheerful time it had been as of late. Though both Emma and her lady's maid had been walking on clouds, this morning meant talking of sadder things.

Emma asked the reason for Anne's silence as she brushed her hair. She was told, between sighs, of the previous day's fright with the cut-up shawl and of her discussion with Simon. Adelina had entered the room with a fragrant bouquet and a well-pleased glance at Emma, and she nodded her sympathies. She pulled out tired stems from yesterday's flowers and promised to keep an eye out for whoever might be trying to intimidate Anne. Adelina, with her kindly ways, was well liked and often confided in. Surely someone would unburden themselves of the facts, even knowing she would set matters straight.

She asked to take a seat near the ladies and

expressed grief over the difficult circumstances of Anne's romance. She reminded her that things do change, especially if one should be determined to make it so. Emma agreed, pointing out how her own life had had such pivotal experiences, something Anne had observed with her own eyes. Just be wise, Adelina told Anne, say many prayers and make careful decisions. Her future happiness lay in her own hands, and she must learn what she could about the man with cautious consideration. Before leaving the room, Adelina spoke one more time, and most kindly. "I have placed your geraniums in your room, now, Anne, as I believe you had forgotten them on the balcony."

That afternoon, the vigilant Miss Darivela ascertained that it was Hattie the nursery maid who, having favored Simon, had cut up the shawl. Dismissed immediately, Miss Hattie said her goodbyes before tea in quite an angry voice and went home to her mother. It was a relief to all to know who had done such a thing and to put it behind them. Few would miss Hattie, least of all Simon.

He and Anne walked out together and purchased a shawl, paid for from Hattie's wages. The disgruntled nursery maid insisted on taking home the shredded shawl so she could finish its decimation. After all, she said, she had paid for it many times over, worst of all with her lost hope of love. The rest of her day was spent with her poor mother in a state of alarm as Hattie roared and ripped the hapless fabric to ribbons, throwing each vehemently cursed piece into the flames below a pot of porridge, pleased at least that it would never warm the shoulders of Anne Amberton again.

Simon insisted Anne, who was every bit a lady, would have the new shawl with a row of lace on the ends, though he must pay out quite a bit for the work of the lace maker. He regretted he could not buy her the gloves to match, but he looked them over well and kept them in mind. The shopkeeper read his thoughts, and he saw her silently slip them into a drawer with a knowing smile.

Their ardent commitment was to wait at least one hundred years for each other, and not a day less, as they tried to arrange matters to remain together.

***

"My dear Miss Carrington," wrote Gabriel a few weeks later, *"It surely is improper for me again to write, but I cannot bear to have no communication. Please forgive my impertinence.*

"I hope you are enjoying the lovely summer weather. Every step out of doors reminds me of our time together in the pleasant sun. I am pleased to know of the outcome for our tearful companion.

"I am happy to hear that you will attend the Midsummer Night's Dream Ball. I, too, shall be there, and I do hope for a dance with you.

"All goes well with me. I hear from my country house that it prospers. My cattle and horses are producing, and my fortunes thus increase. Perhaps someday we will enjoy that house together, however old we may first come to be. I do, though, heartily wish her ladyship good health and a long life.

"Sincerely yours,

Mr. Gabriel Hughes."

Emma was saddened by the letter. It seemed from his words he held hope too dear. She began a note in reply.

"Dear Mr. Hughes,

"I am always pleased to hear from you. And of course, I would be more than delighted to dance with you at the ball, just a few days away. I shall save the

first dance, should that please you, though saving it is hardly necessary in my case. Be assured I am happy to hear of your increasing fortunes, and I hope you will have the happiest future. Please do dance with many ladies at the ball, for I hope you will find a good wife while you are young and subsequently have a lovely family.

    "Yours sincerely,

     Emma Carrington."

Emma had no sooner sent the letter out than Helena and Winifred arrived, relaxed and happy, to sit and stitch. Perhaps now, she thought, would be a good time to ask them some questions? She took a deep breath and prayed for some great amount of courage and then looked to the women.

"Your Grace, and milady, I have concerns about some things that have been previously said. I would like to ask you some questions, for you have kept secrets from me all this time. Please tell me I finally may hear the answers?"

Winnie paused, assuming the topic and at last ready to confess the details. "Yes, dear, do ask."

"I have worn this simple gold ring for nearly three full years, not knowing how it came to be mine. I do notice it shine on my finger insistently, prompting me to indulge in fantasy and fears. Please then, tell me about my shining ring, and whatever you know about my life with regard to it? I have another question, as well. Mr. Gabriel Hughes is said far and wide to be a fine gentleman, and I have heard it from you yourselves. Though I discourage him from waiting for me, I cannot help but reflect on the situation often and wonder—why is it you are so uncommonly concerned that I may further my relationship with him? What could be the deep misfortune in it?"

Winnie sighed, relieved she could at last reply. Helena spoke, though, before her sister could. "My dear Emma, we would like to arrange a meeting with you and Lady Genevieve to discuss these matters. I will contact her as soon as possible to see when this could occur."

Emma stiffened, and her hand flew to cover her chest. Why Genevieve? What had she to do with this? But she agreed and requested her perfumed paper from the footman. He returned within moments to report that her lady's maid knew nothing of any remaining supply in her room.

Helena repented of her own delay, since twenty seconds of inaction had caused Emma to plead for her paper, and with none forthcoming, the desperation mounted. Helena took her quill, and she composed and sent a post. Genevieve returned a letter within the hour, and plans were made to meet that evening at Belgrave.

***

In the meantime, Lady Embry sent out notes asking people to turn their backs on the Holmeshires, should they not conform to society's expectations. It was very important for the good of all that they change their ways, was it not? After all, as she apprised Lady Breyton, the established order could crumble, and the common people could take over the country. Certain anarchy would surely result.

***

Following an early dinner, which worked best for their lordships that evening, Wills approached Emma, offered his arm and walked her up a flight of stairs. They paused on the landing.

"Am I seeing some misery on your…I had best not flatter…on your rather plain face?" He could not help himself. Despite what anguish or despondency he felt,

206

his character could not be repressed.

"I fear you are, and I thank you indeed, sir," she said. She placed her hands on her hips and glared, allowing but a fleeting glimpse of amusement to show. "I do have questions afflicting me, but I believe this situation will soon resolve itself. Whether it is for the good or the bad, I do not know."

"Let me, then, escort you to your destination ere I join the men to leave the house. Perhaps a moment of my presence will improve your state of being."

"You are, to be sure, the best of medicines, and it is admirable that you are liberal in dosing ailing women with your charms. A full moment am I to have?" She shook her head in awe of his ability to entertain. "Please, conduct me to the sitting room, where I will learn of the outcome."

"Suppose I had something important to say?"

Emma dropped her hands from her hips. "A repeat, then, of your momentous musings?"

"Yes, a repeat. And this time there are two most notable matters. First, you must now call me Wills. You must. And I have a question. How many waltzes will you permit me at the ball?"

Pleased at his attention, his engagement having ended, she cocked her head and smiled as they ambled down the hall. "Would you not rather find some less plain girl to step upon?"

He shook his head in feigned irritation. "How you dismay me, when here, I've offered you much."

"One dance is all that is allowed. You well know that, you well-heeled bachelor."

"Is that so? I shall take the matter to Parliament. That will rattle the ton. But look—you are the first lady to the sitting room. See what wonders it does to walk with me? And now you are to be abandoned. On Friday evening, I shall dance with you a dozen times." Wills widened his eyes.

***

The ladies arrived and sat. Remaining uncommonly quiet, they avoided Emma's eyes. She saw an old iron key in the hand of Helena, who tapped it into her palm as they awaited Genevieve.

She had noticed their exchanging impatient glances at the dinner table. It seemed they had struggled, lost in thought, though not unhappy, to carry on conversation with the men. The duke seemed aware of whatever interfered with the pleasantries of the dining hour, and he smiled as he pulled a bit of conversation along with leading questions and thoughtful commentary.

Wills had, at first, carried on with laughable replies as usual and even took up a topic of his own, but it had fallen flat for the ladies' nervous distraction. Before much time had passed, he had begun to feel perplexed and alone in his world of ignorance. He too had become quiet, realizing something of consequence wafted through the air. Apparently, misery had shown on Emma's own face.

She was yet, in the sitting room, trying to imagine what might be the cause of such anxious address. She drew conclusions, but every thought was discarded in the course of trying to fit Genevieve into the puzzle.

The sun was yet required to put in another half hour's time and effort illuminating the sky when Genny arrived at the top of the stairs and was led down the hall to be announced to the ladies, carrying a wooden writing case and paper. She assumed the discussion was to be in regards to their charity efforts.

She sat down with a smile next to Emma and across from the ladies, and she opened her case to expose a sketch she had done of the proposed Shakespearean

Theater of Chenbury. Helena and Winnie were interested in the picture and thus distracted from their purpose, much to the consternation and isolation of poor, dear Emma.

Helena's key tapping wore a hole in the girl's composure. She shifted in her seat and adjusted the shoulders of her gown. Were they to be taken to some room? No, for the key was ancient, too old for this newly built mansion. It appeared they were waiting for some manifestation of a keyhole.

Mercifully, without much more delay, two footmen came in carrying an elaborate, locked trunk. Helena ordered the footmen to leave and to admit no one to the area till the door was opened again.

~Chapter 10~

The Midsummer Night's Dream Ball

London did its part beautifully, painting the skies in brilliant reds and yellows. The Thames splashed and sparkled, reflecting colors from above, and even the air seemed especially fresh. More songbirds huddled in the trees, and more butterflies danced about under them. Aristocratic carriages, filled with diamond-draped fairies and their woodland escorts, rumbled toward Handerton House from every direction.

The long banquet table sparkled, elegantly set, each item placed by measure and waiting. The ballroom dripped with extravagance. It seemed the planners had decided to spend like never before, and Genny's change of heart on the matter had come a bit late.

In the ballroom, lighting was low, only half the chandelier's flambeaus lit to create the nighttime atmosphere. The crystal stars, each with its own tea candle, and the polished silver moon hung from shimmering, silk ribbons stretched across the width of the festive room. Forty potted trees sat on wheeled stands, ready to be pushed from the shining floor when the waltzes began. Musicians played particularly moody, mysterious music.

The ladies were forest nymphs and fairies. Lords and gentlemen were fairy kings and donkeys. Shakespeare was in the air, everyone with a quote or two, and many with theatrical displays of scenes from the theme of the ball they spontaneously performed. People burst into laughter and applauded, sipped champagne, greeted friends and waited for the entrance of the final guests.

The Earl of Holmeshire was announced, and The Right Honorable The Countess of Holmeshire. Their Graces, the Duke of Trent and his duchess were announced.

There was some rabid expectation and unkind intention on the part of a few, but an Emma Carrington did not appear.

Lady Embry dramatized her relief upon noting the girl's absence, gasping gratefully, though it frustrated her retaliatory intentions, and she sidled up to commend Lady Breyton for stopping the flow of servants into society. She floated about, dressed youthfully for a matron of some size with a bodice meant for a smaller bust. Her seamstress dreaded the blow to her own reputation.

Embry presented as an obnoxious figure, assuring one and all she was behind the decision to bring an abrupt halt to this destructive trend on the part of the Holmeshires. After all, the housemaid was not even out in society. Certainly, she said, all would soon be back to normal. The best people's refusing of Emma would restore the senses of the rest, and everyone would be happy again. Even the Holmeshires would eventually thank her.

Winifred used the event as an opportunity to discuss the urgency for an increase in philanthropic efforts. She commended writers like Hannah More to her friends, but said more than writing and preaching was required. There must be a movement among the moneyed to provide help for the desperate. And were they aware of the sentiments of Her Majesty the Queen in this regard?

Wills and Genevieve spoke to many about their charity. Wills approached and prevailed upon the men, and Genny the ladies.

Wills, dapper for a donkey and fascinating in his speech, pointed out the terrible conditions in the workhouses and how families broke up therein. Men go to the men's side, he told them, women to the women's, and children, separated from their parents, might grow up not knowing them. He told them workhouse residents were humiliated, made to wear dreary, identifying garb. His gestures compelled as he spoke of children severely depressed with no will to excel, feeling they could not succeed. How could they someday be workers to support the country's economy? Indeed, they might be dependent their entire lives.

Why would people go there? asked the astonished ignorant, those caught up in leisure. After all, could not their families provide?

Gabriel Hughes, a fairy king, responded. Many families have not the resources, he said. Some of those in the workhouses were simply too old to work, or for other reasons accepted the prison-like plight. Perhaps they were crippled, injured, not of sound mind, and surely this was not by choice.

Many, Gabriel pointed out, even in depressed times, had refused the indignity heaped upon those who entered. They preferred to live in the winter weather, doing what they could to obtain food and clothing. Would one leave this hardship to even their pets?

Could this not be often prevented by building decent homes for temporary shelter with dignity and providing work for the people? Should they be given a start, as the privileged are, surely they could make a living for themselves. London could benefit from the efforts of men and women willing to earn their keep. There was, after all, so much that must be done to enhance the beauty and healthfulness of the Town.

Many of the partiers were duly impressed and vowed to support Wills' work. Promissory notes would be written, events supported, and a talented peer offered a mural to beautify a soon-to-be-built shelter.

Lady Embry, on the other hand, reminded people that able-bodied sloths of the world required correction, that the Lords of Parliament had spoken and that for the government, it would be workhouses. And she was, sadly, right.

"Her Majesty, the Queen." At the announcement, a hush fell over the noisy crowd, and costumed people backed away to form an entrance. The young Queen Victoria stepped in, dressed in a pale lavender gown covered with crystals, giving the appearance of dewdrops on a forested creature at night, and wearing a diamond-studded circlet. She was followed by her mother, the Duchess of Kent, in palest peach. Emma, whose name was not announced, entered last in a deep red gown with the bodice overlaid with lace. She wore a sparkling tiara, her ruby necklace and earrings of diamonds and rubies.

Embry was, of course, horrified and hustled in a quite unseemly manner, and most inappropriately, to the side of the marquess and marchioness. She went fussing and demanding an answer. Had their men gone to sleep at their posts? Why was Emma here, "dressed so outrageously—not in pale color, so out of her class, not in the theme of the ball, and worst of all, following after the queen?" She must have stolen her way in, for she had not even been announced.

She was abruptly shushed by Lady Breyton and pushed aside. The queen, the duchess and Emma, whose steps were the only remaining sound in the room, came to be greeted by the hosts. Though such reception was always accorded the monarch, much of the hush was due to awe and astonishment over the housemaid, Emma. Much attention was on her as she followed the queen. But Lady Breyton, in confusion, pretended to be unaware of her presence, and Emma backed a few steps away. Lord Breyton, on the other hand, moaned and shook his head. He forgot to greet the queen for gaping at the servant girl in diamonds.

The Duke of Trent approached and mentioned to the hostess he would like to make an introduction. Of course, because the queen wished it, and because he was a royal duke, he was allowed. The crowd remained stunned and silent.

The marchioness feared allowing the party to take this uncharted course. She worried what propriety and her friends would demand in such a situation. Time sped as she evaluated what they might require. Though mere seconds passed as she looked from face to face, it seemed a dazed and spinning hour. What was their verdict? There was no reply in their intent, awed stares. What ought she to do? And then, as if in a vision, she saw the duke step forward to speak. She pulled her hands to her chest and froze.

"I will assist our hosts in welcoming you tonight. We are happy to have Her Majesty the Queen with us," he began. "Now that she has arrived, we will soon begin to dance. Have our hosts not provided us with a beautiful, starlit woodland for our festivities this

215

night?"

Everyone applauded, though they looked on past the duke—their minds were not on the setting. "Before the dancing begins," he went on, delighted, "I would like to make an introduction." The crowd held their breath. Breyton stepped back and took his wife's hand as if to protect it in both of his. "Please meet Her Royal Highness, the Princess Emmanuel of Tremeine, niece of His Majesty, King Julian III, who recently contacted Her Majesty in an effort to locate Emmanuel."

The duke paused, Emma stepped to his side and the marquess stood looking at her, numb. "The princess was recently named for her mother, the late Princess Emmanuel of Tremeine, by the king." The duke looked intensely at Breyton. "Perhaps you have heard of her?"

The marquess barely managed to stutter, "Yes, Your Grace." It was as the man had suspected. He bowed in forced homage to the princess. The entire multitude bowed and curtsied as the duke continued.

"The late princess went on holiday in Italy, twenty and some years ago, where she met a viceroy who stopped on his way to India. He was the man who later received the title the Marquess, the Lord Breyton, for heroism in war. They married," he related to loud gasps, "and soon thereafter, Breyton went on to India for his tour of duty. The princess returned home to Tremeine to await their life together, where she realized she was with child. Perhaps you would like to become better acquainted with her daughter and learn from her the rest of her story, should she choose to reveal it. For now, I believe, Her Majesty the Queen is ready to dance." Trent backed into the crowd, leaving the stunning Emmanuel of Tremeine alone, unique in deep red, in the center of the room.

The marchioness, weak and weaving on her feet,

looked at her husband in dismay. He confessed to her that, yes, it was true. Ashamed and humiliated, he tried to explain, "My darling, surely you understand. I was young. One becomes confused about life, you know, in one's youth." He spoke gingerly, touching her shoulder, her arm. Grace pulled away. "And she was royal," he continued. "It was a cardinal opportunity. I was son-in-law to a king. You must understand, my beloved?"

"We were engaged, sir, did you consider that? You had proposed to me before leaving for India. And where is this wife of yours now?"

Genevieve had drifted to Emma's side and curtsied to her, and they were locked in a sisterly embrace before a stunned throng. "You look elegant in your mother's dress, Your Highness," Genny said. "You stand out from the crowd, as you ought. I am so proud to be the only one in this huge assembly allowed to claim you as my sister." She stood back and looked at her again, breaking into a smile. "I know well you have the loveliest white gown in existence, but I am so pleased you wore your mother's regal red."

"My darling sister, I am delighted that you have accepted me so willingly. With much in common, we will enjoy, indeed, a sisterly life." Their smiles gleamed in even the twilight of the stateroom.

Emma promptly searched for the abjuring Mr. Gabriel Hughes. He stood alone, watching with a distant stare at the two women, his arms dropped to his side. Her nod beckoned him to come. He walked toward her with heavy feet but put on a courtier's stance. He approached the princess and bowed deeply.

"Mr. Hughes."

"Your Royal Highness."

"Sir. I believe you had requested of me the first

dance?" She held up her white satin-gloved hand for him to take. They waited in silence for the trees to be waltzed away to somewhere nearer Athens and for the queen to step forward.

"I should be happy for you…and I will be someday," he said, turning toward Emma, and he murmured, "but this is the end of my dear hopes with you. Though you never encouraged me, it is yet hard for me accept the finality, and to dance with a proper smile." She nodded the same sentiments. They went forward and joined in the Grand March following the dukes and duchesses, and then the first waltz.

Afterward, she asked Gabriel to bring her some drink and to sit with her. She graciously postponed several approaching visitors, some delighted at her news, others bearing profuse apologies. Wills and other men with dance requests were acknowledged with a wave. Wills was, however, asked by Emma, "Will you kindly return to me soon?"

Gabriel arrived with lemonade, and they strolled to a terrace to talk. Gabriel kept watch, concerned for her safety.

"I learned but recently," she began, wishing she could sufficiently console him, "that the marquess is my father and the late princess was my mother. What a shock this has been and a great joy, though it has quite overwhelmed me."

"I have no doubt this has been most astonishing and bewildering for you," Gabriel replied.

"It has, sir. I have been informed that my mother came to be with child before returning home from Italy, but her father most angrily refused to accept the marriage. The bloodline of a mere viceroy was not one he had chosen for his grandchildren. He had other intentions for her; marriage to a certain prince, you see, which marriage she had longed to escape."

Emma spoke as she drifted back and forth in front of Gabe across the terrace. "She possibly married to avoid the other match, though her writings indicate she was in love with her husband. Lord Breyton is not royal, so in my grandfather's eyes, he was an outrageous pretender, perhaps intent upon the throne. He told my mother in a dreadful rage he would hide her away till I was born and send me to my father's family. She feared he would in fact keep it all a secret and put me in an orphanage or even have me destroyed without her knowledge so no one could expose the situation. I suppose he expected her to accept his decision, as so many women would feel they must."

"And I am thankful he failed. The world is highly favored with your presence, your life."

"Thank you, sir. I am ever so grateful to have been saved. As it happened, my mother hastened to contact someone she knew, Caroline of Brunswick, who was soon to travel to England. As my mama moved through the continent in Queen Caroline's coach, she dressed as a servant to hide her identity. The queen returned to England, hoping to be crowned alongside His Majesty, King George IV. My mother came with her to hide and wait for her husband's return to the country."

He led her to a marble bench, where they took a seat in the fragrance of night jasmine. "And I know, of course, Caroline was turned away at the coronation and died soon thereafter. What, then, became of your dear mother, should you care to say," he added.

Emma nodded with lowered eyes. "The queen, before her death, commended my poor mother to the care of Her Grace, the Duchess of Trent, who was just returned from abroad. I was born in the duchess' home. The bed I have been sleeping in here is the very bed I was born in. My mother became ill soon thereafter, no doubt as a result of enduring such cruelty and grief. She died when I was but a few weeks old. Alas, I have never known my dear mother, as you have never known yours."

"And I wish we had known both. They are in God's hands."

"They are, indeed, in better hands than those before death. Your poor mother was left to the streets. My dear mother had written to the Lord Breyton that she was ill, the doctors had said she was dying, and I would need him. She also told him about her father's anger, though he already knew. He had received threats from Tremeine, being out of the king's favor. She no doubt hoped he would hurry home to see her before it was too late, and to make provision for my care. He wrote back to the address she had given him. The duke had warned her not to give the Lord Breyton his address in case the letter should be intercepted. In his reply, Breyton said he was not willing to deal with her father and his threats, or to raise the baby after she died. That may have endangered him, I suppose. He ordered her to write to her father that the child had died and then put me in an orphanage. His hope, after all, to have a lofty position in Tremeine was gone. He was soon to accept his grand title and properties in England and to marry a wealthy heiress, Miss Grace Bellingham. To him, it was a relief my mother would die."

"He is, indeed, a scoundrel."

"Had he but kindly told her he was delayed, I could forgive him," Emma said. She waved her vision of the marquess away and bit her lip. She shook her head and went on, "She would have died with less affliction. But he told her he had met another woman and wished to start a new life. In reality, of course, he had been previously engaged. Grace Bellingham was a lifelong friend of Winnie's. He simply did not care for the complications this secret marriage to my mother had created, and certainly not the female issue of it, as a woman cannot inherit the throne of Tremeine. He now felt free to go on about life as though I had never come to be. My mother did not wish him to know she stayed with the Duke and Duchess of Trent, as he might someday try to locate me through them, whatever designs he may have had. The Trents lost all respect for Breyton and agreed to keep their involvement, and my location, a secret. They at first wished to take me as their own child and to say I had been born in Switzerland. The timing was perfect, and they would have done so if not for the question of the British throne."

"To be sure. There was at the time but one heir," Gabriel said, shaking his head. "A child of the duke's would have received the attention of the world and would have been second in line to the throne till Her Majesty had a child."

"Yes, that is it exactly. It just could not be. I am not of the English royal blood. Helena hid us for a short time, but feared we would be hunted in London and found. Lady Holmeshire came to take us to the country. Helena kept my mother's belongings, such as this gown, here with her, so I could not be identified by means of them. But before they left London, my mother began to fear leaving me with nobles, where her father might look and even Breyton might wonder. She told Lady Holmeshire she had decided to leave me with commoners before going up to Holmeshire Hall. She felt nobody would look in such a place for me. The lady recommended the squire's family, so I would always be near her. She admired Mrs. Carrington's goodness and genteel ways. That would be proper training for me. Thus, without telling the Carringtons anything I was placed on the doorstep of their home, in a plain basket with but a little blanket on a warm summer evening. She made one stop with me, though, first. She stopped at a small, ancient chapel on the south side of Holmeshire Village to pray for me. That chapel has, strangely, been a beloved place for all of my life."

"How very interesting. It is almost as if you remember. And did your mother inform the family of your name? For His Grace informed the crowd tonight it was the King of Tremeine who named you Emmanuel."

"No, it was mere coincidence that the Carringtons named me Emma. It was the name of Mrs. Carrington's grandmother. My mother left no note. After leaving me, no doubt with further injury to her poor heart, she was taken up the hill to the home of the Earl of Holmeshire." Emma removed a glove. "She left information about us, and this, her once treasured wedding ring, for me with her ladyship. She asked her to take me in when I was older and raise me as a servant in her household until my grandfather's death, for my protection. This is how I came to be a housemaid."

"But your mother did, then, die?"

"Yes. She died at Holmeshire quite soon after leaving me down the hill. She had used the last of her strength to carry me to a place of safety and to write me a letter, which I now have."

"And are you safe, now?" Gabriel inquired, again looking toward the entrance of the terrace for any sign of danger.

"Thankfully, yes, my grandfather died recently. My

uncle's first act as king was to set out to find my mother and me, should we yet be living. You see, he loved his sister, and he sent a message that her child would be as his own. Her sons and grandsons would be next to him and his son in line of succession to the throne. At least I know who my mother was, and who I am, and that I have a living family. That means more to me than being a princess. I am sure you fully understand such a sentiment."

She looked inside, to where the Breytons were falling apart, and said with a sigh, "And there, I am afraid, is my father. Her Grace, Aunt Helena, and the Countess of Holmeshire felt so badly for Lady Breyton all these many years and were so unhappy with her husband, but they were forced to carry on as usual with him. King George IV was adamant they make a marriage contract for their children. And anything but normal relations would have indicated hidden problems to Lord Breyton. How hard life can be." Gabriel nodded his agreement.

Emma stopped talking for a moment. She tipped her head and looked into Gabe's eyes. A few seconds passed, and she took a bronze coin from inside her glove to give him. "This coin bears a picture of my mother. I have two of these, one for myself and the other for you—a remembrance."

The coin glistened light from a torch as Gabe held it up to be seen. "She is indeed beautiful," he said. "The likeness could be you, you so resemble her. It is no wonder Lord Breyton feared you and treated you as he did. How shocked he must have been when he realized Lady Genevieve was to marry into the family that was raising you and bringing you into society. Yet, he was forced to wait for an excuse to break the engagement. He was indeed quite distressed when you arrived with the queen."

Gabriel looked at the sky. The sun was down, and clouds floated to cover the moon. It seemed light was leaving his life—and the time had come to give up his hope.

"Thank you," he said. "I shall treasure this coin, though its purpose as a memento is of no use. I could never forget." Gabriel looked back at Emma with no strength to smile. "I am quite overcome by all this. Would that my adoption by Caroline of Brunswick, The Princess of Wales, had made me royal."

"I am sorry, Mr. Hughes. I care for you a great deal and have the utmost regard for you, but this makes it the more impossible. You must know, I could not accept this seeming tale at first. It was all but impossible to believe, and I was at pains to sort it out. However, I was invited to Buckingham Palace once I had heard the story. The queen offered me a place to stay as her guest, though I asked to be allowed to remain where I was. That assured me it was, though, the truth."

"And will you go to your uncle?"

"I will go as soon as I can, perchance next summer, as I have people here to receive and things here to accomplish. I dearly wish to meet my uncle, my mother's beloved brother, though, and thank him for having sought me. He must be grieving my mother's death so long ago, as it is recent news to him. Perhaps I will stay for some time to give consolation, and as I do have a nation waiting for me. I hope, at least until then, to stay with Lady Holmeshire."

"And thus I came to know and love a princess of Tremeine. My dear Emma—but forgive my familiarity. I must give up my hopes. The greatest hope of my life, it was, with the saddest ending for me."

The patience of Wills and the crowd that wished to steal Emma away was gone, and a few stepped out onto the terrace.

"I am sorry, my dear Mr. Hughes," she said, her voice breaking. "Life is, for all of us, bittersweet."

They rose to their feet and looked at each other. He kissed her hand, and they backed away from each other, Gabriel touching her fingers as long as he could. He bowed and backed further before turning and leaving the terrace to intruders. Emma excused herself once again and followed him to the ballroom floor. She watched Gabriel bow to the queen, thank Genevieve and escape the company of people happier than he.

Lady Embry developed pneumonia and went home, maintaining adequate strength to drag her husband along by the sleeve.

Though Lady Breyton tried to sustain some composure, she could not stay on her feet for more than a moment at a time. The Lord Breyton busied himself with keeping her fanned and watered and her hands patted. He found himself staring, lost in thought, at his royal daughter, which did not help the disposition of his wife. She finally gave up her struggle, begged for a reprieve and was carried out in her husband's arms. Winnie followed to tend her grieving friend and comfort her.

Emma was more comfortable with Breyton gone for the evening. As Genny said, they could talk to this papa of theirs another day.

Emma had been sensitive to Grace's feelings in the matter of its being exposed at the ball. The duke, however, was indignant at the man for his treacherous behavior, and at the poor treatment of Emma by his friends in the past. In fact, His Grace had continued his relationship with the man for just such a moment, he

225

had said. Should the Lady Breyton have appreciated her friendship with his sister-in-law, he might have reconsidered, but her efforts to appease "the Embry" left him with less mercy to his credit.

The duke was pleased. Breyton was at long last exposed before all the right people, including the queen herself. Perhaps he would learn from it and become more merciful to others? And Emmanuel of Tremeine was introduced and would take her place in society without ever a formal debut. Those who had forbidden Emma from their dinners were sorely shamed, and Winnie's persistence was vindicated.

~Chapter 11~

Wherein Everything, At Last, Comes Together

The Season had ended. Parliament had sat and was back on its feet. The queen had sent condolences to the nation of Tremeine, but had declined sending a representative to the funeral of the late king.

A few days after the Midsummer Night's Dream Ball, coaches and carriages began traveling from London in every direction. They carried wealthy people, exhausted from the Season but eager to return to their country homes to prepare for hunting parties.

One headed toward the Holmeshire moors and pasture grounds carrying a princess and those who most loved her. She brought along her sister that they could come to know each other better, making up for lost years.

Another coach followed with Gwyndolyn, Elizabeth and Adelina Darivela. Adelina had been the lady's maid and dear friend of the late Princess Emmanuel of Tremeine. She had remained those many years working in the household of the Duke of Trent, waiting for little Emma to grow up and come into her position. Grateful to be out of hiding, she rode along to Holmeshire as the new lady's maid for Emma. Master Nicholas did best during the journey shifting from one coach to the next, and riding atop with the coachmen at times.

The queen had sent soldiers on horseback alongside as escorts for the protection of Emmanuel at the request of her uncle.

***

"Ah, the countryside again," sighed a relieved Winnie.

"Ah, the country air again. It can be breathed," Wills replied.

Genevieve quoted her beloved Shakespeare:

"I know a bank where the wild thyme blows,

"Where oxlips and the nodding violet grows,

"Quite over-canopied with luscious woodbine,

"With sweet musk-roses and with eglantine."

"How wonderful it is going to lovely Holmeshire again," she added. "It is perfect in the summer."

"How wonderful to have someone to entertain us along the way," laughed Emma, remembering her prior travels alone. She sat and reflected and said, "How many things have happened since I rode this way before. Just eight months it has been. I never dreamed it...I could never have imagined all this."

"I was certainly stunned at the ball," Wills said, pulling sandwiches from a basket. "Mother never let on to me, not a word. All those years growing up, I never knew. The night of the ball, I was worried. You were not riding with us. Mummy just said you had another ride. I supposed it was with some lady or another. But here I was at the ball, the queen was soon to arrive, and no Emma was to be seen. Doors are shut once the queen has arrived, so I was frantic. Then in you walked with the queen, dressed as the center of the world's attention. It made no sense at all. I supposed you would go to the gallows."

"Your lordships ought to have engaged Lord Holmeshire to Emma at age four, knowing what you knew," Genevieve said to much laughter, "instead of to such a rebel as myself."

Emma took on a pompous bearing and proclaimed, "We would like to announce the engagement of Wilfred, Little Lord Holmeshire, to Emma Carrington, foundling ward of the local squire. She has no money to bring into the marriage, but does possess a fine white blanket." She popped her thumb in her mouth and looked very innocent.

"Imagine—all those years Mama kept quiet, and she worked poor Emma like a slave," Wills said.

"I could not talk about it," Winnie replied. "Should word have gotten out, our Emma might have been killed. As for the work, it was the best of cover-ups. No one would ever have guessed."

"You were right—no one suspected in the least. Your cruelty saved me," Emma replied with a laugh. "And working taught me the plight of the maids, which has blessed me with the virtue of empathy," she said. She rubbed her knees and moaned. "I remember scrubbing floors at the squire's house. He would track it up and be angry with me. I surely know what servants endure, and most surely will speak up for them."

"James, Duke of Trent, had a few encounters with men he suspects were searching for the late princess and her child," Winnie said in a deeper tone, crossing her arms. "At one ball but a year ago, the Ambassador of Tremeine walked about studying the faces of young men and women. Trent was glad to see he was looking at men—it seems to have meant they had not learned of the baby's gender. Trent overheard him asking who a young lady's parents were—he turned and asked if he should be looking to replace his wife. That slowed him down for a time, and he was recalled to retirement at home when His Majesty, King Julian, ascended. I also heard of a man asking about the Breytons. Genny, you were suspected of being the daughter of the late Emmanuel. I worried for you, that you might be in danger. For this I cannot forgive your father."

Genny's eyes widened, and she gasped, "Oh, milady, I now understand frightful mysteries of my life. I have been followed for quite some time. I was indeed alarmed and asked Father for protection. Perhaps you understand why there were extra footmen along wherever I went. Mother was terrified for me, and neither of us could make the least sense of it."

Winnie turned to Emma and said, "We had to watch out for you, too, once we brought you to London and allowed Breyton to see your face. You have no idea how we had you watched over. That is why Helena sent a note down to Mr. Hughes when he took you out walking. She wrote him to protect you with his very life—not that the mandate was needed."

It dawned upon all aboard the swaying coach what a great reprieve had been granted with the new king's coming to the throne of Tremeine. It was no wonder he had searched for the two and, having discovered his niece, requested protection for her. Emma sighed with relief and took Genny's hand.

***

There was much excitement at the Holmeshire Village Inn. People rejoiced, laughed and bought each other ale. Charles was confused, sitting at a table over a hearty plate of mutton and bread, wondering what was

230

being celebrated. Lucy cleaned tables and brought plates and bowls of soup to exuberant villagers, but puzzled, stopped and asked what the fuss was about. "Our Emma," she was told, "our Emma is a princess from Tremeine!" "The squire never knew of it." "She is on her way here now."

Lucy looked over at Charles, her hand flying to her mouth. He shot up from the table. "Paw needs ta know. I gotta find Paw," he blurted as he rushed to the door, crashing past the table. His mutton fell forgotten to the floor. He ran for the noisy pub across the way where Benedict had just heard the news. "Paw!"

"Charles!"

"You heard? You heard about Emma? What do we do?" Charles shifted from side to side, dragging the fingers of both hands through his hair.

"I do not know. What do we do? I gotta think here," Benedict replied. It was hard to think when he could not stand for as long as it takes to snatch a money bag.

"We gotta get a message to your solicitor, Paw. Maybe he can tell us what ta do. This could make us very, very rich."

"Now you're getting it, boy—what took you so long? Find my walking stick. Where'd I put it?"

People bustled around them, clanging mugs and spilling ale, celebrating and yelling, "Our Emma, a princess!" The squire had been hurried into town by raucous, cheering men, and they picked him up and rode him about on their shoulders. He cheered about "his darling daughter" and sang, unrestrained, as if it was all his own doing. This surely was the reason Lady Holmeshire had taken her from him and her "deeply saddened sisters."

Gradually it dawned on the men that they must

hurry home. Their wives and children must be cleaned, combed and dressed in their Sunday best to welcome their very own princess back to town.

Charles tried to stop people, pushing into their paths for advice on sending a message to London, but they hurried about him, cheering and rejoicing, and hardly felt him grab at their arms. When only the pub keeper remained, he chased them from the building to lock it up.

"How do we get a message to London fast?" Charles begged of him outside the door.

"Go send a telegram," he called back, running down a narrow lane to his home.

"Telegram, Paw? What's a telegram?"

"I do not know, son, it's something they have just in Holmeshire."

***

Lady Embry, in her floral-papered boudoir, refused visitors, sending down messages that she was stricken with colic, typhus or pneumonia. She could never remember what she had informed the last caller. Under the influence of a bit of laudanum, she sent out letters stating she had heard Tremeine was not a Christian nation, and there was doubt as to the authenticity of the claim of Emma's family to the throne.

That was before it came out in the Times that the queen's father, the Duke of Kent, had been close friends with the King of Tremeine's grandfather, and that the current king regularly visited and went hunting with King Leopold of Belgium, the widower of the beloved Charlotte of Wales. Lady Breyton did not reply to Embry's notes about how deceitful The Countess of Holmeshire had been, and how she had chosen to humiliate her dear friends rather than tell the truth about the girl in the first place.

Grace was depressed. She had abandoned her lifelong friend Winnie and listened to all the wrong people. Winnie had warned her about the man, had she not? How it humiliated her that she had banned Emma from the ball as a servant. Facing people had become difficult.

But things were certainly worse for the marquess. A man with such a reputation would be avoided by many in polite society. His wife was in shambles, and she asked him repeated questions. How could her fiancé have married another woman and never mentioned it, Lady Breyton asked. How could he have denied his own motherless child?

She was much more pained by his anger at the birth of Genevieve, merely a daughter, than she had been in the past. She scolded and turned her back because of his rage at her and her doctors when she could have no more children. Had he been the perfect husband? Lady Breyton formed an opinion. The marquess was unwelcome on the upper floors, and it would be quite some time before that was to change.

He began to spend late hours in his study. Only a few short nights had passed since the ball before everyone climbed into their coaches and left. He had not spoken with his newly discovered daughter. Someday we will, she had said. Nor had he felt able to refuse Genevieve permission to go along to Holmeshire Hall.

Before leaving, Genny had gone upstairs to comfort her anguished mother. She had brought her flowers and promised her devoted support in the form of a letter every few days and a pleasant future together. Would her mother like to assist at Chenbury? Upon receiving a weeping, but solidly affirmative reply, Genny had sent a note to Helena, who had stayed in Town to tend the dear lady. It would be appreciated, she'd said, if the two could oversee things at Chenbury until she returned, and many gracious thanks.

***

A telegram made its way up the hill to Holmeshire Hall, and the household laughed and cheered at length. Even the stolid Barreby danced in circles for a moment. But things must be polished like never before, the windows quickly rewashed, and the dog bathed and trimmed. Not one person was to put a foot out of line. Extra birds and a lamb were slaughtered, and potatoes were boiled, for even the servants would eat well that night. Horses were brushed and brought to attention in the courtyard with their uniformed grooms, a classy backdrop for the welcome home. Every living thing at Holmeshire was well turned out.

Barreby looked below and saw the village dressed and waiting. At last coaches appeared in the distance. The household went to the front and lined up on the cobblestones to wait. Sitting with Barreby was the spaniel, whimpering with excitement, though she had no idea why.

***

The passengers pulled their curtains aside and strained to see through dusty windows ahead to the town. They heard shouting and the music of a band striking up a well-known melody. Scottish men joined with their bagpipes. As the coach drew near, the travelers saw hastily made, old fabric banners and crowds of people stretching to wave. Children were hoisted to see them enter the village.

Emma waved and waved, smiling hugely, out the window at her dear village friends as they passed through the town. Nicky slept through it all. And soon they arrived at the entrance of Holmeshire Hall, where

234

the servants just could not stand straight and still as they ought.

***

"Did you see the princess?" Lucy asked as she took off her cap to let down her hair. "I'm so tired." She dropped her cap on a table and leaned against the cool brick wall, her arms dropped at her sides.

"No, Lucy, we did not. We had to find us a telegraph office," Charles replied.

"What's that?" she said with a shrug, turning up her palms.

"It is amazing, girl, you can send a message to London quick as a flash of lightning," he said.

"No,"she scowled at Charles the Liar, and her hands went to her hips.

"You can—it is new, a new invention. They clack up some words, a message, and there it goes. It's gone. And then you get a reply."

Lucy postponed believing his words. "And what message did you send to London?" she asked in a suspicious tone.

"Well," Benedict broke in, shoving his way to bottles and goblets on a ledge. "We had to wait till the fool princess went by for the telegraph men to return to their shop, and then we sent a message off to John Brown to find out just how much of this kingdom we can have for ourselves." He and Charles broke out laughing. "The telegraph men didn't like that at all."

Charles joined in the drinking. "Imagine us slugging down scotch in fine smoking jackets," he said, "with servants waiting on us day and night."

Lucy, her hands on her hips, stood back shaking her head.

***

Morning came, and Winnie showered gifts on her

servants. Ribbons and pretty, initialed kerchiefs she gave the dazzled girls, and the men accepted paper and wax seals with a gracious nod. Few mistresses were so generous.

Wills asked Barreby to call his mother to the dark bookcases, leather-bound books and white walls of the library. Down the hall the butler went to find her talking and laughing about events in London with Emma and Genevieve, but she happily rose and went to meet her son. She found him on a ladder reaching for a book on Chancery law.

"You called for me, son?" She had embroidery in her hands and continued her work.

"Yes, Mama—thank you for coming." He climbed down to the floor and motioned her to a silk divan. His brow furrowed as he came and sat beside her. "You know, do you not," he began, "that before we left London, I filed papers to become the legal guardian of Nicholas?" He looked at her while tapping a hand on his leg.

"Yes, I do," she replied.

"I have been kept up to date on Lord Breyton's pursuit of the Chancery matter. I just received a telegram stating there are others making a claim for him. Do you have any idea who that could be?"

Winnie leaned back, looking at the ceiling, and then took him by the arm. "I'm sorry, son, but I do believe it might be the father or brother of Alexander." He thought and nodded agreement. She remembered the letter from Barreby she had received while in London. "Oh dear, I do believe they are here in the village, and I know they have asked for positions in the household. I forgot to tell you, but I never thought of them trying to take Nicholas."

"And they may have the right, Mama. That is the

horrid thing. Wentby is looking into it for me."

***

Emma took Genevieve walking in the late summer sunlight, pointing out her favorite trees and laughing over revealed memories. Going on about the grounds, she showed Genny where she thought Wills might put a pond with the lily pads she fancied for a lovely Italian garden. Genevieve replied with thoughts about the garden and plans for her own, with every flower white, at Chenbury.

Emma asked Genny to travel with her to Tremeine when she would eventually go. "The king, dear Genny, is your relative, too, after all."

"So he is, dear Ems," she giggled. "Though I fear he will not at all approve of my lineage."

"That is possible, but it is the same as mine, is it not, the line he may not approve. Still, he wishes me to come, and so you will be accepted, too. Should there be an uprising," she said with a laugh, "I shall protect you. I will see that you are fed regularly and not thrown into a dungeon." Emma became pensive. After a quiet moment, she stopped walking and said, "Genny, I wish to tell you a secret of mine. Please prepare yourself. You have another unknown relation, dear sister. You see...." She took a deep breath and slowly let it out. "Nicholas is my son."

"Your son? Oh Emma." Genevieve stared into her sister's eyes and tightened her grip on a branch. She had never imagined this. How should she respond, she wondered? Who was the father? Why had she not guessed, with Nicky so close to the family? Genny stood with a hand over her opened mouth.

Wills and Winnie approached to bring unpleasant news to Emma, and they heard what had been said. Wills spoke to reassure Genny and rescue Emma's reputation. "You see," he said, "Emma came as a servant. Mother knew the truth, but allowed Ems to work on her knees scrubbing floors as a disguise." He raised his eyebrows at Winnie and snatched her embroidery. He turned back to Genevieve. "We also had a wonderful and very handsome stable hand named Alexander."

Winnie interrupted. "I never dreamed they would marry, but bad little Emma and Alex—they did. I do suppose scrubbing floors was not the life a young girl would choose." She straightened a bow on Emma's sleeve with a smile and patted it into place. "Without marriage, it would seem to have been her only future," she said in a soothing tone. "They married, and somehow they spent time together. Lovers manage those things, do they not? He did have a room over the stables." She gave Emma a teasing glance, and she blushed as Winnie continued her tale.

"They made plans to go to London, Genny, where Alex thought he could have a better income and free her from service. Here I thought I had protected her so well. I thought I had kept her tidy for her future as a princess, but you just cannot watch someone all the time, can you? I could not yet inform them of Emma's position, but I offered Alex better pay to stay. Barreby has never understood why I wanted the lad paid so well. He frets to this day." Everyone laughed, imagining the scene.

"I made Emma's life more leisurely, more pleasant," Winnie went on. "I made her my companion. I credit her generous and kindly nature with keeping the other servants from becoming jealous. I am surprised, though, none of them ever suspected the truth about her and Alex."

"We could not let the staff know, to be sure," Wills

said.

"Letting servants marry would have set a terrible precedent, but I could not let this princess disappear, could I?" Winnie said, "So, only the official who married them knows, and the official's witnesses, and they are sworn to never speak of it."

"That will not be a matter of concern, now, as the facts will be revealed," Wills added. "Mama had Emma stay upstairs more, as we needed to seclude her from the normal day-to-day life with the servants. She felt sick in the mornings," he said in a near whisper.

"Furthermore, I needed to make a princess of her— a princess with a stable-hand husband," Winnie said, and everyone smiled. "And the difficulty continued until now, as I feared just a month past she would again wish to marry a commoner."

"Marry again?" Genny turned to Emma and took her arm. "What has become of Alexander? I have never met him." She looked with expectation at Wills and back to Emma. "Is he living?"

Wills explained. "I had to go to London a few weeks after we learned of it. I wished to go on horseback, so I brought Alex to care for the horses. We had a pleasant ride and stayed in inns along the way. We spent a few days in London and then headed back. We were riding through open country, enjoying the wind in our faces, when my horse spooked. She reared and bolted. Alex rode to my side as she tried to throw me and flung himself on her neck to settle her." Emma dropped her face into her hands. Winnie reached over to stroke her arm, and Wills said, "I was saved, but Alexander was killed." Genevieve put an arm around Emma and looked at the ground, shaking her head.

Wills gave out, and Winnie picked up the story. "We let his family know, and meant to help them, but they screamed abuses at our solicitor so severely he could not discuss it with them. We could not locate them again after that occurrence. Back here at home, Emma was in her second month with child. We mourned terribly over Alex, but I was forced to move Emma away to have her baby in secret. I sent her to my former governess, who was retired in her own home. I used the excuse of finishing Ems for her new role as my companion. It was perfect—it freed her from caring for me during her pregnancy, and it helped ready her for her role as a princess. We planned to bring the child here, not saying whose he was so he would be safe even if Emma were found. Wills brought little Nick, in Emma's own white blanket, home with him one day. Emma stayed in London for a good bit of time, sad, no doubt, to be parted from her tiny chap, but she was glad he would grow up in our home. It was helpful, as well, to assure that Emma would choose to stay here with us until we could tell her of her position. Such a loyal companion she became," Winnie said with a smile.

Emma replied, "I do love it here. I love everyone and everything here, so leaving was never a consideration. And I loved that my son would have a good life. He might have been the child of a widowed servant girl, perhaps in the almshouse, destined for hardship. How thankful I was he was to be the ward of Lord Holmeshire instead. Few people know whose child Nicky is, which created quite a stir in London recently." She tipped her head and half-smiled at Genny.

"You have me to thank for that, indeed. It had me distraught," Genny said with a sigh. "But I am quite happy now."

"It is fine. It does not matter," Wills said, comforting Genny as well as himself over the

240

memories of dinner at Handerton. "We knew it would be hard for you to accept a child as your own under such conditions." He lifted his chin, fanned himself with Winnie's embroidering hoop and said, "The King of Tremeine has but one heir in his family ahead of Nicky."

Winnie took back her work and tucked the needle in securely. "Females are unable to ascend Tremaine's throne," she said. "The son of a king's daughter or granddaughter can, and Nick is second in line after the Crown Prince. Our queen has informed him of Nicky's birth, and the king has responded by announcing it to his country."

"And he is a legitimate son," Emma stated with a firm nod. "I have the physician's statement. Nicky is a prince in good standing."

"Now, however," Wills said to Emma as he reached out and took her hand, "it appears that Alexander's father or brother is trying to claim him in Chancery."

"Oh, no," Emma cried, "so he did tell his family I was expecting a child. This on top of Lord Breyton's efforts."

"They sought work here this summer, Mama says. At first, they likely but wished to ascertain whether Nicky is yours and find a means to make money from the situation," Wills said, "with Nicky's being in my care and all. Perhaps they intended to blackmail me. The 7th Earl of Holmeshire had taken in the child of a housemaid who had quietly left the home, you know. What would people assume? Now that it will become known he is yours, and that he is a prince, they cannot blackmail me, and they wish to take him. Perhaps they believe they will have more money from the king than they might ever have had from me, or perhaps they expect to be given a grand home and an income to raise him. They likely have the right to him. He is in England and under English law."

"No," Emma cried out, "I could not bear that." She looked around, worried, and covered her face with shaking hands.

The group comforted her, for though it was English law, her circumstances were unusual. Perhaps they would succeed in court, they assured her, or if it must be, she and little Nick could don poor clothing and flee to Tremeine. Each of them promised to do what they could. They were most thankful the queen had sent guards for Emma and Nicky, who was safe in his bed.

***

Down in the village, Benedict stumbled about knocking on doors. He busied himself, breaking the news to everyone he found that he was the father of Alexander Scott, and the princess was his daughter-in-law. Best of all, he said, the future King Nicholas of Tremeine was his grandchild, and soon he would have enough money off it to buy drinks for the lot of them—and that more than once. Surely he would have their support. The people, though, did not believe him, and their protective feelings for their Emma took form. They began to watch this inebriate's every move.

***

An English widow had no right to her husband's property or even to his child, and Alexander had not left a will. Chancery would establish a male guardian for Nicky. Wills hoped to be that guardian, but he had not brought Chancery into the matter previously, which might now work against him. More than ever, he hoped to find a way to keep Nick at Holmeshire Hall, and he prayed with all his heart that he had. He approached the women who were commiserating at their tea.

242

"Hello Mama, Emma, Genny," Wills said, attempting to raise the spirits of the women. "Do you have something here for me to eat? Hmmm, let me see what is on Mama's plate." He took all that was there and left only crumbs.

"Hence, the menfolk are not brought to tea," his mother responded, grateful for his efforts to cheer, but now without a tart.

Wills ignored her. "Ems, or rather, Your Highness, would you be so kind as to come have a walk-out in the garden with me?"

Emma set down her china, shook her head at the incorrigible Wills and quit the drawing room at his side. They left the house through the western door, passing through the wisteria-enclosed landing. They walked down the terrace stairs and entered a secluded area surrounded by privet hedges. The garden around them was filled with sweet-smelling red roses, white petunias and elegant sculptures brought out from the crates.

They took the time to breathe, to allow some of nature's good into their day. Wills offered Emma a seat on a stone bench, and he sat down beside her.

Emma had in her hands the letter her mother once wrote and left with Winnie to be given to her when her grandfather died. She shared it with Wills. It explained many things, including that Breyton was Emma's father. She wrote that she had left the matter in the hands of Helena and Winnie because the Duke of Trent had kindly helped her. She felt she could entrust all her precious things, most of all the destiny of her newborn daughter, to them. She had written a bit of her own life story to Emma and told her to seek out her Uncle Julian's help, and to trust him, as soon as she knew of her grandfather's death.

Wills was pleased to hear the letter read, and said, "I am happy for you, dear Emma, and I know you must be eager to see your uncle."

"The fact is, Wills," she replied, "my life has been here, and it has been delightful. I very much wish to continue here. I realize I have a position in Tremeine, but I hope the king and the people will understand my circumstances. I shall surely visit there and spend a good bit of time. My only concern is that Nicky might be taken from me before I can go."

"Ems," he suggested, "I am so happy to know you care to stay here. It would break my heart to see you leave us. That hope expressed, I see a possible solution to the threat of Nicholas being given to the Scotts." Wills went to his knee on the ground and looked up at Emma with a most devoted expression. "Though it is inappropriate for an earl to propose to a princess, this is a matter of gravest importance. Would you consent to marry me? I do love you, you see, with all my heart. I have loved you for a very long time, even much before I ought to have."

Hoping to persuade her, he forgot the required position and moved up to the bench. Saying, "If I might," he took her hands. "As for Nicky, we could prove that I, an earl, would be married to the mother of the child, a princess, and the courts may see fit to leave him with us. That is, dear Emma, should you accept me as your husband, and should the King of Tremeine allow it."

For a moment, Emma was unable to speak. She closed her eyes, and she trembled. It was as if all the world had been wrapped in pretty fabric, tied with a ribbon and handed to her. She could not tell whether she was happier because of the solution to the custody case or the hope of a future in Will's arms.

How many years she had longed to be with Wills. Her infatuation with him had begun as a child. Her regard had developed while she served in the house, and it had become devotion as she had watched him with Nick. Was she, indeed, to have everything a girl could ever dream of having? She squeezed Wills' hands and accepted his proposal. Wills, however, regarded her hesitation as conflict in her mind.

***

Winnie told the family at dinner that night the grave of the Princess Emmanuel of Tremeine was sadly common and neglected. She had been laid in her grave with but a small, stone plaque. It was necessary, at the time, she revealed, to maintain secrecy, to bury her as a stranger and a pauper. Something should now be done.

The following day, they made up floral bouquets. A team of horses was readied and the group went down the road to the village. Emma was led to the grave marker, now nearly hidden under the grass, that read, "A Young Traveler." She was at last knowingly near the remains of her mother, and she stood silent with tearing eyes, breathing thanks for the loving care and wise decisions that had brought her safely to where she was this day. She laid down flowers, followed in turn by the others, and stood back. Soon a fine memorial would replace the old stone over the grave of a princess who had been buried in a servant's dress.

***

Barreby had ordered the room with precision, and the family was ready to dine. They were seated and reaching for samples of saddle of mutton and pies when a kitchen maid ran up to the dining room, calling out between heavy breaths, "Excuse me, sir, Mr. Barreby, sir, those horrid men are back. They're at the door, but this time they have come with others from the village.

The people have them by the neck." Her eyes were huge, looking back and forth from Barreby to the door.

Barreby spun around, knocking over a bottle of wine. Torn between wine on the floor, the family's dinner and leaving, he realized there was no wishing this away. He threw up his hands and took off down to the servants' hall. He was followed by the Holmeshires, Emma and Genny. There was hardly room for those crinolined skirts in such a crowd, but no one much cared about creases for the moment. The villagers had flooded into the house, and they yelled out to Wills once they saw him.

"My lord," they cried, "we have a case against this man and his son. They've been stealing from us, and we have the proof. They're a disgrace to the memory of Alexander Scott." They divulged tales of missing money and stolen goods, how they were discovered and how it was proven—in the excitement everyone spoke at once. The Scotts' designs upon the princess had raised the ire of enough women they could have hung the thieves themselves. Wills called for order and quiet, ascertained what had happened and addressed the Scott men.

"How good for you that punishment for theft is no longer a capital matter, as it was a few years ago. Your lives are spared. The good people of Holmeshire, however, have been abused by your stay in this town, and you must pay. You shall remain in my dungeon till the police come for you."

"You will now be allowed in this house, young man," Barreby added, "and you shall have dinner this time. Bread and stale ale. But you will, neither one, step foot in here again." A swoop of his hands toward the lower floor sealed their fate.

***

The marquess, as of yet unaware of Nicky's parentage, had gone to Chancery on behalf of the good people of England to have the child, probably an urchin from the streets of London, sorted through the proper channels. He had tried to brand him a pauper, but establishing the child's parentage seemed impossible. He had asked that Nicholas be raised in a workhouse where he would be "with people of his own class and learn to be a hard worker."

Breyton's solicitor had been told to find the best barrister in the land to manage this case in court. This was no ordinary Chancery case, he had told the man, but an affront to the Crown, raising such children into the society of courtiers. He had even tried to move the case from Chancery into common law for the sake of the future of social class structure.

The barrister who had received the case to argue "for the Crown", as it turned out, had been a stray kitten on the streets himself at one time, unbeknownst to Breyton and his lawyer. He had known the boy's identity, once revealed in whispers by the child's mother. The barrister, now Sir Gabriel Hughes, had refused the case, arguing that this was, in fact a Chancery case, that he was no Chancery lawyer and that he was, in fact, a friend of the boy's mother.

Lord Holmeshire, of course, had provided proof of the identity of the child to the defense to win his case. This would work to the benefit of the people of England even better, he had said, as public funds would not be required to provide for him.

Lord Breyton's new barrister now lost his argument to the defense before a packed court, and it was there publicly exposed that the child the marquess was trying to ruin was the one and only heir to his own title and fortune. Even Breyton's dream of a legacy was compromised, for though Nicky inherited the title The 2nd Marquess of Breyton, created to be inherited through his daughter, he was widely known as Nicholas, Prince of Tremeine, and he and his sons would be thought of as that, first and foremost, forever.

***

Wills was reading a paper in his leather-furnished study when he saw Emma pass through the hall. He had, for some time, postponed the discussion he felt they must have, and even now hesitated, but he rose to his feet and called out to her. She came to the Tudor arch doorway to hear his thoughts, hands clasped and concerned at his sad countenance.

"Emma, I received a telegram from my solicitor, and he has been able to ascertain from Chancery that it was indeed the Scotts trying to take Nicholas. They are, of course, no longer a threat. The threat from Lord Breyton has also ended."

He walked to the door where she stood. "I mean to say, Emma, should you wish to be freed from our engagement, which you so hesitated to accept, the danger to Nicholas is past. I did not mean to take advantage of the situation, should it have seemed so. I truly meant but to help. As a princess, perhaps you wish to find an alliance through your uncle the king."

Emma stepped into the study and pushed the door shut behind her. "Dearest Wills," she said, distressed at not having replied more clearly, "I assumed you knew how I felt. I adore you." Emma drew near Wills and took his hands. "I had always fancied you. But my feelings for you grew so very deep after Alexander's accident, when I saw you were so pained. And you so worried how I would be affected by his death. You worked to give a poor, grieving girl comfort and security. Even without knowing your mother's secret,

248

you took my son to raise as your own that you might keep him near me and give him the advantages of your high birth. The day you came to take Nicholas from my arms and bring him to Holmeshire, I knew he was in the most loving hands on earth. It made me love you hopelessly, and I longed to tell you how I felt. But life was quite twisted about, and you were engaged to another. Thinking at the time I was a commoner, I could not speak of it." She reached out to Wills. "I believe, though, that I see true love for me in your eyes, and I wish to know by your words if that should be true."

Wills reached back to Emma, putting an arm around her waist. "I have, indeed, long had the deepest, most wishful, loving feelings for you. It seemed Mr. Gabriel Hughes might someday have what I desired most, while I was to be married to another. I was terribly saddened, but I did not wish to interfere with your happiness, or Genny's. Now, however, you cannot marry a commoner, should you have ever hoped to, a fact which I believe Mr. Hughes has realized. And it is you who are above me now in station, and you must say. I have received the king's permission, and nothing could make me happier than if you should wish to be my wife."

Emma pulled him closer. "Dearest Wills, I am convinced I have been more fortunate in life than any other and have somehow captured the hearts of the best of the men in this world, one of whom I married, and another I refused. But now, a life with you is all I ask. Married to you, I would have all the treasures of the world. I would have the man I loved for many years as my adored husband. I would have the most caring father for my dear son. So, yes, please, I would very much like to marry you."

The happiest of men wrapped his arms around the beautiful Emmanuelle of Tremeine and tenderly kissed her.

***

Emma was greatly relieved at the rapid conclusion of the matter in Chancery. "It is now possible for us to do something I have wanted to do for many months," she told Wills.

***

Genevieve having said, "I must away," she had returned to her work at Chenbury. Wills, Winnie and Emma went up to the sparsely decorated nursery to see how their lad was doing. Barreby was there talking to Gwyn, and the two backed away and stood silent. Nicky had been readied for bed and was having a look at a book of drawings in his room. Emma sat down beside him for a serious talk.

"Nicky, I have something I wish to tell you," she began, and she declared to him the secret she had once shared with Mr. Gabriel Hughes. "Nicky, I am your mummy."

"I know," he said, and turned another page.

"Look at me—you do? You know?"

He looked up. "Yes, I know. Nanny Bowen told the nursery maid." All faces showed surprise, and Gwyn cringed.

"I have been asked to marry Lord Holmeshire, Nicky," Emma continued, "and the King of Tremeine has agreed to it, so he will be your papa. You may soon call him Papa."

"Yes, I will. I will call him Papa." He looked back at his book.

"Well, I have one more thing to tell you. I am a princess, and it makes you a prince," she said. "And it may be, not likely, but perhaps, you would even become a king someday."

"I know," he said, and he crawled off of the bed.

"You know," Emma laughed. "Where are you going?"

"I got a crown."

"You have a crown?" Wills chimed in.

"Yes." With that, Nicky ran to a shelf with the box holding the marble horses Wills had bought him. He pulled out of it Winnie's sapphire and emerald bracelet and put it on top of his head. "You see? I am a king."

Emma's mouth flew open. "Why did you take that bracelet?" she asked.

"I wished to be a king."

Barreby buried his face in his hands.

Debra Brown

Epilogue

The workhouse arrangement would continue for decades, degrading people and ruining any happiness they may have had. But there was a strengthened resolve among many of the privileged with sympathetic hearts to enable the poor to help themselves as best they could by providing the means and necessities while they struggled upward.

Chenbury came to be a well-organized hub for philanthropic work. Nobles and middle-class persons participated generously in fund-raising ventures. Many men and women in want of income were grateful to be hired to work in various aspects of the charity.

Mr. Simon Jones had been hired as personal assistant to Lord Holmeshire at Chenbury. He sat in their shared office organizing workers and planning for more even before the Handerton Ball. His skills proved invaluable, and he came to be responsible for managing most aspects of the charity. Anne stayed behind to marry Simon and to work as a seamstress at Belgrave Square for but ten hours a day. This, she pointed out, she could do well from her own home, like her mum, should she need to leave to care for a child. Simon and Anne's twin daughters grew up to become seamstresses in one of the first fashion houses of London.

Henry Smith eventually became administrator of numerous well-maintained and successful temporary homes. His experience living on the streets gave him an empathetic approach. His mother organized donated clothing and food for people in the homes. Little Wilfred Smith grew up a strong and happy lad, frequently pushing a broom through the halls of Chenbury for a coin or two.

Genevieve was delighted her father had an heir, freeing her to live her life as she pleased, working for the good of the country. She lived out her life at Chenbury, controlling the house, decorating and entertaining just as she pleased. She had much of the house for living quarters, as only the ground floor was needed for the charity.

She provided homes on the upper floors for other single women who had chosen to lead humanitarian lives, but who had not been granted houses of their own. These women came to be her close friends. Along with them, her mother, her sister and other companions, Genny lived a long, happy and rewarding life. She was warmly welcomed in the Kingdom of Tremeine, where she was created a countess, and enjoyed many a holiday there, basking in the love of the people. She left Chenbury to her nephew, Nicholas of Tremeine.

As the grandson of the first Princess Emmanuel of Tremeine, Nicholas inherited properties and money there. The Duke of Trent left something to him and, dearly loving both Nicky and his mother, Winifred left him her settlement house and monies. The entailed holdings and the title of the Earldom of Holmeshire went to his younger brother, Alexander. Nicholas of Tremeine became a great philanthropist in the two countries to which he belonged.

As it turned out, Benedict Scott was transported for hard labor in Tasmania, and his son, Charles, was imprisoned for several years. Their intent to claim Nicholas and his probable wealth was derailed. Wills received a good report on Lucy. Though she wished to continue her work at the Inn, in honor of her brother-in-law Alexander, he gave her a cottage near the village for the rest of her life to see her through. Lucy worked hard and saved money that she willed to her nephew's charities, though she kept her husband, Charles, in a comfortable bed and well fed as long as he lived.

It was a surprise, after many years, to learn that Sir Gabriel Hughes had not only left money and modest homes to the children of his happy marriage and to three children whom he had adopted from the streets of London, but he had also left Nicholas a small fortune to be used in his charitable work.

Author's Notes

I love English history. It has a unique loveliness despite realities that are often left unmentioned in stories. There are many fascinating scenes a reader from other countries can slip into vicariously. Over the two thousand years since Roman rule of the island, dramatic changes have occurred, leaving art, writings and structures from each era. There is much to be learned about each if a reader is to understand a novel, as it is not the author's intent to teach history but to tell a story. For much information about British history, you might be interested in my multi-author blog, English Historical Fiction Authors at http://englishhistoryauthors.blogspot.com.

The Companion of Lady Holmeshire is set in an imaginary part of Northumbria, England, near the Scottish border. I have done my best to create realistic conditions as they might have been. Economic conditions were difficult in the early years of Victoria's reign. During the preceding decade, laws had brought about changes, some beneficial to the working poor and, of course, the dreadful workhouses for the destitute. The upper classes were, however, beginning to see the need to take the lower classes into account, and humanitarian concerns developed. Queen Victoria herself did have concern for the poor as my story indicates.

I did knowingly fudge on one point; there are a few years difference in actual chronology between the death of Charlotte of Wales and the birth of Victoria. It worked better if I could ignore the passage of a few years in the backstory.

Some of the characters were real persons, namely Queen Victoria, Albert her future husband, Victoria's mother, George IV (formerly the Prince Regent) and his hated wife, Caroline of Brunswick (formerly the Princess of Wales) as well as their daughter Charlotte and Leopold, Charlotte's husband. I tried to make those characters ring true to their real personalities, going easy on the reputations of both George IV and his wife as that did not play into the story. Caroline of Brunswick really did adopt children. Fictional characters include Emma and the Carringtons, the Holmeshires, His Grace James The Duke of Trent and the Duchess, the Breytons, Mr. Gabriel Hughes and all surrounding characters in the village and at dinners and the ball.

Engagement rings were not yet in vogue when Wills gave the ring to Genevieve, and so it was not meant for that purpose. No doubt, however, a man might give a gift to a woman to whom he proposed, as Albert gave Victoria a ring, starting the fashion.

In England, though not everywhere, titles and property went to the eldest surviving son. If there was none, rather than the inheritance going to a daughter or her sons as is done in some countries, the family tree would be climbed backward until a male relative was found who had descended from the original title or property holder. This was done to keep property in the direct family, as a woman's property went to her husband. Passing the title or property through a woman would move an estate into the hands of a different family. There were, however, various differences in such matters if they were stipulated as part of the original creation of the title. Henry VIII created a title which he said could be passed through the daughter of the peer. I took advantage of that precedent in allowing the creation of the title Marquess of Breyton to pass through his daughter, who turned out to be not Genevieve, as was originally expected, but her older sister.

Indulging Your Inner Aristocrat~
British Period Novels

Meet Author Debra Brown

I grew up with my nose in books. I loved period stories, mysteries and surprise endings. I especially loved the Victorian houses my favorite sleuths tiptoed around in. In school, I was handed a copy of Great Expectations, which I could not put down. Miss Havisham was an incredible character. For the rest of my life, I wanted to be a mouse in the wall watching her live her strange life.

During my years of self-employment in the jewelry field, I watched period movies while I worked on my creations. I was in love with the characters, the plots, the historical realities. I became acquainted with the rigidly structured class system, the customs of the times and the required polite behaviors with the policy of shunning anyone who stepped out of line.

I ran out of movies.

With the economic difficulties of recent years, my jewelry business slowed. I began to write my own little story as a hobby, never intending to publish it. It developed in my mind faster than I could get it down on my word processor, and I stayed up later than I should have typing away. It didn't let me sleep when I did go to bed. It developed so beautifully that I decided to put it out there into the world. I am grateful to those that have helped me in various ways with this happy project. You know who you are. I am thankful to World Castle for accepting my book for publication.

And my second book now keeps me from sleeping. Please watch for my historical fantasy, <u>For the Skylark.</u>

www.ingramcontent.com/pod-product-compliance
Lightning Source LLC
Chambersburg PA
CBHW021958170626
46808CB00001B/205